DEBBIE MACOMBER

BRENDA NOVAK

SHERRYL WOODS

I'LL BE HOME FOR CHRISTMAS

mira

Recycling programs
for this product may
not exist in your area.

ISBN-13: 978-0-7783-3401-9

I'll Be Home for Christmas

First published in 2017. This edition published in 2023.

Copyright © 2017 by Harlequin Enterprises ULC

Silver Bells
First published in 1996. This edition published in 2023.
Copyright © 1996 by Debbie Macomber

On a Snowy Christmas
First published in 2009. This edition published in 2023.
Copyright © 2009 by Brenda Novak

The Perfect Holiday
First published in 2002. This edition published in 2023.
Copyright © 2002 by Sherryl Woods

For questions and comments about the quality of this book, please contact us
at CustomerService@Harlequin.com.

Mira
22 Adelaide St. West, 41st Floor
Toronto, Ontario M5H 4E3, Canada
BookClubbish.com

Printed in U.S.A.

CONTENTS

Praise for the authors

#1 *New York Times* Bestselling Author Debbie Macomber

"Macomber is a skilled storyteller." —*Publishers Weekly*

"Debbie Macomber tells women's stories in a way no one else does."
—*BookPage*

"Debbie Macomber is one of the most reliable, versatile romance
writers around." —*Milwaukee Journal Sentinel*

New York Times Bestselling Author Brenda Novak

"[Novak] deftly integrates topics such as coming to terms with
one's past and the importance of forgiveness into another beautifully
crafted, exceptionally poignant love story."
—*Library Journal* on *Discovering You*

"With great sensitivity and an exquisite flair for characterization,
Novak explores the ideas of redemption, forgiveness, and the
healing power of love. *This Heart of Mine* is a potently emotional,
powerfully life-affirming contemporary romance."
—*Booklist* (starred review)

#1 *New York Times* Bestselling Author Sherryl Woods

"Sherryl Woods gives her characters depth, intensity and the
right amount of humor." —*RT Book Reviews*

"A surprisingly pleasant read, and sure to satisfy fans."
—*Publishers Weekly* on *A Chesapeake Shores Christmas*

SILVER BELLS

DEBBIE MACOMBER

ONE

"Dad, you don't understand."

"Mackenzie, enough."

Carrie Weston hurried through the lobby of her apartment complex. "Hold the elevator," she called, making a dash for the open doors. Her arms were loaded with mail, groceries and decorations for her Christmas tree. It probably wasn't a good idea to rush, since the two occupants appeared to be at odds—which could make for an awkward elevator ride—but her arms ached and she didn't want to wait. Lack of patience had always been one of her weaknesses; equally lacking were several other notable virtues.

The man kept the doors from closing. Carrie had noticed him earlier, and so had various other residents. There'd been plenty of speculation about the two latest additions to the apartment complex.

"Thanks," she said breathlessly. Her eyes met those of the teenager. The girl was around thirteen, Carrie guessed. They'd moved in a couple of weeks earlier, and from the scuttlebutt Carrie had heard, they'd only be staying until construction on their new home was complete.

The elevator doors glided shut, as slowly as ever, but then the people who lived in the brick three-story building off Seattle's Queen Anne Hill weren't the type to rush. Carrie was the exception.

"What floor?" the man asked.

Carrie shifted her burdens and managed to slip her mail inside her grocery bag. "Second. Thanks."

The thirtysomething man sent her a benign smile as he pushed the button. He stared pointedly away from her and the teenager.

"I'm Mackenzie Lark," the girl said, smiling broadly. The surly tone was gone. "This is my dad, Philip."

"I'm Carrie Weston." By balancing the groceries on one knee she was able to offer Mackenzie her hand. "Welcome."

Philip shook her hand next, his grip firm and solid, his clasp brief. He glared at his daughter as though to say this wasn't the time for social pleasantries.

"I've been wanting to meet you," Mackenzie continued, ignoring her father. "You look like the only normal person in the entire building."

Carrie smiled despite her effort not to. "I take it you met Madame Frederick."

"Is that a real crystal ball?"

"So she claims." Carrie remembered the first time she'd seen Madame Frederick, who'd stepped into the hallway carrying her crystal ball, predicting everything from the weather to a Nordstrom shoe sale. Carrie hadn't known what to think. She'd plastered herself against the wall and waited for Madame Frederick to pass. The crystal ball hadn't unnerved her as much as the green emeralds glued over each eyebrow. She wore a sort of caftan, with billowing yards of colorful material about her arms and hips; it hugged her legs from the knees down. Her long, silver-white hair was arranged in an updo like that of a prom queen straight out of the sixties.

"She's nice," Mackenzie remarked. "Even if she's weird."

"Have you met Arnold yet?" Carrie asked. He was another of the more eccentric occupants, and one of her favorites.

"Is he the one with all the cats?"

"Arnold's the weight lifter."

"The guy who used to work for the circus?"

Carrie nodded, and was about to say more when the elevator came to a bumpy halt and sighed loudly as the doors opened. "It was a pleasure to meet you both," she said on her way out the door.

"Same here," Philip muttered, and although he glanced in her direction, Carrie had the impression that he wasn't really seeing her. She had the distinct notion that if she'd been standing there nude he wouldn't have noticed or, for that matter, cared.

The doors started to shut when Mackenzie yelled, "Can I come over and talk to you sometime?"

"Sure." The elevator closed, but not before Carrie heard the girl's father voice his disapproval. She didn't know if the two of them were continuing their disagreement, or if this had to do with Mackenzie inviting herself over to visit.

Holding her bags, Carrie had some difficulty unlocking and opening her apartment door without dropping everything. She slammed it closed with one foot and dumped the Christmas ornaments on the sofa, then hauled everything else into her small kitchen.

"You'd been wanting to meet him," she said aloud. "Now you have." She hated to admit it, but Philip Lark had been a disappointment. He showed about as much interest in her as he would a loaf of bread in the bakery window. Well, what did she expect? The fact that she expected *anything* was because she'd listened to Madame Frederick one too many times. The older woman claimed to see Carrie's future and predicted that, before the end of the year, she'd meet the man of her dreams when he moved into this very building. Yeah, right. She refused to put any credence into that prophecy. Madame Frederick was a sweet, rather strange old lady with a romantic heart.

Carrie pulled out the mail, scanned the envelopes and, except for two Christmas cards and a bill, threw the rest in the garbage. She'd just started to unpack her groceries when there was a knock at the door.

"Hello again," Mackenzie Lark said cheerfully when Carrie opened the door. The quickness of her return took Carrie by surprise.

"You said I could come see you," the teenager reminded her.

"Sure, come on in." Mackenzie walked into the apartment, glanced around admiringly and then collapsed onto the sofa.

"Are you still fighting with your dad?" Carrie asked. She'd had some real go-rounds with her mother before Charlotte married Jason Manning ten years earlier. At the time, Carrie and her mother had been constantly at odds. Carrie knew she was to blame, in part, but she was also aware that her mother had been lonely and unhappy.

Hindsight told her that the root of their problem had been her parents' divorce. Carrie didn't remember a lot about her father—her parents had separated when she was four or five. As she grew older, she came to resent that she didn't have a father, and for reasons that were never clear, she'd blamed her mother.

"Dad doesn't understand." Mackenzie lowered her eyes, her mouth turned down.

"About what?" Carrie asked gently.

The girl stood and walked over to the kitchen and watched Carrie put away groceries. She folded her arms on the counter and then rested her chin there. "Everything. We can't talk without fighting. It's tough being a teenager."

"You might find this difficult to believe, but it's just as difficult raising one," Carrie said.

Mackenzie sighed. "It didn't used to be like this with Dad

and me. We got along really well. It wasn't easy when Mom left, but we managed."

"So your parents are divorced?" Although she didn't mean to pry, she was definitely curious.

Mackenzie wrinkled her nose. "It was awful when they split."

"It always is. My parents divorced when I was just a kid. I barely remember my dad."

"Did you see him very much afterward?"

Carrie shook her head. It had bothered her when she was younger, but she'd made her peace with it as an adult. She'd felt hurt that her father didn't want to be part of her life, but ultimately she'd decided that was his choice—and his loss.

"I'm spending Christmas with my mom and her new husband." Mackenzie's eyes brightened. "I haven't seen her in almost a year. She's been busy," she said. "Mom works for one of the big banks in downtown Seattle and she's got this really important position and has to travel and it's hard for her to have me over. Dad's a systems analyst."

Carrie heard the pain in Mackenzie's voice. "You're fifteen?" she asked, deliberately adding a couple of years to her estimate, remembering how important it was to look older when one was that age.

Mackenzie straightened. "Thirteen, actually."

Carrie opened a bag of fat-free, cheese-flavored rice cakes and dumped them onto a plate. Mackenzie helped herself to one and Carrie did, as well. They sat across from each other on opposite sides of the kitchen counter.

"You know what I think?" Mackenzie said, her dark eyes intense. "My dad needs a woman."

The rice cake stuck midway down Carrie's throat. "A... woman?"

"Yeah, a wife. All he does is work, work, work. It's like he can forget about my mother if he stays at the office long enough." She grabbed another rice cake. "Madame Frederick said so, too. *And* she says he's going to meet someone, but she couldn't be any more specific than that."

"Madame Frederick?"

"She looked into her crystal ball for me and said she saw lots of changes in my future. I wasn't too happy—except for the part about my dad. There've been too many changes already with the move and all. I miss my friends and it's taking way longer to build the new house than it was supposed to. Originally we were going to be in for Christmas, but now I doubt it'll be ready before next Thanksgiving. Dad doesn't seem to mind, but it bugs me. I'm the one who's going to a strange school and everything." She frowned, shaking her head. "I want my life back."

"That's understandable."

Mackenzie seemed caught up in a fantasy world of her own. "You know, I think Madame Frederick might've stumbled on something here." Her voice rose with enthusiasm.

"Stumbled on something?" Carrie repeated cautiously.

"You know, about a relationship for my dad. I wonder how I could arrange that?"

"What do you mean?"

"Finding a new wife for my dad."

"Mackenzie," Carrie said and laughed nervously. "A daughter can't arrange that sort of thing."

"Why not?" She seemed taken aback.

"Well, because marriage is serious. It's love and commitment between two people. It's…it's…"

"The perfect solution," Mackenzie finished for her. "Dad and I've always liked the same things. We've always agreed on everything…well, until recently. It makes sense that I should be the one to find him a wife."

"Mackenzie…"

"I know what you're thinking," she said, without a pause.

"That my dad won't appreciate my efforts, and you're probably right. I'll have to be subtle."

Carrie laughed. "I can't believe this," she whispered. This girl was like a reincarnation of herself eleven years earlier.

"What?" Mackenzie demanded, apparently offended.

"Take my advice and stay out of your father's love life."

"Love life?" she echoed. "That's a joke. He hasn't got one."

"He doesn't want your help," Carrie said firmly.

"Of course he doesn't, but that's beside the point."

"Mackenzie, if you're not getting along with your dad now, I hate to think what'll happen when he discovers what you're up to. My mother was furious with me when I offered Jason money to take her out and—"

"You were willing to *pay* someone to date your mother?"

Carrie didn't realize what she'd said until it was too late. "It was a long time ago," she murmured, hoping to leave it at that. She should've known better. Mackenzie's eyes grew huge.

"You actually paid someone to date your mother?" she said again.

"Yes, but don't get any ideas. He refused." Carrie could see the wheels turning in the girl's head. "It was a bad idea, and like I said, my mother was really mad at me."

"Did she ever remarry?"

Carrie nodded.

"Anyone you knew?"

Again she nodded, unwilling to tell her it was the very man she'd tried to bribe.

Mackenzie's gaze met hers and Carrie looked away. "It was *him*, wasn't it?"

"Yes, but I didn't have anything to do with that."

Mackenzie laughed. "You offered him money to date your mother. He refused, but dated her anyway. That's great! How long before they got married?"

"Mackenzie, what happened with my mother and Jason is…
unusual."

"How long?" she repeated stubbornly.

"A few months."

She smiled knowingly. "They're happy, aren't they." It was
more of a comment than a question.

"Yes."

Carrie only hoped she'd find a man who'd make her as truly
contented as Jason Manning had made her mother. Despite ten
years of marriage and two children, her mother and stepfather
behaved like newlyweds. Carrie marveled at the strength of
their love. It inspired her and yet in some ways hampered her.
She wanted that kind of relationship for herself and wasn't willing to settle for anything less. Her friends claimed she was too
picky, too demanding when it came to men, and she suspected
they were right.

"My point exactly," Mackenzie declared triumphantly. "You
knew your mom better than anyone. Who else was more quali-
fied to choose a husband for her? It's the same with me. I know
my dad and he's in a rut. Something's got to be done, and Madame Frederick hit the nail on the head. He needs a love interest."

Carrie's smile was forced. "Madame Frederick is one of my
favorite people, but I think it's best to take what she says with
a grain of salt."

"Well, a little salt enhances the flavor, right?" Mackenzie
added. Excited now, she got to her feet. "What about you?"
she asked.

"Me?"

"Yeah, you. Would you be willing to date my dad?"

TWO

"She's pretty, isn't she, Dad?"

Philip Lark glanced up. He sat at the kitchen table, filling out an expense report. His daughter sat across from him, smiling warmly. The way her eyes focused on him told him she was up to *something*.

"Who?" he asked, wondering if it was wise to inquire.

"Carrie Weston." At his blank look, she elaborated. "The woman we met in the elevator. We talked this afternoon." Mackenzie rested her chin in her hands and continued to gaze at him adoringly.

Philip's eyes reverted to the row of figures on the single sheet. His daughter waited patiently until he was finished. Patience wasn't a trait he was accustomed to seeing in Mackenzie. She usually complained when he brought work home, acting as though it was a personal affront. He cleared his mind, attempting to remember her question. Oh, yes, she wanted to know what he thought of Carrie Weston. For the life of him, he couldn't remember what the woman looked like. His impression of her remained vague, but he hadn't found anything to object to.

"You like her, do you?" he asked instead, although he wasn't convinced that pandering to Mackenzie's moods was a smart thing to do. She'd been impossible lately. Moody and unreasonable. Okay, okay, he realized the move had been hard on her; it hadn't been all that easy on him, either. But they'd be here for only six to eight weeks. He'd assumed she was mature enough to handle the situation. Evidently, he'd been wrong.

Mackenzie's moods weren't all he'd miscalculated. Philip used to think they were close, but for the past few months she'd been a constant source of frustration.

Overnight his sane, sensible daughter had turned into Sarah Bernhardt—or, more appropriately, Sarah Heartburn! She hadn't whined this much since she was three. Frankly, Philip didn't understand it. Even her mother's defection hadn't caused this much drama.

"Carrie's great, really great."

Philip was pleased Mackenzie had made a new friend, although he would have been more pleased if it was someone closer to her own age. Still, as he kept reminding her, the situation was temporary. Gene Tarkington, a friend of his who owned this apartment building, had offered the furnished two-bedroom rental to him for as long as it'd take to complete construction on his Lake Washington house. The apartment wasn't the Ritz, but he hadn't been expecting any luxury digs. Nor, truth be told, had he expected the cavalcade of characters who populated the building, although the woman with the crystal ball looked fairly harmless. And the muscle-bound sixty-year-old who walked around shirtless, carrying hand weights, appeared innocuous, too. He wasn't as certain about some of the others, but then he didn't plan on sticking around long enough to form friendships with this group of oddballs.

"Dad," Mackenzie began in a wistful voice, "have you ever thought of remarrying?"

"No," he answered emphatically, shocked by the question.

He'd made one mistake; he wasn't willing to risk another. Laura and the twelve years they were together had taught him everything he cared to know about marriage.

"You sound mad."

"I'm not," he said, thrusting the expense report back inside his briefcase, "just determined."

"It's because of Mom, isn't it?"

"Why would I want to remarry?" he asked, hoping to put an end to this conversation.

"You might want a son someday."

"Why would I want a son when I have you?"

She grinned broadly, obviously approving his response. "Madame Frederick looked into her crystal ball and said she sees another woman in your life."

Philip laughed at the sheer ridiculousness of that. Remarry? Him? He'd rather dine on crushed glass. Wade through an alligator-infested swamp. Or jump off the Space Needle. No, he wasn't interested in remarrying. Not him. Not in this lifetime.

"Carrie's a lot like me."

So *this* was what the conversation was all about. Carrie and him. Well, he'd put a stop to that right now. "Hey." He raised his hand, palm out. "I guess I'm a little slow on the uptake here, but the fog is beginning to lift. You're playing matchmaker with me and this—" person he couldn't recall a single thing about "—neighbor."

"Woman, Dad. Carrie's young, attractive, smart and funny."

"She is?" He hadn't noticed that earlier, but then how could he? They'd met for about a minute in the elevator.

"She's perfect for you."

"Who says?" As soon as the words left his lips, Philip knew he'd made a strategic error. He'd all but invited an argument.

Mackenzie's smile blossomed like a rose in the sun. "Madame Frederick, for one. Me for another. Just think about it,

Dad. You're in the prime of your life and all you do is work. You should be enjoying the fruit of your labors."

"I'm building the house," he said, wondering where she'd heard *that* expression.

"Sure, to impress Mom, just so she'll know what a mistake she made leaving you."

His daughter's words brought him up short. Philip sincerely hoped that wasn't true. He wanted a new home for plenty of reasons, none of which included his ex-wife. Or so he believed.

"Why would your mother care about a home I'm building?"

"Think about it, Dad."

"I am."

She shot him a knowing look, one tempered with gentle understanding, which only irritated him further. "Let's leave Laura out of this, all right?" His feelings for Mackenzie's mother were long dead. He'd tried to make the marriage work, as God was his witness. Even when he discovered she was having an affair—the first time—he'd been willing to do whatever was necessary to get them back on track. It'd worked for a few years, but for the most part he'd been deluding himself.

The divorce had come well after there was any marriage left to save. He'd berated himself for a long time before, and since. He had his daughter and his dignity, and was grateful for both. The last thing he intended to do at this point was risk that hard-won serenity.

"I want you to ask Carrie out."

"What?" He couldn't believe her nerve. "Mackenzie, for heaven's sake, would you stop? I'm *not* dating Carrie Westchester or anyone else."

"It's Carrie Weston."

"Her, either." He stalked into the kitchen and poured himself a cup of coffee. He took one sip, cringed at the bitter taste and dumped the rest in the sink.

"Please? She's in Apartment 204."

"No! Case closed! I don't want to hear another word about this, understand?" He must have added just enough authority to his voice because she didn't pursue the subject again. Philip was grateful.

The next time he glanced at his daughter, he saw her sitting in the middle of the living room, her arms folded tightly around her. The sour look on her face could have curdled cream.

"Say, why don't we go out and buy a Christmas tree?" he suggested. Despite what Mackenzie might think, he didn't enjoy fighting with her.

She turned to stare at him disdainfully and consider his proposal. With what seemed to require an extraordinary amount of effort, she said, "No thanks."

"Fine, if that's the way you want to be."

"I thought you said a Christmas tree would be too much trouble this year."

It would be, but he was willing to overlook that if it'd take his daughter's mind off her present topic of interest. "We could put up a small one." He figured a compromise would go a long distance toward keeping the peace.

"She likes you," Mackenzie said with a righteous nod.

Philip didn't need to ask who she was talking about. He pressed his lips together to keep from saying something he'd later regret. Such as...how did this Carrie person know enough about him to either like or dislike him?

"She told me what happened to her when she was about my age," Mackenzie continued undaunted. "Her parents divorced when she was around five and her mother didn't date again or anything. She closed herself off from new relationships, just the way you're doing, so Carrie felt she had to take matters into her own hands. And who could blame her? Not me, that's for sure." She paused long enough to draw in a breath. "By the time Carrie was a teenager, her mother had shriveled into this miserable, unhappy shrew." She stared pointedly at him before saying, "Sort of like what's happening to you."

"Come on now!"

"So," she went on, ignoring his outburst, "Carrie felt she had to do something. She offered to pay this guy to date her mother. Out of her own meager savings from babysitting jobs and walking the neighbor's dog. She took everything she'd managed to scrape together to pay this man. She told me she would've done anything to give her love-starved mother a second chance at happiness."

Philip restrained himself from rolling his eyes at her melodramatic rendition. All she needed was a violin playing softly in the background. "How noble of her."

"That's not the end of the story," Mackenzie informed him.

"You mean there's more?"

She paid no attention to his sarcasm. "When her mother found out what she'd done, she was furious with Carrie."

"I can well imagine." Philip crossed his arms and leaned against the doorjamb. He glanced at his watch, indicating that there was only so much of this he was willing to listen to and he was already close to his limit.

"But she withstood her mother's outrage. Knowing she was right, Carrie gladly accepted the two-week restriction her mother placed on her."

The strains of the violin grew distinctly louder.

"Carrie didn't pick just any Tom, Dick or Harry for her mother, though. She carefully, thoughtfully surveyed the eligible men around her and chose this really cool guy named James...or something like that. His name isn't important—what *is* important is that Carrie knew her mother well enough to choose the perfect man for her. She chose the very best."

Now his daughter was beginning to sound like a greeting-card commercial. "This story does have a point, doesn't it?"

"Oh, yes." Her eyes gleamed with triumph. "Not more than

three months later, four at the most, Carrie's mother married Jason."

"I thought you said his name was James."

"I also said his name doesn't matter. The point is that he married her and they're both happy."

"That must have cost her a pretty penny, since Carrie had already paid him everything she'd saved just for that first date."

"He married her for free."

"Oh, I see, she was on sale."

Mackenzie frowned at him. "You're not funny. Carrie told me that meeting Jason was the best thing that ever happened to her mother. Once a year, on the anniversary of their first date, her mom sends her flowers out of gratitude that her daughter, the very one she'd restricted for two whole weeks, had cared enough to find the man of her dreams."

As her voice rose victoriously, the violin faded and was replaced with a full choral arrangement of *God Bless America*. Philip could just about hear it. His daughter was Sarah Heartburn during her finest hour.

"Now," she said, "will you ask Carrie out? She's perfect for you, Dad. I know what you like and what you don't, and you're gonna like her. She's really nice and fun."

"No." He yawned loudly, covering his mouth.

"I've never said anything, but I'd really love to be a big sister, the way Carrie is to her two half brothers."

"Thanks, but no thanks." The kid was actually beginning to frighten him. Not only was she telling him he should date a woman he'd barely met, now she was talking about them having children together.

"Don't do it because I asked it of you. Do it for yourself. Do it before your heart turns into a hardened shell and you shrivel up into an old man."

"Hey, I'm not dead yet. I've got a good forty or fifty years left in me."

"Maybe," Mackenzie challenged. "*If* you're lucky." With her nose pointed at the ceiling she exited the room with all the flair and drama of an actress walking offstage after the final curtain call.

Grinning to himself, Philip opened his briefcase. He removed a file, then hesitated, frowning. It was one thing to have his daughter carry on like a Shakespearean actress and another for an adult woman to be feeding her this nonsense. While he couldn't remember much about Ms. Carrie Weston, he did recall that she'd appeared interested in him, judging by the intent way she'd studied him. Perhaps he'd better set the record straight with her. If she intended to use his daughter to get to him, then she was about to learn a thing or two.

He slammed his briefcase shut and marched toward the door.

"Where are you going?" Mackenzie asked, returning—of course—at that very instant.

"To talk to your friend," he snapped.

"You mean Carrie?" she asked excitedly. "You won't be sorry, Dad, I promise you. She's really nice and I know you'll like her. If you haven't decided where to take her to dinner, I'd suggest Henry's, off Broadway. You took me there for my birthday, remember?"

Philip didn't bother to inform his daughter that inviting Carrie to dinner wasn't exactly what he had in mind. He walked out the door and nearly collided with the old biddy clutching the crystal ball.

"Good evening, Mr. Lark," Madame Frederick greeted him with a tranquil smile. She glanced at him and then at the crystal ball and her smile grew wider.

"Keep that thing away from me," he told her in clear tones. "I don't want you doing any of that hocus-pocus around my daughter. Understand?"

"As you wish," she said with great dignity and moved past

him. Philip glared at her, then sighed, exasperated. He headed for the stairs, running down to the second floor.

When he reached Carrie Weston's apartment, he was winded and short-tempered. She answered his knock almost immediately.

"Mr. Lark." Her eyes widened with the appropriate amount of surprise, as though she'd spent the past five minutes standing in front of a mirror practicing.

"It seems you and I need to talk."

"Now?" she asked.

"Right now."

THREE

Carrie Weston was lovely, Philip realized. For reasons he didn't want to analyze, he hadn't noticed how strikingly attractive she was when they'd met in the elevator. Her eyes were clear blue, almost aquamarine. Intense. Her expression warm and open.

It took him a moment to recall why he'd rushed down here to talk to her. Maybe, just maybe, what Mackenzie had been saying—that he was shriveling up emotionally—contained a grain of truth. The thought sobered him.

"I need to talk to you about Mackenzie," he stammered out.

"She's a delightful young lady. I hope I didn't keep her too long." Carrie's words were apologetic as she reached into the hallway closet for her coat.

"It's about your discussion with her this afternoon."

"I'm sorry I can't chat just now. I feed Maria's cats on Wednesdays and I'm already late."

It could be a convenient excuse to escape him, but he was determined to see this through. "Do you mind if I tag along?"

She looked mildly surprised, but agreed. "Sure, if you want." She picked up a ten-pound bag of cat food. Ten pounds? Philip knew the older woman kept a ridiculous number of animals. Gene had complained to him more than once, but the retired schoolteacher had lived in the building for fifteen years and paid her rent on time. Gene tolerated her tendency to adopt cats, but he didn't like it.

"You might want to get your coat," she suggested as she locked her apartment.

"My coat?" She seemed to imply that the old lady kept her apartment at subzero temperatures. "All right," he muttered.

She waited as he hurried up the stairs. Mackenzie leaped to her feet the second he walked in the door. "What'd you say to her?" she demanded.

"Nothing yet." He yanked his coat off the hanger. "I'm helping her feed some cats."

The worry left his daughter's eyes. "Really? That's almost a date, don't you think?"

"No, I don't think." He jerked his arms into the jacket sleeves.

"She asked me if I wanted to bake Christmas cookies with her and her two brothers on Saturday. I can, can't I?"

"We'll talk about that later." Carrie Weston was wheedling her way into his daughter's life. He didn't like it.

Mackenzie didn't look pleased but gave a quick nod. Her worried expression returned as he walked out the door.

Philip wasn't sure why he'd decided to join Carrie. He needed to clarify the situation, but it wasn't necessary to follow her around with a bag of cat food to do so.

"Maria has a special love for cats," Carrie explained as they entered the elevator and rode to the ground floor. "I just don't feel it's a good idea for her to be going out alone at night to feed the strays."

So *that* was what this was all about—feeding stray cats.

"Maria calls them her homeless babies."

Philip sure hoped no one at the office heard about this. They stepped outside and his breath formed a small cloud. "How often does she do this?" he asked, walking beside Carrie.

"Every day," she answered. Half a block later she turned into an almost-dark alley. Carrie had said she didn't think it was safe for Maria to venture out alone at night. Philip wasn't convinced it was any less risky for her. He glanced about and saw nothing but a row of green Dumpsters.

They were halfway down the dimly lit alley when he heard the welcoming meow of cats. Carrie removed a cardboard container from a Dumpster and left a large portion of food there. The cats eagerly raced toward it. One tabby wove his way around her feet, his tail slithering about Carrie's slender calf. Squatting down, she ran her gloved hand down the back side of a large male. "This is Brutus," she said, "Jim Dandy, Button Nose, Falcon and Queen Bee."

"You named them?"

"Not me, Maria. They're her friends. Most have been on their own so long that they're unable to adapt to any other way of life. Maria's paid to have them neutered, and she nursed Brutus back to health after he lost an eye in a fight. He was nearly dead when she found him. He let her look after him, but domesticated living wasn't for Brutus. Actually, I think he's the one that got Maria started on the care and feeding of the strays. I help out once a week. Arnold and a couple of the others do, too. And we all contribute what we can to the costs of cat food and vet care."

All this talk about cats was fine, but Philip had other things on his mind. "As I explained earlier, I wanted to talk to you about Mackenzie."

"Sure." Carrie gave each of the cats a gentle touch, straightened and started out of the alley.

"She came back from her visit with you spouting some ridiculous idea about the two of us dating," Philip continued.

Carrie had the good grace to blush, he noted.

"I'm afraid I'm the one who inadvertently put that idea in her head. Mr. Lark, I can't tell you how embarrassed I am about this. It all started with an innocent conversation about parents. My parents got divorced, as well—"

"When you were four or five, as I recall," he said. He hated to admit it, but he enjoyed her uneasiness. Knowing Mackenzie, he was well aware of the finesse with which his daughter manipulated conversations. Poor Carrie hadn't had a chance. "Mackenzie also said you paid a man to date your mother."

"Oh, dear." She closed her eyes. "No wonder you wanted to talk to me." She glanced guiltily in his direction. "Jason was far too honorable to accept my offer."

"But he did as you asked."

"Not exactly… Listen, I do apologize. I'd better have another talk with Mackenzie. I'll try to set the record straight. I was afraid she might do something like this. Actually, I should've realized her intent and warned you. But I didn't think she'd race right upstairs and repeat every word of our conversation."

"My daughter has a mind of her own. And she's taken quite a liking to you." For that, Philip was grateful. Mackenzie needed a positive female role model. Heaven knew her mother had shown little enough interest in her only child. Philip could do nothing to ease the pain of that, and it hurt him to hear Mackenzie make excuses for Laura's indifference.

As they chatted, Carrie led him into a nearby vacant lot. He learned quite a bit about her in those few minutes. She worked for Microsoft, had lots of family in the area and doted on her two half brothers.

The minute they stepped onto the lot, ten or so stray cats eased out of the shadows. They'd obviously been waiting for Carrie. Talking softly, issuing reassurances and comfort, she distributed the food in a series of aluminum pie plates situated about the area.

"I saw a lot of my teenage self in Mackenzie," she said when she rejoined him. She looked at him, but didn't hold his gaze long. "It wasn't just the fact that my parents were divorced— broken homes were prevalent enough—but I'd been cheated out of more than the ideal family. In some ways I didn't have a mother, either."

"Are you trying to say I'm not a good father?" he asked tightly.

"No, no," she said automatically. "I think I should keep my mouth shut. I do apologize for what happened with Mackenzie. Don't worry, Mr. Lark, I have no intention of using your daughter to orchestrate a date with you."

"Do you still want her to come over to bake cookies?" he asked. He'd be in trouble with Mackenzie if she didn't.

"You don't mind?"

"Not if you and I are straight about where we stand with each other. I'm not interested in a relationship with you. It's nothing personal. You're young and attractive and will make some man very happy one day—it just won't be me."

"I wouldn't… You're not—" She stopped abruptly and glared up at him. "Rest assured, Mr. Lark, you have nothing to fear from me."

"Good. As long as we understand each other."

Carrie removed her gloves and viciously shoved them into her pockets. She hung her coat in the closet and sat down, crossing her arms and her legs. She uncrossed both just as quickly, stood and started pacing. She couldn't keep still.

Philip Lark actually believed she'd tried to use his daughter to arrange a date with him! Talk about an egomaniac! This guy took the prize as the most conceited, egotistical, vain man she'd ever had the displeasure of meeting. She wouldn't date him now if he were the last man on the face of the earth.

The phone rang and she frowned at it, then realized she was being ridiculous and picked up the receiver.

"Carrie?" Her name was whispered.

It was her stepfather, Jason Manning. "Yes?" she answered. "Is there a reason you're whispering?"

"I don't want your mother to hear me."

"Oh?" Despite her agitation with Philip Lark she grinned.

"I ordered Charlotte a Christmas gift this afternoon," he boasted. From years past, Carrie knew buying gifts didn't come naturally to Jason, since he'd been a confirmed bachelor until he met her mother. The first Christmas after they were married he'd bought Charlotte a bowling ball, season tickets to the Seattle Seahawks and a vacuum cleaner. After that, Carrie had steered him toward more personal things.

"You know how your mother likes to go to garage sales?"

"I'm not likely to forget." Jason had given her mother a lot of grief over her penchant to shop at yard sales. He liked to joke that Charlotte had found priceless pieces of Tupperware in her search for treasure.

"Well, a friend of mine started a limousine service and I hired him to escort your mother to yard sales on the Saturday of her choice. What do you think?" His voice rose in excitement. "She'll love it, won't she?"

"She will." Carrie couldn't keep from smiling. "She'll have the time of her life."

"I thought so," he said proudly. "Jeff's giving me a twenty-percent discount, too."

"I also think it's really sweet that you're taking Mom Christmas shopping in downtown Seattle on Saturday."

"Yeah, well, that's the price a man pays to please his wife." He didn't sound very enthusiastic.

"Doug and Dillon are coming to stay with me. We're baking cookies."

"I can't believe I'm voluntarily going Christmas shopping. There isn't another person in the world who could drag me into the city during the busiest shopping season of the year. Your mother's got to know I love her."

"She does know." Carrie had never doubted it, not from the first moment she'd seen her mother and Jason together. Rarely had any two people been more right for each other. While Jason might not be the most romantic man alive—she smiled whenever she recalled the look on her mother's face when she unwrapped that bowling ball—he was a devoted husband and father.

Jason Manning loved and nurtured Carrie as if she'd been his own child. A teenager couldn't have asked for a better stepdad. After some of the horror stories she'd heard from other girls in her situation, she appreciated him even more.

She heard a persistent pounding. "There's someone at my door," she told Jason.

"I'll let you go, then," he said. "Promise me you won't say anything to your mother."

"My lips are sealed." A limo to escort her to garage sales! Carrie smiled. She replaced the receiver and hurried across the living room to answer the door. It'd been a long day and a busy evening; she was hungry, tired and in no mood for company.

"Hi," Mackenzie said, her eyes wide. "So how'd it go with my dad?"

Carrie frowned.

"That bad, huh?" The girl laughed lightly. "Don't worry, it'll get better once he gets used to the idea of dating again."

"Mackenzie, listen, you and I need to talk about this. Your father's—"

"Sorry, I can't talk now. Dad doesn't know I'm gone, but I just wanted to say don't be discouraged. All he needs is time." She beamed her another wide smile. "This is going to be so great! Wait until Jane hears about how I found my dad a wife. Jane's my best friend. I'll see you Saturday." Having said that, she promptly disappeared.

Carrie closed the door and shut her eyes, feeling mildly guilty at what she'd started.

There was an abrupt knock at the door.

"Now what?" she demanded, her patience gone.

Madame Frederick smiled back at her. Arnold, muscles bulging in his upper arms, stood beside her. Both regarded her with open curiosity.

"Has she met him yet?" Arnold asked. "Has she met the man of her dreams—and do you know who it is?"

Madame Frederick's face glowed. "You can see for yourself." She lifted her crystal ball and ran her hand over the smooth glass surface. "One look should tell you."

But Carrie couldn't see anything at all.

FOUR

A thin layer of flour dusted her small kitchen. Carrie fanned her hand in front of her face in an effort to clear the air. The scent of baking gingerbread men drifted through the apartment, smelling of spices and fun.

Dillon stood on a chair, leaning over the electric mixer, watching intently as it stirred the cookie dough. Doug was at the counter, his sleeves up past his elbows, a rolling pin in his hand. Mackenzie used a spatula to scoop the freshly baked cookies from the baking sheet and placed them on the wire rack to cool.

"Do you think anyone will taste the eggshell?" she asked.

"The recipe said two eggs," Dillon muttered defensively, "and Carrie said the whole egg. How was I supposed to know she didn't mean the shell?"

"You just should," his older brother informed him with more than a hint of righteousness.

"I already said we don't need to worry about it." Carrie inserted, hoping to soothe Dillon's dented ego. She'd gotten most of the shell out and the remainder had been pulverized to the point that it was no longer distinguishable.

Mackenzie rolled her eyes expressively, but it was clear she was enjoying herself. More and more she reminded Carrie of herself eleven years earlier. She'd taken to Doug and Dillon immediately and they were equally enthralled with her. Within an hour they were the best of friends.

"I want to decorate the cookies, too," Dillon cried, when he saw that Carrie had finished making the frosting.

"You can't lick the knife," his older brother remarked snidely. "Not when we're giving the cookies to other people."

"There'll be plenty of frosting for everyone," Carrie reassured them.

"Who's going to taste the first gingerbread man?"

The three kids looked at one another. "Dillon should," Doug said.

"Okay." Her youngest brother squared his shoulders bravely. "I don't mind. Besides, Carrie said no one would be able to taste the eggshell, anyway." He climbed off the chair and reached for a cookie. "Maybe you should put a little frosting on, just in case," he said to Carrie.

She slathered some across the cookie and handed it back to him. Dillon closed his eyes and opened his mouth while the others waited for the outcome. One bite quickly became another.

"Maybe I should eat two just to make sure," the six-year-old told her.

Carrie winked and handed her youngest brother a second cookie, also slathered with frosting.

"I better try some, too," Doug said and grabbed one. He gobbled it up, head first, then nodded. "Not bad," he mumbled, his mouth full of cookie. "Even *without* the frosting."

"We're saving some for us, aren't we?" Dillon asked, reaching across the counter for the frosting knife.

"Of course, but I promised a plate to Arnold, Maria and Madame Frederick."

"Can I frost now?" Dillon asked, pulling the chair closer to the counter where Carrie stood.

"I want to decorate, too."

"Me, too," Mackenzie chimed in.

An hour later, Carrie was exhausted. Doug and Dillon finished drying the last of the dishes and threw themselves in front of the television to watch their favorite DVD. Carrie sat on a bar stool, her energy gone, while Mackenzie painstakingly added tiny red cinnamon candies to the cookie faces.

"Dad's late," she said with a knowing sigh as she formed a pair of candy lips, "but then he's always longer than he says he's going to be. He has no life, you know." She glanced up from her task to be sure Carrie was paying attention.

"We agreed," Carrie reminded the girl, wagging her index finger.

"I remember." Carrie had insisted Mackenzie keep Philip Lark out of the conversation. It seemed drastic, but was necessary, otherwise Mackenzie would use every opportunity to talk about her poor, lonely father, so desperate for female companionship that he was practically shriveling up before her eyes. Carrie could repeat the entire speech, verbatim.

It had taken the better part of two days to convince the girl that Carrie wasn't romantically interested in Philip, no matter how perfectly matched they appeared to be in Mackenzie's estimation.

Carrie suspected that Mackenzie was hearing much the same thing from her father. Philip wasn't thrilled with the idea of his daughter playing matchmaker any more than she was. In the three days since their first meeting, they'd made an effort to avoid seeing or talking to each other. The last thing Mackenzie needed was evidence that her plan was working.

"It's a real shame," Mackenzie said, eyeing her carefully. "Madame Frederick agrees with me and so do Arnold and Maria."

"Enough!" Carrie said, loudly enough to draw the boys' attention away from the TV screen.

When Mackenzie had finished decorating the last of the cookies, Carrie set them on three plastic plates, covered each with clear wrap and stuck a bright, frilly bow to the top.

"I want to deliver Arnold's," Doug told her. The oldest of her brothers had developed an interest in the former weight lifter. Arnold fit the stereotype. From his shiny bald head to his handlebar mustache and bulging muscles, everything about him said circus performer. Sometimes, as a concession to holidays or other special occasions, he even wore red spandex shorts over his blue tights. Doug was entranced.

"Will Maria let me pet her cats?" Dillon wanted to know.

"Of course she will."

"I guess that leaves me with Madame Frederick," Mackenzie said, not sounding disappointed. She cast a look toward the kitchen and Carrie guessed she wanted to make sure there'd be enough cookies left to take home to her father. Carrie had already made up a plate for the Larks, and told her so.

"Thanks," Mackenzie said, her eyes glowing.

All three disappeared, eager to deliver their gifts, and Carrie collapsed on the sofa. She rested her head against the cushion and closed her eyes, enjoying the peace and quiet. It didn't last long.

Doug barreled back in moments later, followed by Mackenzie. Dillon trailed behind.

"She's in here," Carrie heard her brother explain as he entered her apartment. Philip walked with him.

Carrie was immediately aware of how she must look. Flour had dusted more than the kitchen counters. She hadn't bothered with makeup that morning and had worn her grungiest jeans. She'd hardly ever felt more self-conscious in front of a man. She probably resembled a snowman—snow woman—only not so well dressed.

"Dad!" Mackenzie cried, delighted to see him.

Carrie stood and quickly removed the apron, certain the domestic look distracted from any slight air of sophistication she might still possess. Perhaps it was her imagination, but it seemed Philip's gaze zeroed in on her.

"I should've knocked," he said, and motioned to Dillon, "but your friend here insisted I come right in."

"Oh, that's fine." Each word seemed to stick to the roof of her mouth like paste. She clasped her hands together, remembering how uneasy her mother had been around Jason those first few times. Carrie had never understood that. Jason was the easiest person in the world to talk to.

Now she understood.

"Mackenzie behaved herself?" Once again the question was directed to Carrie.

"Dad!" Mackenzie burst out. "Way to embarrass me."

"She was a big help," Carrie assured him.

"Mom didn't call, did she?" Mackenzie advanced one step toward her father, her eyes hopeful.

Philip shook his head, and Carrie watched as disappointment settled over the girl. "She's really busy this time of year," Mackenzie explained to no one in particular. "I'm not surprised she didn't call, not with so much else on her mind... and everything."

Carrie resisted the urge to place her arm around Mackenzie's shoulders.

"How about a movie?" Philip suggested abruptly. "I can't remember the last time we went together."

"Really?" Mackenzie jerked her head up.

"Sure. Any one you want."

She mentioned the current Disney picture. "Can Doug and Dillon come, too?"

"Sure." Philip smiled affectionately at his daughter.

"And Carrie?"

"I...couldn't," she interjected before Philip could respond.

"Why not?" Doug asked. "You said we're all done with the cookies. A movie would be fun."

"You'd be welcome," Philip surprised her by adding. His eyes held hers and the offer appeared genuine. Apparently he felt that with three young chaperones, there wouldn't be a problem.

"You're positive?"

"Of course he is," Mackenzie said. "My father doesn't say things he doesn't mean, isn't that right, Dad?"

"Right." He sounded less confident this time.

Carrie was half tempted to let him take the kids on his own but changed her mind. Doug had a point; a movie would be a great way to relax after the hectic activity of the morning.

The five of them would be at the show together—and what could be more innocent? But the moment they entered the theater and had purchased their popcorn, the three kids promptly found seats several rows away from Philip and Carrie.

"But I thought we'd all sit together," Carrie said, loudly enough for Doug and Dillon to hear. Desperation echoed in her voice.

"That's for little kids," six-year-old Dillon turned around to inform her.

With the theater filling up fast, the option of sitting together soon disappeared. Carrie settled uneasily next to Philip. Neither spoke. He didn't seem any happier about this than she was.

"Do you want some popcorn?" Philip offered, tilting the overflowing bucket in her direction.

"No, thanks," she whispered, and glanced at her watch, wondering how much longer it would be before the movie started. "I certainly hope you don't think I arranged this," she whispered.

"Arranged what?"

"The two of us sitting together." She'd hate to have him accuse her of anything underhanded, which, given his apparent penchant for casting blame, he was likely to do. On the other hand, she was the one who'd unwittingly put the matchmaking notion in Mackenzie's head. What a fool she'd been not to realize the impressionable teenager would pick up on the ploy she'd used on her own mother.

"Why would I blame you?" he asked, sounding exasperated.

"Might I remind you of our last conversation?" she said stiffly. "You seemed to think there was some danger of me, uh, seducing you."

Philip laughed out loud and didn't look the least bit repentant. "It wasn't myself I was worried about," he explained. "I was afraid of Mackenzie making both our lives miserable. If I seemed rude earlier, I apologize, but I was protecting us from the wiles of my headstrong daughter."

That wasn't how Carrie remembered it…

"I'm not going to let my daughter do my courting for me," he said, as though that explained everything. "Now relax and enjoy the movie." He tilted the popcorn her way again, and this time Carrie helped herself.

The theater lights dimmed as twenty minutes of previews began.

Somewhat to Carrie's surprise, she loved the movie, which was an animated feature. She was soon completely immersed in the plot. Philip laughed in all the places she did and whatever tension existed between them melted away with their shared enjoyment.

When the movie ended, Carrie was sorry there wasn't more. While it was true that she'd enjoyed the story, she also found pleasure sitting with Philip. In fact, she liked him. She'd almost prefer to find something objectionable about him—a nervous habit, a personality trait she disliked, his attitude. *Something.* Anything that would distract from noticing how attractive he was.

He'd made it as plain as possible that he wasn't interested in a relationship with her. With anyone, if that was any comfort. It wasn't. She wanted him to be cold and standoffish, brusque and businesslike. The side of him she'd seen at the movie was laid-back and fun-loving. But she knew Philip hadn't developed a sudden desire to escort his daughter to the movies. He'd offered because of Mackenzie's disappointment over her mother's lack of sensitivity. He loved his daughter and wanted to protect her from the pain only a selfish parent could inflict on a child.

"This was a nice thing you did," she said as they exited the theater. The kids raced on ahead of them toward the parking lot. "It helped take Mackenzie's mind off not hearing from her mother."

"I'm not so sure it was a good idea," he muttered, dumping the empty popcorn container in the garbage can on their way out the door.

"Why not?"

He turned and stared at her. "Because I find myself liking you."

Her reaction must have shone in her eyes, because his own narrowed fractionally. "You felt it, too, didn't you?"

She wanted to lie. But she couldn't. "Yes," she whispered.

"I'm not right for you," he said.

"In other words, I'm wrong for you."

He didn't answer her for a long time. "I don't want to hurt you, Carrie."

"Don't worry," she answered brightly, "I won't let you."

FIVE

"What do you think?" Mackenzie proudly held up a crochet hook with a lopsided snowflake dangling from it. "Carrie's whole tree is decorated with snowflakes she crocheted," she added. "Her grandma Manning taught her to crochet when she was about my age." She wound the thread around her index finger and awkwardly manipulated the hook.

"It's lovely, sweetheart."

"Mom'll be pleased, won't she." Mackenzie turned the question into a statement, so certain was she of his response.

"She'll be thrilled." Philip's jaw tightened at the mention of Laura. His ex-wife had contacted Mackenzie and arranged a time for their daughter to visit her. Ever since she'd heard from her mother, Mackenzie had been walking five feet off the ground. Philip didn't know what he'd do if Laura didn't show. He wouldn't put it past her, but he prayed she wouldn't do anything so cruel.

"Carrie's been great," Mackenzie continued. "She taught me everything." She paused long enough to look up at him. "I like her so much, Dad."

The hint was there and it wasn't subtle. The problem was that

Philip had discovered that his feelings for Carrie were similar to those of his daughter. Although he avoided contact with Carrie, there was no escaping her. Mackenzie brought her name into every conversation, marching her virtues past him, one by one.

Carrie had become a real friend to Mackenzie. It used to be that his daughter moped about the apartment, complaining about missing her friends—although she spent plenty of time on the phone and the Internet with them—and generally making his life miserable. These days, if she wasn't with Carrie, she was helping Maria with her cats, having tea with Madame Frederick—and having the leaves read—or lifting weights with Arnold.

"I'm going to miss the Christmas party," she said matter-of-factly. "It's in the community room on Christmas Eve." She glanced up to be certain he was listening. "Everyone in the building's invited. Carrie's going, so is Madame Frederick and just everyone. It's going to be a blast." She sighed with heartfelt regret. "But being with Mom is more important than a party. She's really busy, you know," Mackenzie said, not for the first time.

"I'm sure she is," Philip muttered distractedly. He'd forgotten about the Christmas party. He'd received the notice a day or so earlier, and would've tossed it if Mackenzie hadn't gone into ecstasies when she saw it. From her reaction, one would think it was an invitation to the Christmas ball to meet a bachelor prince. As for him, he had better things to do than spend the evening with a group of friendly oddballs—and Carrie.

Philip reached for his car keys and his gym bag. "I'll only be gone an hour," he promised.

"It's okay. It'll take me that long to finish this." She looked up. "Oh, I almost forgot," she said, putting everything aside and leaping out of the chair as if propelled upward by a loose spring. She ran into her bedroom and returned a moment later with a small white envelope. "It's for you," she said, watching him eagerly. "Open it now, okay?"

"Shouldn't I wait until Christmas?"

"No." She gestured for him to tear open the envelope.

Inside was a card in the shape of a silver bell.

"Go ahead and read it," she urged, and would have done so herself if he hadn't acted promptly. The card was an invitation to lunch at the corner deli. "I'm buying," she insisted, "to thank you for being a great dad. We've had our differences this year and I want you to know that no matter what I say, I'll always love you."

"I feel the same way, and I don't tell you that enough," he murmured, touched by her words. "I'll be happy to pay for lunch."

"No way," she said. "I've saved my allowance and did a few odd jobs for Madame Frederick and Arnold. I can afford it, as long as you don't order the most expensive thing on the menu."

"I'll eat a big breakfast," he said and kissed her on the cheek before he walked out the door. He pushed the button for the elevator and caught himself grinning. He'd been doing a lot more of that lately. In the beginning he thought moving into the apartment had been a mistake. No longer. The changes in Mackenzie since meeting Carrie had been dramatic.

The elevator arrived and he stepped inside, pushing the button for the lobby. It stopped on the next floor and Carrie entered, carrying a laundry basket. She hesitated when she saw he was the only other occupant.

"I don't bite," he assured her.

"That's what they all say," she teased back. She reached across him and pushed the button for the basement, then stepped back. The doors closed sluggishly. Finally the elevator started to move, its descent slow and methodical, then it lurched sharply, dropping several feet.

Carrie gasped and staggered against the wall.

Philip maintained his balance by bracing his shoulder against the side. Everything went dark.

"Philip?" Carrie inquired a moment later.

"I'm here." It was more than dark, it was pitch-black inside. Even straining his eyes, he couldn't see a thing. "Looks like there's been a power outage."

"Oh, dear." Her voice sounded small.

"Are you afraid of the dark?"

"Of course not," she returned indignantly. "Well, maybe just a little. Everyone is— I mean, it wouldn't be unusual under these circumstances to experience some anxiety."

"Of course," he agreed politely, putting his gym bag down beside him.

"How long will it take for the power to come back on?"

"I don't know." He shrugged, although he realized she couldn't see him. "Give me your hand."

"Why?" she snapped.

"I thought it would comfort you."

"Oh. Here," she murmured, but of course he couldn't see it. He thrust his arm out and their hands collided. She gripped his like a lifeline tossed over the side of a boat. Her fingers were cold as ice.

"Hey, there's nothing to be afraid of."

"I *know* that," she responded defensively.

He wasn't entirely sure who moved first, but before another moment passed, he had his arm around her and was holding her protectively against him. He'd been thinking about this since the day they'd attended the movie. He hadn't allowed himself to dwell on the image, but it felt right to have her this close. More right than it should.

Neither spoke. He wasn't sure why; then again, he knew. For his own part, he didn't want reality interrupting his fantasy. Under the cover of the dark he could safely lower his guard. Carrie, he suspected, didn't speak for fear she'd reveal how truly frightened she was. Philip felt her tremble and welcomed the opportunity to bring her closer into his embrace.

"It won't be long."

"I hope so," she whispered back.

Without conscious thought, he wove his fingers into her hair. He loved the softness of it, the fresh, clean scent. He tried to concentrate on other things and found that he couldn't.

"Maybe we should talk," she suggested. "You know, to help pass the time."

"What do you want to talk about?" He could feel her breath against the side of his neck. Wistful and provocative. In that instant Philip knew he was going to kiss her. He was motivated by two equally strong impulses—need and curiosity. It'd been a long time since he'd held a woman. For longer than he wanted to remember, he'd kept any hint of desire tightly in check. He'd rather live a life of celibacy than risk another failed marriage.

He would've ended their embrace then and there if Carrie had offered any resistance. She didn't. Her lips were moist and warm. Welcoming. He moaned softly and she did, too.

"I thought you wanted to talk," she whispered.

"Later," he promised and kissed her again.

At first their kisses were light, intriguing, seductive. This wouldn't be happening if they weren't trapped in a dark elevator, Philip assured himself. He felt he should explain that, but couldn't stop kissing her long enough to form the words.

"Philip…"

He responded by brushing his moist lips against hers. His gut wrenched with sheer excitement at what they were doing.

Carrie wrapped her arms around his neck, clinging tightly. He eased her against the wall, kissing her ravenously.

That was when the lights came back on.

They both froze. It was as if they stood on a stage behind a curtain that was about to be raised, revealing them to a waiting audience.

But the electricity flashed off as quickly as it had come on.

Philip plastered himself against the wall, his hands loose at his sides as he struggled to deal with what they'd been doing. He wasn't a kid anymore, but he'd behaved like one—like a love-starved seventeen-year-old boy.

For the first time since his divorce, Philip felt the defenses around his heart begin to crack. The barriers had been fortified by his bitterness, by resentment, by fear. This—falling in love with Carrie—wasn't what he wanted. After the divorce, he'd vowed not to get involved again. Carrie was young and sweet and deserved a man who came without emotional scars and a child in tow.

He was grateful that the electricity hadn't returned; he needed these few additional minutes to compose himself.

"Are you all right?" he asked, when he could speak without betraying what he felt.

"I'm fine." Her voice contradicted her words. She sounded anything but.

He thought of apologizing, but he couldn't make himself say the words, afraid she'd guess the effect she'd had on him.

"You can't blame a guy for taking advantage of the dark, can you?" he asked, callously and deliberately making light of the exchange.

The electricity returned at precisely that moment. He squinted against the bright light. Carrie stood with her back against the wall opposite him, her fingers fanned out against the panel, her eyes stricken. The laundry basket rested in the far corner where she'd dropped it, clothing tumbled all around.

"Is that all this was to you?" she asked in a hurt whisper.

"Sure," he responded with a careless shrug. "Is it supposed to mean anything more?"

Before she could answer, the elevator stopped at the lobby floor and the doors opened. Philip was grateful for the chance to escape.

"Obviously not," she answered, but her eyes went blank and she stared past him. Then she leaned over and stabbed the basement button again. She crouched down to collect her laundry as he stepped out, clutching his gym bag.

He felt guilty and sad. He hadn't meant to hurt Carrie. She'd touched Mackenzie's life and his with her generosity of spirit.

Philip cursed himself for the fool he was.

"Go after her," a voice behind him advised.

Irritated, he turned to find Maria and Madame Frederick standing behind him.

"She's a good woman," Maria said, holding a fat calico cat on her arm, stroking its fur. "You won't find another like her."

"You could do worse." Madame Frederick chuckled. "The fact is, you already have."

"Would you two kindly stay out of my affairs?"

Both women looked taken aback by his gruff, cold response to their friendly advice.

"How rude!" the retired schoolteacher exclaimed.

"Never mind, dearie. Some men need more help than we can give them." Madame Frederick's words were pointed.

Disgusted with the two busybodies, and even more so with himself, Philip hurried out of the apartment building, determined that, from here on out, he was taking the stairs. Without exception.

SIX

"Did I ever tell you about Randolf?" Madame Frederick asked as she poured Carrie a cup of tea the next Saturday morning. "We met when I was a girl. All right, I was twenty, but a naive twenty. I knew the moment our eyes met that I should fear for my virtue." She paused, her hand holding the lid of the teapot in place, her eyes caught in the loving memory of forty years past. Laughing softly, she continued. "We were married within a week of meeting. We both knew we were meant to be together. It was useless to fight fate."

"He was your husband?" Although Madame Frederick had obviously loved him deeply, she rarely talked about her marriage.

"Yes." She sighed. "The man who stole my heart. We had thirty happy years together. We fought like cats and dogs and we loved each other. Oh, how we loved each other. One look from that man could curl my toes. He could say to me with one glance what would take three hundred pages in a book."

Carrie added sugar to her tea and stirred. Her hand trembled slightly as her mind drifted back to the kisses she'd shared with Philip in the elevator. She'd taken the stairs ever since.

She'd been kissed before, plenty of times, but it had never felt like it had with Philip. What unsettled her was how perfectly she understood what her neighbor was saying about Randolf.

"I didn't remarry after he died," Madame Frederick said as she slipped into the chair next to Carrie. "My heart wouldn't let me." She reached for her teacup. "Not many women are as fortunate as I am to have found a love so great, and at such a tender age."

Carrie sipped her tea and struggled to concentrate on Madame Frederick's words, although her thoughts were on Philip—and his kisses. She wanted to push the memories out of her mind, but they refused to leave.

"I wanted to give you your Christmas present early," Madame Frederick announced and set a small, wrapped package in her lap.

"I have something for you, too, but I was going to wait until Christmas."

"I want you to open yours now."

The older woman watched as Carrie untied the gold ribbon and peeled away the paper. Inside the box was a small glass bowl filled with dried herbs and flowers. Despite the cellophane covering, she could smell the concoction. Potpourri? The scent reminded her a bit of sage.

"It's a fertility potion," Madame Frederick explained.

"Fertility!" Carrie nearly dropped the delicate bowl.

"Brew these leaves as a tea and—"

"Madame Frederick, I have no intention of getting pregnant anytime soon!"

The woman smiled and said nothing.

"I appreciate the gesture, really I do." She didn't want her friend to think she wasn't grateful, but she had no plans to have a child within the foreseeable future. "I'm sure that at some point down the road I'll be brewing up this potion of yours." She took another drink of her tea and caught sight of the time.

"Oh, dear," she said, rising quickly to her feet. "I'm supposed to be somewhere in five minutes." Mackenzie had generously offered to buy her lunch as a Christmas gift. Philip's daughter had written the invitation on a lovely card shaped like a silver bell.

"Thank you again, Madame Frederick," she said, downing the last of the tea. She carefully tucked the unwrapped Christmas gift in her purse and reached for her coat.

"Come and visit me again soon," Madame Frederick said.

"I will," Carrie promised. She enjoyed her time with her neighbor, although she generally didn't understand how Madame chose their topics of conversation. Her reminiscences about her long-dead husband had seemed a bit odd, especially the comment about fearing for her virtue. It was almost as if Madame Frederick knew what she and Philip had been doing in the darkened elevator. Her cheeks went red as she remembered the way she'd responded to him. There was no telling what might have happened had the lights not come on when they did.

Carrie hurried out of the apartment and down the wind-blown street to the deli on the corner. It was lovely of Mackenzie to ask her to lunch and to create such a special invitation.

The deli, a neighborhood favorite, was busy. Inside, she was greeted by a variety of mouthwatering smells. Patrons lined up next to a glass counter that displayed sliced meats, cheeses and tempting salads. The refrigerator case was decorated with a plastic swag of evergreen, dotted with tiny red berries.

"Over here!" Carrie heard Mackenzie's shout and glanced across the room to see the teenager on her feet, waving. The kid had been smart enough to claim a table, otherwise they might've ended up having to wait.

Carrie gestured back and made her way between the tables and chairs to meet her. Not until she reached the back of the room did she realize that Mackenzie wasn't alone.

Philip sat with his daughter. His eyes revealed his shock at seeing Carrie there, as well.

"Oh, good, I was afraid you were going to be late," Mackenzie said, handing her a menu. "Tell me what you want, and I'll get in line and order it."

Briefly Carrie toyed with the idea of canceling, but that would've disappointed Mackenzie, which she didn't want to do. Philip had apparently reached the same conclusion.

"Remember I'm on a limited budget," Mackenzie reminded them, speaking loudly to be heard over the hustle and bustle of the deli. "But you don't have to order peanut butter and jelly, either."

"I'll take a pastrami on whole wheat, hold the pickle, extra mustard."

Carrie set her menu aside. "Make that two."

"You like pastrami, too?" Mackenzie asked, making it sound incredible that two people actually found the same kind of sandwich to their liking.

"You'd better go line up," Philip advised his daughter.

"Okay, I'll be back before you know it." She smiled before she left, expertly weaving between tables.

Carrie unwound the wool scarf from her neck and removed her jacket. She could be adult about this. While it was true that they hadn't expected to run into each other, she could cope.

The noise around them was almost deafening, but the silence between them seemed louder. When she couldn't stand it any longer, she said, "It's very sweet of Mackenzie to do this."

"Don't be fooled," he returned gruffly. "Mackenzie knew exactly what she was doing."

"And what was that?" Carrie hated to be defensive, but she didn't like his tone or his implication.

"She set this up so you and I would be forced to spend time together."

He made it sound like a fate worse than high taxes. "Come on, Philip, I'm not such a terrible person."

"As far as I'm concerned, that's the problem."

His words lifted her spirits. She took a bread stick from the tall glass in the middle of the table and broke it in half. "Are you suggesting I actually tempt you?" she asked.

"I wouldn't go that far, so don't flatter yourself."

"I'm not." She knew a bluff when she heard one. "If anyone should be flattered it's you. First, I'm at least eight years younger than you, with endless possibilities when it comes to finding myself a man. What makes you think I'd be interested in an ill-tempered, unfriendly, almost middle-aged grump?"

He blinked. "Ouch."

"Two can play *that* game, Philip."

"What game?"

"I almost believed you, you know. You were taking advantage of the dark? Really, you might've been a bit more original."

His eyes narrowed.

"But no one's that good an actor. You're attracted to me, but you're scared to let go of the rein you've got on your emotions. I'm not sure what your problem is, but my guess is that it has to do with your divorce. So be it. If you're content to spend the rest of your days alone, far be it from me to stop you." She took a bite of the bread stick, chomping down hard.

Mackenzie had their order. She carried the tray above her head as she reversed her previous journey among the tables. Her eyes were bright with excitement when she rejoined them.

She handed one thick ceramic plate to Carrie. "Pastrami on whole wheat, no pickle and extra mustard."

"Perfect," Carrie said, taking the plate from her. She was grateful Mackenzie had returned when she did, unsure she could continue her own bluff much longer. As it was, Philip had no opportunity to challenge her statement, which was exactly the way she wanted it.

Mackenzie distributed the rest of the sandwiches, set the tray aside and flopped down in the seat between Carrie and Philip. "Don't you just love the holidays?" she asked before biting into her sandwich.

Philip's eyes locked with Carrie's. "Sure do," he said, but Carrie saw that he was gritting his teeth.

From the way Philip tore into the sandwich, anyone would think he hadn't eaten in a week. It was as though they were taking part in a contest to see who'd finish first.

Philip won. The minute he swallowed the last bite, he stood, thanked his daughter and excused himself.

"He's going back to work," Mackenzie explained sadly as she watched her father leave. "He's *always* going back to the office."

"Inviting us both to lunch was very thoughtful of you," Carrie said, "but your father seems to think you asked us to suit your own purposes."

Mackenzie lowered her gaze. "All right, I did, but is that such a bad thing? I like you better than anyone. It's clear that my dad's never going to get married again without my help. My parents have been divorced for three years now and he's never even gone out on a real date."

"Mackenzie, your father needs time."

"Time? He's had more than enough time! He can't keep going through life like this. He's put everything on hold while he tries to forget what my mother did. I want him to marry you."

"Mackenzie!" Carrie exhaled sharply. She couldn't allow the girl to believe that dealing with human emotions was this simple. "I can't marry your father just because you want me to."

"Don't you like him?"

"Yes, I do, very much, but there's so much more to marriage than me liking your father."

"But he cares about you. I know he does, only he's afraid to let it show."

Carrie had already guessed as much, but that could be because she wanted to believe it so badly.

"My mom is really pretty," Mackenzie said, and she lowered her gaze to her hands, which clutched a paper napkin. "I think she might've been disappointed that I look more like my dad's side of the family than hers. She's never said anything, but I had the feeling maybe she would've stayed married to my dad if I'd been prettier."

"I'm sure that isn't true." Carrie's heart ached at the pain she heard in the girl's voice. "I used to feel those kinds of things, too. My dad never wanted anything to do with me. He never wrote or sent me a birthday gift or remembered me at Christmas, and I was convinced it was something I must have done."

Mackenzie raised her eyes. "But you were a little kid when your parents divorced."

"It didn't matter. I felt that somehow I was the one to blame. But it didn't have anything to do with me. And your parents didn't divorce because you took after your father's side of the family. Your parents' problems had nothing to do with you."

Mackenzie didn't say anything for a long moment. "This is why I want you to marry my dad. You make me feel better. In the past couple weeks you've been more of a mom to me than my real mother ever was."

Carrie reached out and silently squeezed Mackenzie's hand.

The girl squeezed back. "I didn't mention it last Saturday, but that was the first time I've ever baked homemade cookies. Dad helped me bake a cake once, but it came in a box."

Carrie had suspected as much.

"I like the way we can sit down and talk. You seem to understand what's in my heart," Mackenzie murmured. "I'm probably the only girl in my school who knows how to crochet, even though all I can do is those snowflakes. You taught me that. The house is going to be finished soon, and Dad and I are going to move away. I'm afraid that if you don't marry my dad, I'll never see you again. Won't you please, please marry my dad?"

"Oh, sweetheart," Carrie whispered and wrapped her arm around the girl's neck. She leaned forward, resting her forehead on Mackenzie's head. "It isn't as simple as that. Couldn't I just be your friend?"

Mackenzie sniffled and nodded. "Will you come visit me when we move?"

"You bet."

"But Madame Frederick says my dad's going to meet someone and—"

Carrie groaned inwardly. "Madame Frederick means well, and she's a dear, dear person, but I'm going to tell you something that's just between you and me."

"Okay." Mackenzie stared at her intently.

"Madame Frederick can't really see anything in that crystal ball of hers."

"But—"

"I know. She says what she thinks *should* happen or what she *hopes* will happen, and in doing so puts the idea in people's minds. If her predictions come true, it's because those people have steered the course of their lives in the direction she pointed."

"But she seems so sure of things."

"Her confidence is all part of the act."

"In other words," Mackenzie said after a thoughtful moment, "I shouldn't believe anything she tells me."

SEVEN

If Carrie hadn't seen it with her own eyes—and dozens of times at that—she wouldn't have believed any two boys could be so much like their father. Doug and Dillon sat on the sofa next to Jason, watching the Seahawks football game. Three pairs of feet, each clothed in white socks, were braced on the coffee table, crossed at the ankles. Jason had the remote control at his side, a bowl of popcorn in his lap. Each one of his sons held a smaller bowl. So intent were they on the hotly contested play-off game that they gave Carrie little more than a hurried nod of acknowledgment.

The sight of Jason with his sons never ceased to amaze her. The boys were all Manning, too. Smaller versions of their father in both looks and temperament.

Carrie found her mother in the kitchen, whipping up a batch of fudge for the Manning family pre-Christmas get-together. "Carrie, this is a pleasant surprise." Charlotte's face relaxed into a smile when she saw her daughter.

"I came for some motherly advice," Carrie admitted, seeing no need to tiptoe around the reason for her impromptu visit. She'd left Mackenzie less than an hour before and hadn't been able to stop thinking about their conversation, or about Philip's reaction to her being there. It was as though he couldn't escape fast enough.

"What's up?" Charlotte stirred the melted chocolate.

Carrie pulled a padded stool over to the countertop where her mother was working. "I'm afraid I'm falling in love."

"Afraid?"

"Yes." She'd purposely chosen that word. That was exactly the way she felt about it.

"This wouldn't have anything to do with your friend Mackenzie, would it?"

Carrie nodded, surprised her mother even knew about the thirteen-year-old girl. But the boys must have said something. "Do you remember how it was when you first started dating Jason?" she asked.

Her mother paused and a hint of a smile lifted the edges of her mouth. "I'm not likely to forget. I wasn't sure I wanted anything to do with the man, while you were busy inventing excuses to throw us together."

"You really weren't interested in him at first?"

Charlotte chuckled softly. "That's putting it mildly, but gradually he won me over. He was endlessly patient..."

Carrie realized there was a lot more that her mother wasn't telling her. She'd long suspected that in the early days, her mother's relationship with Jason had been anything but smooth.

Charlotte resumed stirring. "As I said, his patience won me over. His patience and his drop-dead kisses," she amended. "If ever a man had a talent for kissing, it's your stepfather." She grinned shyly and looked away.

"Philip has the same gift," Carrie whispered, feeling a bit shy about sharing this aspect of their relationship with her mother.

Charlotte didn't say anything for a long moment. "So you've been seeing Mackenzie's father."

"Not as much as I'd like," she said. "He's been divorced for three years and according to Mackenzie he hasn't gone out on a single date." She assumed that well-meaning friends had tried to set him up. His own daughter had made the effort, too. With Carrie.

"So he comes with a load of emotional trauma. Has he ever talked about what went wrong in his marriage?"

"No." Carrie hated to admit how little time they'd spent together. Feeding Maria's homeless cats was as close as they'd come to an actual date. She wasn't sure how to measure the time in the elevator. Although she'd managed to make him think his callous attitude afterward hadn't fooled her, in truth she didn't know what his reaction had been.

"You're afraid he's coming to mean more to you than is sensible, after so short an acquaintance."

"Exactly. But, Mom, he's constantly on my mind. I go to bed at night, close my eyes and he's there. I get up in the morning and take the bus to the office and all I can think about is him."

"He's attracted to you?"

"I think so... I don't know anymore. My guess is that he is, but he's fighting it. He doesn't *want* to care for me. He'd rather I lived across the city—or the country—than in the same building with him. We try to avoid each other—we probably wouldn't see each other at all if it wasn't for Mackenzie. The girl's made it her mission in life to make sure we do."

Charlotte dumped the warm fudge into a buttered cookie sheet. "This is beginning to sound familiar."

"In what way?"

Charlotte giggled. "Oh, Carrie, how soon you forget. You're the one who pushed, pulled and shoved me into a relationship with Jason. It would've been horrible if he was a different kind of man. But he was patient and nonthreatening. Like Philip, I came into the relationship with more than my share of emotional trauma. But he was exactly the man I needed. You've always been a sensitive, intuitive child. Out of all the men you might have picked for me, you chose the one man who possessed the qualities I needed most." She reached over and stroked the side of Carrie's face, her expression warm and tender. "In my heart of hearts, I'm confident you've done the same thing for yourself. Philip needs you just as much as I needed Jason. Be patient with him, Carrie. Your heart—and your ego—may take a few jabs before this is finished. Be prepared for that, but don't be afraid to love him. Mackenzie, too. I promise you, it'll be worth the wait."

How wise her mother was, Carrie mused as she left the family home. How wise and wonderful. Not for the first time, Carrie was grateful for a mother she could talk to, a mother she could confide in, a mother who didn't judge, but listened and advised.

"What are you doing here?" Gene Tarkington asked, stepping into Philip's office. He leaned against the doorjamb, striking a relaxed pose. The entire floor was empty. Row upon row of desks stretched across the floor outside his office.

"I thought I'd come in and run these figures one last time," Philip murmured, staring at the computer screen. Although he considered Gene one of his best friends, he'd prefer to be alone just then.

"Hey, buddy, it's almost Christmas. Haven't you got anything better to do than stop by the office?"

"What about you?" Philip challenged. He wasn't the only workaholic in this company.

"I came to get some papers and saw the light on in your office. I thought you were having lunch with Mackenzie this afternoon. A little father-daughter tête-à-tête. That kid's a real sweetheart."

"We had our lunch," Philip muttered, "but it turns out I wasn't the only one Mackenzie invited."

"You mean she brought along that neighbor friend of yours? The woman who works for Microsoft?"

"That's her." Philip frowned anew, remembering how upset he'd been when he discovered what Mackenzie had done. From the way she'd acted, he should've guessed she'd try something like this. What distressed him even more was the way his heart had responded when Carrie walked into the deli. The joy and excitement he'd felt...

But he didn't want to feel these things for her. It'd taken effort to steel himself against those very emotions. He'd been burned once, badly enough to know better than to play with fire. Carrie Weston wasn't some little innocent, either. Every time he was with her, he felt as if he was holding a book of matches.

"Mackenzie's pretty levelheaded. What have you got against this neighbor woman? She's not ugly, is she?"

"No." He recalled what a shock it was when he realized how lovely Carrie was.

"If you want my opinion, I'd say count your blessings. Generally, the divorced guys I know would welcome a woman their daughters like. Remember what happened to Cal? His daughter and second wife hate each other. Any time they're out together, Cal has to keep them from coming to blows."

"I'm not Cal."

"It seems to me that if your daughter's that keen on this neighbor, you should take the time to find out what she likes so much. I'm no expert on women or romance, but—"

"My thoughts exactly," Philip said pointedly. He'd come to the office to escape Carrie, not to have her name thrown in his face. "I appreciate what you're trying to do."

Gene rubbed the side of his face. "I doubt that. But I hate to see you wasting time in this office when Christmas is only a few days away. If you want to hide, there are better places than here."

Although Gene's tone was friendly enough, the words made Philip's jaw tighten. It was all he could do to keep from blaming his friend for his troubles. Gene owned the apartment complex, and it was because of him that Philip and Mackenzie were living there.

"Well, I've got to get back to the car. Marilyn's waiting. You know how it is the last weekend before Christmas. The malls are a madhouse and naturally my wife thinks this is the perfect time to finish the shopping. She wouldn't dream of going alone. I told her there should be a Husband of the Year award in this for me," he said, and chuckled. "But she promised me another kind of reward." From the contented, anticipatory look on his friend's face, one would think Gene was headed for the final game of the World Series, not a shopping mall.

"See you later," Philip said.

"Later," Gene returned. "Just promise me you won't stay here long."

"I won't."

Gene left, and the office had never seemed emptier. The place seemed to echo with loneliness, a constant reminder that Philip was by himself. His friend was right; it was almost Christmas, yet he was at the office hiding. While Gene was out fighting the Christmas crowds with his wife, Philip had crept in here, the way he always did whenever life threatened to offer him something he couldn't handle. Even a gift.

Because that was what Gene had more or less told him Carrie was. A woman Mackenzie not only liked, but championed. Like Gene, lots of guys would advise him to count his blessings. But instead of thanking his daughter for lunch, he'd chastised her for using it as an opportunity to get him together with Carrie.

Carrie.

Every time he thought of her, a chill raced through his blood. No, that wasn't it. His blood didn't go *cold*, it heated up. Carrie was charming, generous, delightful, kind—and more of a mother to his daughter than her own had ever been.

Philip rolled his chair away from his desk, stood and walked over to the large picture window. The view of downtown Seattle and Puget Sound was spectacular from his twentieth-story viewpoint. Breathtaking. The waterfront, the ferry dock, Pike Place Market, all alive with activity. Philip couldn't count the number of times he'd stood exactly where he was now and looked out and seen nothing, felt nothing.

He went back to his desk and turned off his computer, feeling more confused than when he'd arrived. It was a sad day, he thought wryly, when he was reduced to accepting his thirteen-year-old daughter's advice, but in this case, Mackenzie was right. She'd told him to get a life. Instead, Philip had dug himself deeper into his rut, fearing that any life he got would include putting the past behind him. It wasn't that the past held any allure for him. The reverse, in fact. He'd married too young, unwisely. He was terrified of repeating the same mistake. Terrified of what that would do to him—and Mackenzie.

Locking up, Philip went back to the apartment building. He parked in the garage across the street and was just walking toward the entrance when he saw Carrie. There was a natural buoyancy to her step, a joy that radiated from inside her. He sometimes wondered what she had to be so happy about. That no longer concerned him, because he wanted whatever it was.

"Carrie!" Unsure what he'd say when he caught up with her, Philip hurried across the street.

Carrie paused midway up the steps and turned around. Some of the happiness left her eyes when she saw him. She waited until he'd reached her before she spoke. "I had no idea Mackenzie had invited us both to lunch," she told him.

"I know that," he said, regretting his angry mood earlier.

"You do?"

Every time he saw her it was a shock to realize how beautiful she was. Her intense blue eyes cut straight through him. "I was wondering… I know it's last-minute and you've probably got other plans, but…" He paused. "Would you go Christmas shopping with me?" He was afraid that if he invited her to dinner or a movie she'd turn him down and he wouldn't blame her. "For Mackenzie," he said, adding incentive. "I could do with a few suggestions."

His invitation had apparently taken her by surprise because she frowned at him before asking, "When?"

"Is now convenient?" he asked hopefully. He was as crazy as his friend Gene to even consider going shopping today.

"Now," she repeated, then smiled, that soft, sweet smile of hers. "Okay."

Okay. It was crazy how one small word could produce such exhilaration. If this were the theater, he'd break into song about now. A Christmas carol maybe—something like "Joy to the World."

She walked down the three or four steps to join him on the sidewalk. That little bounce of hers was back. The bounce that said she was glad to be alive and glad to be with him.

He was the one who should be grateful, Philip thought. He tucked her arm in his and led her back to the parking garage.

Life was good. It had been a long time since he'd believed that, but he did now.

EIGHT

A few hours earlier, Carrie had been telling her mother that she barely knew Philip Lark and now she doubted there was any man she knew better. They sat in an Italian restaurant, Christmas packages around their feet, and talked until it seemed there was nothing more to say. Their dinner dishes had long since been removed and Philip poured the last of the red wine into her goblet.

The room swayed gently from side to side, but her light-headedness wasn't due to the pinot noir. Philip was the reason. He'd told her things she'd felt it would take him months if not years to reveal. He'd spoken of his marriage and his feelings about fatherhood. She listened, a lump in her throat, as he heaped the blame for the failure of his marriage on his own shoulders. She doubted very much that he was entirely responsible, but she admired his gallantry.

"You're friends with Laura?" she asked at one point.

"Yes. Beyond anything else, she's Mackenzie's mother. I made mistakes in this marriage, but my daughter wasn't one of them. I'll always be grateful to my ex-wife for Mackenzie."

Tears formed in the corners of Carrie's eyes at the sincerity with which he spoke. How easy it would be for him to blame his ex-wife for all their problems. Carrie was sympathetic to his side, and knew from things Mackenzie had told her that Laura wasn't exactly a loving or attentive mother. Carrie suspected she hadn't been much of a wife, either.

"What are you doing tomorrow?" Philip asked unexpectedly.

"Sunday." Carrie propped her elbows on the white linen tablecloth. "The Mannings are getting together. Mom and I married into this large, wonderful family. Jason has four brothers and sisters. There are so many grandchildren these days it's difficult to keep track of who belongs to whom. Why don't you and Mackenzie come along and meet everyone?" Carrie couldn't believe she'd impulsively tossed out the invitation. While she did want him to attend, there'd certainly be speculation...

"You're sure?"

"Positive. Just... Never mind," she said, stopping herself. Her gaze held his. "It would mean a great deal to me if you'd come."

"Then we will." He reached for her hand with both of his.

Philip had given up the effort of remembering everyone's names. He'd cataloged the first ten or so relatives Carrie had introduced him to, but the others became lost in the maze.

Mackenzie had disappeared almost the minute they arrived. Doug and Dillon had greeted him cheerfully and then quickly vanished with his daughter. Holding a cup of eggnog, Philip found himself a quiet corner.

From this vantage point, he watched Carrie interact with her family. His eyes followed her as she moved across the room, apparently to find her mother so she could introduce her parents to Philip. He couldn't take his eyes off Carrie. Her face was flushed with happiness, her eyes glowing with excitement.

She'd married into this family, but it was clear they thought of her as one of their own.

"Do you mind if I join you?" a woman unexpectedly asked him.

"Please do." He stood to offer her his seat.

"No, no. Sit down, please. I can only stay a moment. You're Philip, aren't you?"

"Yes. Philip Lark." The dark-haired beauty had to be Carrie's mother. "You're Charlotte Manning?"

"How perceptive of you. Yes." She held out her hand, which he shook.

He was astonished that he hadn't recognized the resemblance sooner. Charlotte and Carrie had the same intense blue eyes, the same joyous energy and a gentleness of spirit that was unmistakable.

They spoke for a few minutes about unimportant matters. Small talk. Although Philip had the impression he was being checked out, he also had the feeling that he'd passed muster. He liked Charlotte, which made sense, since he definitely liked Carrie.

"So this is Carrie's young man." Charlotte's husband, Jason Manning, joined his wife and slipped his arm around her waist. "Welcome. Where's Carrie? She's left you to fend for yourself?"

"I gather she went in search of you two."

The three of them spoke for a while before Jason glanced over his shoulder and called out, "Paul, come and meet Carrie's friend."

Soon a large group had gathered around Philip, more faces than he could ever remember. He stood and shook hands with Carrie's two uncles. Once again he felt their scrutiny.

Soon a loud, "Ho, ho, ho," could be heard in the background. Jason's father had donned a Santa suit and now paraded into the room, a bag of gifts swung over his shoulder. The children let out cries of glee and crowded around Santa.

Philip was grateful that everyone had begun to watch the scene taking place with Santa Claus. He sat down in his chair again and relaxed, grateful not to be the center of attention. Soon Carrie was with him. She sat on the arm and cast him an apologetic look.

"Sorry, I got sidetracked."

"So I saw." He patted her hand. "I met your stepfather and two uncles."

"Aren't they great?" Her eyes gleamed with pride.

"I need a degree in math to keep track of who's married to whom."

"Don't worry, it'll come. Be thankful not everyone's here."

"You mean there are even more?"

Carrie grinned and nodded. "Taylor and Christy both live in Montana. Between them they have six children."

"My goodness." Adding ten more names to his list would have overwhelmed him. "Mackenzie certainly seems to fit right in."

"Doug and Dillon think she's the best thing since cookie-dough ice cream. Knowing her gives them the edge over their cousins."

While the youngsters gathered around their grandfather in his red suit, Mackenzie made her way toward him and Carrie. Philip understood. At thirteen she was too old to mingle with the kids who believed in Santa Claus, and too young not to be caught up in the excitement, even though Santa wouldn't have a gift for her.

"Are you having fun?" Philip whispered when she sat down on the chair's other arm, across from Carrie.

"This is so great," she whispered. "I didn't know families could get this big. Everyone's so friendly."

Santa dug deep into his bag, produced a package and called out the name. Doug leaped to his feet and raced forward as if he had only a limited amount of time to collect his prize.

Santa reached inside his bag again and removed another gift. "What's this?" he asked, lowering his glasses to read the tag. "This is for someone named Mackenzie Lark. I do hope Mrs. Claus didn't mix up the gifts with those of another family."

"Mackenzie's here!" Dillon shouted. He stood and pointed toward Philip and Carrie.

"Me?" Mackenzie slid off the chair. "There's a gift in there for *me?*"

"If your name's Mackenzie, then I'd say this present is for you."

His daughter didn't need a second invitation. She hurried over to Santa, as eager as Doug had been.

Philip's questioning gaze sought out Carrie's. "I'm sure my mother's responsible for this," she told him.

"I met her," he said. "We talked briefly."

Carrie's eyes widened. "What did she have to say?"

"She was very pleasant. It was your stepfather who put the fear of God into me."

"Jason? Oh, dear. Listen, whatever he said, disregard it. He means well and I love him to death, but half the time he's thinking about sports statistics and he doesn't know what he's saying."

Philip smiled. He'd never seen Carrie more unnerved. Even when they were trapped in the elevator, she'd displayed more composure than this.

"Carrie, good grief, what do you think he said?"

She clamped her mouth shut. "I—I'm not sure, but it would be just like him to suggest you take the plunge and marry me."

"Oh, that, well…"

"Are you telling me he actually—"

Philip had to make an effort not to laugh out loud. "He didn't, so don't worry about it."

Mackenzie had claimed her gift and was walking back, clutching the package in both hands.

"You can open it," Carrie assured her.

"Now?" She tore into the wrapping as though she couldn't

wait a second longer. Inside was an elegant vanity mirror with a brush and comb set. "It's perfect," she whispered, holding the brush and comb against her. "I've always wanted one of these sets. It's so...so feminine."

"How'd your family know?" Philip asked. He'd never have thought to buy something like this for his daughter.

"I have one," Carrie whispered. "She's used it a number of times."

"Oh." More and more he felt inadequate when it came to understanding his daughter. She was in that awkward stage, and it was difficult to know exactly where her interests lay. Half the time she talked about wanting a horse and ballet lessons; the rest of the time she listened to music he'd never heard before and gossiped about celebrities who seemed completely irrelevant to him. Part girl, part woman, Mackenzie traveled uneasily from one desire to the next. It wasn't just her interests that confused him, either. One minute she'd be her lighthearted self and the next she'd be in tears over something he considered trivial. He wished Laura had taken more interest in her. Often he felt at a loss in dealing with Mackenzie's frequent mood swings.

Philip had enjoyed himself, but he was exhausted and felt relieved when the party ended. He thanked the elder Mannings for having him and Mackenzie.

"You're welcome anytime," Elizabeth Manning said, clasping his hand between both of her own. In what seemed an impulsive gesture, she leaned forward and kissed his cheek. "You'd be a welcome addition to our family," she whispered in his ear. "Just promise me one thing?"

"What's that?" he asked.

"I want a nice, big wedding," she said, this time loudly enough for half the room to hear.

Philip heard a murmur of approval behind him. "Ah..."

"Thanks again, Grandma," Carrie said, saving him from having to come up with a response.

Carrie hugged the older couple and led the way outside. Jason, Charlotte, Doug and Dillon followed them to the driveway for a second round of hugs and farewells. This had to be one of the most outwardly affectionate families Philip had ever met, but it didn't bother him. The opposite, in fact. He liked everything about them. These were good people, hardworking and family-oriented. He'd never seen himself in that light, although it was what he wanted to be. However, neither he nor Laura had been raised that way.

They sang Christmas carols on the drive home. Carrie's voice blended smoothly with that of his daughter. His own was a bit rough from disuse and slightly off-key, but no one seemed to mind, least of all Mackenzie, whose happiness spilled over like fizz in a soda bottle. He parked in the garage and they walked across the street to the apartment building, still laughing and chattering excitedly.

"I had a wonderful time," his daughter told Carrie, hugging her close as they waited for the elevator.

"I did, too."

"I'm so glad your family get-together was tonight instead of tomorrow. I'll be with my mother, you know."

"I do," Carrie said. "You'll miss the party here, but I'll tell you all about it."

"Do you think Madame Frederick will made a prediction for me, even if I'm not there?"

"I'm sure she will," Carrie answered.

"She'll have to make one for me in absentia, as well," Philip said.

"You aren't coming?" This news appeared to catch Carrie by surprise. She'd asked him about the Christmas party earlier and he'd managed to avoid answering one way or the other.

"No," he said, pushing the button to close the elevator door.

"But I thought… I hoped…" Her disappointment was evident.

Philip didn't want to say anything negative, but as far as he was concerned, the majority of people living in the building complex were oddballs and eccentrics. He didn't have anything against them, but he didn't want to socialize with them, either.

"Talk him into it," Mackenzie said when the elevator stopped on Carrie's floor.

He wished now that he hadn't said anything. "Would you like a cup of coffee?" Carrie asked.

What he'd like was time alone with Carrie.

"Sure he would," Mackenzie answered for him, and shoved him out of the elevator. The doors closed before he could respond.

"I guess I would," he said, chuckling.

Carrie's eyes shyly met his. "I was hoping you would."

She unlocked her door and walked inside, but he stopped her from turning on the light. With his hand at her shoulder, he guided her into his arms. "I've been waiting for this all night," he whispered and claimed her lips.

He meant it to be a soft, gentle kiss. One that would tell her he'd enjoyed her company, enjoyed their evening together. But the minute his mouth settled over hers he experienced a desire so strong it was all he could do to keep it in check. No woman had ever affected him like this. He wove his fingers into her hair and tilted her head to one side in order to deepen their kisses.

She groaned softly. Then again, it could be the sound of his own pleasure that rang in his ears. The hot, breathless kisses went on. And on...

"Why won't you come to the party tomorrow night?" she asked minutes later.

The building's Christmas party was the last thing on Philip's mind. He led her through the darkened living room, sat down and drew her into his lap. "Let's talk about that later, all right?" He didn't give her time to say anything, but directed her lips back to his.

"Why later?" She nibbled the side of his neck, sending delicious shivers down his back.

"I'm not sure I trust Madame Frederick."

She laughed and he felt her breath against his skin. "She's completely harmless."

"So they say." He placed his hands on either side of her face and brought her lips down to meet his again. The kiss was long and deep, and it left him breathless.

"The people in this building are a bunch of oddballs. Half of them are candidates for the loony bin," he said when he'd recovered sufficiently to speak.

Carrie stiffened in his arms. "You're talking about my friends."

"No offense," he said. But surely she recognized the truth when she heard it.

Carrie squirmed out of his lap and stood in front of him. "I live in this apartment complex. Is that how you think about me?"

"No." He sighed. "If it means so much to you, I'll attend this ridiculous party."

"No, thanks," she muttered. "I wouldn't want you to do me any favors."

From her tone of voice, Philip realized he'd managed to offend her, which he regretted. Yesterday's conversation with Gene had made him understand that she was a blessing in his life. A gift.

A gift he wanted to accept...

"Carrie, I'm sorry. I spoke out of turn."

"Is that what you really think of us, Philip?" she asked, her voice uncertain.

He didn't respond right away, afraid anything more he said would only make things worse.

"That's answer enough. I'm tired... I'd like you to leave now."

"Carrie, for heaven's sake, be reasonable."

She stalked over to the door and opened it, sending a harsh shaft of light across his face. Philip squinted and did as she asked. "We'll talk about this later, all right?"

"Sure," she said in a sarcastic murmur.

Rather than wait for the elevator, Philip took the stairs to his apartment a floor above Carrie's. He'd discuss this with Mackenzie, get her advice on how to handle it. Ironic that he was turning to his thirteen-year-old daughter for help with the very situation she'd engineered...

The apartment was dark and silent when he entered. He switched on the light and walked down the hall to Mackenzie's bedroom. Her bed was slightly mussed as if she'd sat on it.

"Mackenzie!" he called.

No response.

He checked the other rooms and found a note from her on the kitchen table.

Dad,
Mom left me a message. She said she wouldn't be coming for me, after all, and that I couldn't spend the holidays with her. I guess I should've known she'd be too busy for me. She has time for everything else but me. I need some time alone to think.

Mackenzie

NINE

Carrie didn't understand why Philip's comment about Madame Frederick and the others had distressed her so much. While it was true they were her friends, she couldn't deny that they *were* all a bit weird. But they were also affectionate, warmhearted people and it hurt to have Philip dismiss them with such carelessness. She was still figuring out her feelings when there was a knock at the door. Whoever it was seemed impatient, because there was another knock immediately afterward.

"Just a moment," she called out.

To her surprise it was Philip. "Have you seen Mackenzie?" he demanded.

"Not since we returned from the party."

He exhaled and rubbed his hand along the back of his neck. "Her mother left a message for her saying she won't be bringing Mackenzie to her place for Christmas after all," he explained.

Carrie saw a muscle beside his jaw jerk with the effort it took to control his anger.

"She was looking forward to spending Christmas with Laura," he continued. "It was all Mackenzie could talk about."

Carrie knew that. She'd spent time with the girl, discussing her hairstyle and wardrobe for the impending visit. Mackenzie had wanted everything to be perfect for her mother. She'd wanted to impress Laura with how grown-up she was, how stylish. She'd wanted to make herself as attractive as possible, hoping her mother would notice and approve.

"Mackenzie wrote me a note that said she needed time alone." He checked his watch, something Carrie knew he'd probably done every five minutes since discovering the note. "That was an hour ago. Where on earth would she go?"

"I don't know," Carrie whispered. Her heart constricted as she imagined the pain the girl must be suffering. These few days with Laura had meant so much to Mackenzie.

"I thought maybe she'd come to you." He shook his head. "I've tried her cell, but it's off. I've called her girlfriends, but none of them have heard from her. Now I don't know where to look. Think, Carrie."

"She probably doesn't want to be around people just yet," she murmured, trying to clear her head of worry and fear in order to be of help.

Philip nodded. "Do you think she went for a walk? Alone in the dark?" He cringed as he said the words.

"I'll go out with you to look."

His eyes told her he was grateful. Carrie grabbed her coat and purse, and they both rushed out of the building.

Soon after she'd graduated from high school, when Carrie was eighteen, she'd decided to seek out her father. It had been a mistake. He'd seemed to think she wanted something from him, and in retrospect, she knew she had. She'd wanted him to love her, wanted him to tell her how proud he was of the woman she'd become. It had taken her the better part of a year to realize that Tom Weston was selfish and immature and incapable of giving her anything. Even his approval.

In the five years she'd known Jason Manning, at that point, he'd been far more of a father than her biological one would ever know how to be. She hadn't had any contact with Tom Weston since. It had hurt that the man responsible for her birth wanted nothing to do with her, but after a few months she'd accepted his decision. If anything, she appreciated his honesty, hurtful as it'd been at the time.

Not really knowing where they were going, they walked quickly from one spot to another, trying to guess where Mackenzie might have gone. Their fears mounted, but they both struggled to hide them. Instead, they offered each other reassurances neither believed.

"I hate to think of her out in the cold, alone and in pain," Philip finally murmured, his hands in his coat pockets.

"Me, too." The cold air stung her cheeks.

"I could hate Laura for doing this to her," Philip said defiantly, "but I refuse to waste the energy. She can treat me any way she pleases, but not Mackenzie."

Carrie knew it was pointless to remind him that he had no control over his ex-wife. Laura would behave as she chose.

"Perhaps I should've said something to Mackenzie," Philip was saying, "warned her not to count on anything her mother promised. I didn't because, well, because I didn't want Mackenzie to think I'd try to influence how she thinks about her mother."

"I find that admirable. And wise."

"I don't feel either of those things just now." His voice revealed his anger and frustration.

"Mackenzie's smart enough to figure out what her mother's really like. She won't need you or me to tell her," Carrie said.

His eyes met hers under a streetlamp decorated with silver bells. "I hope you're right."

They searched everywhere they could think of, without success. By the time they returned home, it was almost midnight. The building was dark and silent, alarming them even more.

"You don't think she'd do anything stupid, do you?" a worried Philip asked. "Like run away and find her mother on her own?"

"I...don't know."

When they stepped into the lobby, Carrie noticed that the door leading to the basement party room was open. As she came closer, she could hear voices below.

"Let's check it out," Philip suggested.

Carrie followed him down the stairs. As they descended, the sound of voices became more distinct. She recognized Madame Frederick, chatting away with Arnold. Carrie guessed they were putting the finishing touches on the decorations for the Christmas party, which was to take place the following night.

They found Mackenzie busy pinning green and red streamers in the center of the ceiling, fanning them out to the corners. The girl didn't so much as blink when she saw Carrie and Philip.

"Oh, hi, Dad. Hi, Carrie," she said, climbing down from her chair.

"Just where have you been, young lady?" Philip demanded gruffly.

Carrie placed her hand on his arm, pleading with him to display less anger and more compassion. She felt some of the tension leave his muscles and knew it took a great deal of determination not to cross the room and hug the teenager fiercely.

"Sorry, Dad. I forgot to tell you where I was."

"I've been searching for hours! Then Carrie helped me look. We walked through the whole neighborhood."

"Sorry," Mackenzie returned contritely. "I sat in here by myself for a while, then these guys came down to decorate and—" she shrugged "—I decided to pitch in."

"Are you okay?" Carrie asked. "I mean, about not being able to spend the holiday with your mother?"

Mackenzie hesitated and her lower lip trembled slightly. "I'm disappointed, but then as Madame Frederick said, 'Time wounds all heels.'" She laughed and wiped her forearm under her nose. "Mom's got to make her own decisions about what role I'll play in her life. All I can do is give her the freedom to choose. I've got my dad and my friends." Her gaze moved about the room, pausing on each person.

Arnold was there with his spandex shorts and twinkling eyes. Madame Frederick with her crystal ball and her sometimes corny wisdom. Maria with her tenderhearted care for the neighborhood's cats. And, Carrie realized, she was there, too. They were Mackenzie's friends.

The girl wrapped her arms around her father's waist and hid her face in his chest. "I'll be here for the party," she said. "But you don't have to come, Dad. I'll understand."

"I want to come," he said, his eyes on Carrie. He held out his hand to her and their fingers locked together. "It takes moments like this for a man to recognize how fortunate he is to be blessed with good friends."

Mackenzie smiled and glanced over her shoulder at Madame Frederick.

"What did I tell you?" the older woman said, smiling just as broadly. "The crystal ball sees all."

"It didn't help me decide which mutual fund to invest in," Arnold reminded her. "And it didn't help me pick the winning lottery numbers, either. You can take that crystal ball of yours and store it in a pile of cow manure."

"I told you it wouldn't help you for personal gain," Madame Frederick said with more than a hint of defensiveness.

"What good is that silly thing if it doesn't make your friends rich?"

"It serves its purpose," Philip surprised everyone by responding. He slid his arm around his daughter's shoulders. "Now, I'd say we've had enough excitement for one evening, wouldn't you?"

Mackenzie nodded. "Night, everyone."

"Good night," Arnold called.

"Sleep well," Madame Frederick sang out.

"Good night, sweetie. You stop by and visit me tomorrow, you hear?" Maria said.

"I will," Mackenzie promised.

Carrie left with Philip and his daughter. "I'm baking cookies for the party in the morning," she said when the elevator reached her floor.

"Do you need any help?" Mackenzie asked eagerly. "You won't have to worry about eggshells getting in the dough this time."

"I'd love it if you came by."

Content that all was well, Carrie entered her apartment and got ready for bed. As she slipped on her nightgown, the phone rang. It was Philip.

"I know I was with you less than ten minutes ago, but I wanted to thank you."

"For what? I didn't do anything." She'd shared his helplessness in searching for Mackenzie, his frustration and anger.

"You helped me find my daughter—in more ways than one."

"No, your love for her did that."

"I was wrong about your friends."

She'd wondered how long it would take him to admit that.

"They're as terrific as you are." He paused. "Not spending time with her mother was a big blow to Mackenzie. She was devastated when Laura put her off once again. I don't know what Madame Frederick really said, but it was obviously what Mackenzie needed to hear. For all her strangeness, Madame has good instincts about people."

"You're a fast learner."

Philip's amusement echoed over the phone line. "Don't kid yourself. I was with the slow reading group in first grade. I'm not exactly a speed demon when it comes to relationships, either. My marriage is a prime example."

"You'll come to the Christmas party?"

"With bells on." He chuckled. "The thing is, I'll probably fit right in."

EPILOGUE

Six months later

"This is the most exciting day of my life!" Mackenzie declared, waltzing around the small dressing room in her slender full-length pale green dress. A wreath of spring flowers adorned her head. "You're actually going to be my stepmother, just like Madame Frederick said."

Only Carrie and Mackenzie were still in the room, as Carrie made her final preparations.

"It's an exciting day for me, too." Carrie pressed her hands against her stomach to calm her jittery nerves. The church was full of family and friends, waiting for her to make her appearance. Jason, dressed in a tuxedo, would soon escort her down the aisle. Her step-aunts, Christy and Taylor, were also in her wedding party, and so were her two closest friends from college. Gene was Philip's best man.

"Dad was so cute this morning," Mackenzie said, laughing. "I thought he was going to throw up his breakfast. He's so much in love he can hardly eat."

Carrie closed her eyes. She hadn't even attempted breakfast, and applauded Philip for making the effort. As for being in love, she was crazy about him and Mackenzie. This day was a dream come true, worthy of the finest fairy tale.

"Madame Frederick, Maria and Arnold are here, and lots of people from the office," Mackenzie said, peering out at the church. "I didn't think that many people knew my dad." Gracefully she waltzed her way around Carrie. "You're going to be the most beautiful bride ever. That's what Dad said, and he's right."

"Thank you, sweetie."

"It's extra-special that you're letting me be in the wedding party. Not everyone would do that. My first wedding," she said, and her eyes held a dreamy, faraway look.

"You're a good friend, Mackenzie."

"You probably wouldn't be marrying my dad if it wasn't for me," Mackenzie reminded her in a low voice. "But then, Madame Frederick's the one who gave me the idea, so I guess I should give her the credit."

"Remember what I told you about Madame Frederick and her crystal ball."

"I remember. It's just that you and Dad really do seem perfect for each other. Madame Frederick couldn't have known that."

"I'm pleased *you* think so."

"If I were to pick someone to be my mother, I'd choose *you*." Her eyes grew dark. "My dad needs you almost as much as I do. You're perfect for both of us. I'd rather spend time with you than anyone, except for Les Williams." She sighed deeply. "But then, Les doesn't know I'm alive."

"Don't be so sure of that."

"Are you two ready?" Jason called from outside the dressing room.

Carrie drew in a breath. "Ready as I'll ever be."

Mackenzie handed her the bouquet and Carrie opened the door. Jason was working his black tie back and forth in an effort to loosen it. He stopped in midaction and his jaw sagged.

"You…you look lovely."

"Don't act so surprised," Carrie teased.

"You look so much like your mother on our wedding day, it's hard to believe. I can't get over it…"

Mackenzie threw her a smile and hurried to join the wedding party for the procession down the aisle.

"Be happy," Jason said, his voice suspiciously low. He tucked her hand in the crook of his arm.

When Carrie glanced his way, she noticed a sheen of tears in his eyes.

"You'll always be my daughter," he murmured, fidgeting with his tie again. "I couldn't be prouder of you than I am right this minute."

"Thanks, Dad," she whispered.

They stood at the back of the church and waited for their cue, which came when Mendelssohn's "Wedding March" began. Carrie took a step forward. Toward Philip. Toward love. Toward their life together.

★ ★ ★ ★ ★

ON A SNOWY CHRISTMAS

———

BRENDA NOVAK

ONE

Adelaide Fairfax had been apprehensive about taking this flight from the very beginning. For one thing, she preferred not to be in such close proximity to her election opponent. Maxim Donahue, the man who'd filled her husband's state senate position via special election two years ago, was working on his laptop across the aisle and slightly in front of her. He was the only other person on the seven-seater Cessna except for the pilot and, although he refused to show it, he couldn't be happy that she'd been the one to claim Franklin Salazar's endorsement at their meeting this morning. A very wealthy developer, Franklin would not only be a generous campaign benefactor, he'd be a strong influence on other key supporters.

But, despite the awkwardness of their association, it wasn't being cooped up on a private plane with Donahue that'd tempted her to stay in Tahoe and forgo the governor's fundraiser in Los Angeles. Neither was it the Christmas music that filtered through the speakers, reminding her of a season she preferred, for the third year, to forget. It was that she'd always hated flying. The newspaper article she'd read last week, detailing the shocking number of uncharted plane wrecks in the

Sierra Nevadas, didn't help. This range contained some of the highest mountains in the northern hemisphere—craggy, rocky peaks that soared above the timberline.

Those same craggy peaks were now lurking somewhere below them in the blizzardlike weather. How close, Adelaide didn't know. But she had a feeling it was too close.

She knew the instant they were going to crash, but because of her fear, she couldn't really describe it as a premonition. It was more of a gut instinct, a sudden prickly sensation that told her something terrible was about to happen—the same sensation she'd experienced right before she'd received the call notifying her of her husband's fatal car accident.

She opened her mouth to ask the pilot if everything was okay but didn't have a chance to voice the words. One of the powerful downdrafts they'd been battling almost since takeoff jerked the plane, and it lost altitude at such a rate her stomach jumped into her throat.

Senator Donahue looked back at her, his expression, for once, devoid of the contempt he typically reserved for her. It was an honest "Oh, my God" moment when their eyes met and they understood without speaking that the primary they both wanted to win so desperately the following June no longer mattered. Chances were they wouldn't see Christmas.

The impact of the crash rattled Adelaide's teeth and threw her against the harness of her seat belt, like a one-two punch to the stomach and chest. At the same time, a heavy object fell from above, striking her on the temple. It hit hard enough to disorient her, but she didn't lose consciousness. She sat, eyes wide open, staring at nothing but darkness. The Christmas music was gone, replaced by a low hissing sound.

The smell of gasoline registered simultaneously with the pain she felt from the landing. She had to climb out, get away from the fuselage. But how? If there were emergency lights, they hadn't come on.

Could she find the exit? If she did, could she open it? She was shaking so violently she doubted she had the strength to move even a small piece of luggage out of her way.

How had this happened? The pilot had promised they'd be able to get through. And God owed her a small break, didn't He? She'd barely been able to function since Mark died. The coming election, and her decision to enter the race—what should've been Mark's race—had given her a reason to go on.

Ironically, it was also thanks to the coming election that her life was now at risk.

She struggled to get her bearings, but the creaks and groans of the plane and the heavy dust-filled darkness worked against her. Never had she imagined herself in such a situation, where survival depended entirely on her own ingenuity and instincts. A pilot, a flight attendant, a firefighter—she'd always assumed there'd be Someone In Charge in case of an emergency. Someone *else*.

Had the senator or pilot survived? What were the chances?

Not good, surely. She didn't hear anything—no movement, no groans. Was she completely on her own?

She held her breath. The howling wind gusted into the cabin as if a hole had been ripped in the metal, or the hull had broken apart. Maybe she wouldn't need to open the door. Maybe she was mere inches from freedom and didn't know it. But if she made it out alive, how long would she survive in conditions like this? Were there any emergency supplies on board? Flares?

I'm going to die.

That realization made her shake. But what did dying mean, exactly? As a foster child who'd been bounced around so many homes she'd lost track, she hadn't stayed in touch with any of her "parents." She had no children. She'd already turned her business over to the woman who'd worked for her almost from the beginning, so she could campaign.

For the briefest of moments, she allowed herself to fantasize about seeing Mark again, touching him. He'd been the one constant in her life, the only person who'd ever made her feel loved. She missed his appreciation for fine wine and good books and old architecture and modern art, missed the way he laughed and made her laugh. Was he still the same in some other dimension, maybe living in heaven, as so many organized religions taught?

The possibility calmed her. If heaven existed, maybe she wouldn't be alone for Christmas, after all. Lord knew she'd trade her money, her company and her hopes of winning a state senate seat for some kind of contact with Mark—would do it in a heartbeat. No more forcing herself to meet each new day without the husband she'd lost. No more aching loneliness. Only someone with a fierce will to survive could come out of an accident like this. And that wasn't her. She'd fought enough battles. It was better to give up right away, let go—

A moan interrupted her thoughts. She was almost reluctant to acknowledge what that moan meant. Another survivor complicated her desire to slip away without a struggle.

It had to be Maxim Donahue, she decided. He opposed her in everything.

But it wasn't Donahue. The sound came from the pilot. She could tell because Maxim called out to him a second later, his voice so scratchy and strained it made her wonder if he'd been seriously injured. "You…okay, Mr. Cox?"

Cox. That was the pilot's name. They'd been introduced when Adelaide came on board, but she'd been too busy keeping to herself to concentrate on someone she'd likely never meet again. A friend of the governor's had provided the plane and the pilot. Governor Bruce Livingston wasn't about to let bad weather beat him out of what he had planned for his biggest fundraiser of the year. He'd invited Donahue as a way to show his continued support; he'd invited her as a way to reach her wealthy supporters. She knew it was a calculated move, but her acceptance was every bit as calculated. Although most folks expected the governor to stand by Donahue, her inclusion in this event signaled that he wouldn't be entirely opposed to seeing her take over. It was a perfect strategy—playing the middle ground, as Livingston did so well.

"Mr. Cox?" Donahue called, a little louder.

The moaning stopped. "Get out…now!" the pilot rasped.

Other than that hissing she'd noticed earlier, silence fell, as absolute as the darkness.

"Adelaide?" Donahue said next.

It was odd even in such a desperate moment for this man, who'd only ever addressed her as *Ms.* Fairfax—lately with a starched courtesy that bordered on rudeness—to use her first name. But at least he sounded more coherent than he had a minute or two before. She knew that should've brought relief. Instead, she experienced an unmistakable reluctance to give up her hope of seeing Mark again.

"Hey, you still with us?" he persisted.

Don't answer. She knew what she was in for, couldn't face it. They'd freeze to death even if they got out.

And yet, despite all the odds stacked against them, despite the possibility of Mark waiting for her in heaven, the drive to go on, to live, finally asserted itself.

"I'm here." Unfortunately. Why couldn't it have happened quickly? Why couldn't it be over already?

"Where's here?"

In her seat. She hadn't budged because she'd assumed it was pointless. She didn't know where to go or what to do. Her head hurt, and a wet substance rolled down the side of her face, but it couldn't be tears. She was too shocked to cry.

"Answer me, damn it," he snapped while she was puzzling over her own reaction.

The force of his demand, and the same instinct that had led her to answer the first time, drew another response. "Where I was when w-we crashed."

That information was enough to guide him to her. A moment later she felt him touch her. His hands ran over her head, her face and then her body. They moved briskly, purposefully— and they missed *nothing*.

Mark... The yearning nearly overwhelmed her.

"I don't feel any major injuries," he said. "Can you walk?"

Not Mark. Mark's replacement. Mark's old acquaintance turned political enemy. "I th-think so." Why weren't his teeth chattering? How could he remain calm, even through *this*?

She should've expected it. She'd often said he was made of stone. His wife, already ailing with cancer, had died by suicide two years ago, six months after Mark's death. But Maxim Donahue had never shown so much as a hint of regret. She could still remember the implacable expression he'd worn when he appeared on television on a completely unrelated matter only days after Chloe Donahue's funeral.

Adelaide had always resented him for the ease with which he'd been able to return to business as usual. He made carrying on look simple. Probably because he cared about nothing as much as his own ambition. That was part of the reason she'd decided to run against him. What Donahue had said about her late husband provided the rest of her motivation.

"Let's get out of here," he said.

The pilot didn't utter another sound. *Cox*. Adelaide knew she'd never forget his name again. Not if she lived to be a hundred.

"Wh-what about M-Mr. Cox?"

Light appeared. At last. But it wasn't the emergency lights.

It was the blue glow of flames licking across the cockpit. The flicker illuminated the slumped figure of the pilot.

"Get your hands out of the way!" Maxim Donahue shoved her fumbling fingers aside, unlatched her seat belt and half dragged her to the door, where he pulled the barely visible emergency latch. But the door wouldn't open. They were trapped. Unless they could discover where that wind was getting in…

Grabbing her shoulder, he shoved her toward the back. "Find the opening. I'll get Cox."

Find the opening. Adelaide could feel the wind, the cold, even the wet snow seeping through the wreckage, but her head injury left her dizzy, stupefied. She couldn't think. Especially when she heard Donahue behind her, his gruff voice carrying a terrible note of finality. "He's gone."

"Gone?" she repeated, unable to absorb his meaning.

He didn't clarify. He pushed past her and kicked at the walls and windows. But the fire in the cockpit yielded more smoke than light. Flames stole along the floor, threatening to destroy the only hope they had.

Adelaide's nose and throat burned. And the sticky substance, the blood, coming from the wound on her head kept running into her eyes. She wiped at it and blinked and blinked and blinked, but it made no difference. She couldn't see. She couldn't breathe. She couldn't imagine how they'd live another five minutes.

Suddenly, the plane shifted, and a great gust of ice and snow blew back her hair.

Donahue had found an opening. He'd widened it. That brought a poignant burst of hope. But at the same time, metal screeched against rock, echoing miserably against the night sky. Then the plane tilted at a crazy angle and the floor beneath their feet gave way.

TWO

The frigid blast of air that represented escape hit Maxim Donahue just as the plane plummeted down the side of the mountain. Had he not already lunged for the opening, he would've experienced a second crash—and Adelaide Fairfax would've gone down with him. As it was, the movement of the plane jerked her so hard he nearly lost hold of her. Numb from the cold and blinded by swirling snow, he wasn't sure he'd managed to pull her out until her hand patted its way across his chest as they lay, prone, in the snow. Maybe she wanted to confirm that he was still with her. Or maybe she was just seeking warmth. They were both going to need it. He wondered if they'd last long enough to be rescued.

"I'm here," he yelled above the raging storm. "You okay?"

"That depends on how…you define okay." The wind made it difficult to communicate, but at least she seemed to be making sense. The shock of the crash had caused her to react with a sort of stunned lethargy. He was under the impression that she'd still be sitting in her seat if he hadn't unbuckled her restraint and prodded her to get moving. But that didn't surprise him. There'd actually been studies showing that only a small fraction of the people involved in plane wrecks got themselves out. Another small percentage grew hysterical. The majority did neither. They simply stayed put and allowed themselves to die.

A bang resounded far below, indicating that the plane had come to rest.

The pilot was still inside.

The image of Cox's body, now probably as mangled as the twisted metal that encased it, made Maxim sick. But he couldn't change what was, couldn't turn back time. His only choice was to do what he'd done with Chloe's death—bury the shock and grief in some other part of his brain so he could function. If the panic he held at bay ever took root, it'd spread so fast he wouldn't be able to stop it. Just as Adelaide had remained buckled in her seat, watching flames devour the cockpit, he'd find himself lying in the snow, unable to move or even think. And if ever he needed to keep his wits about him, it was now. Together with a wing and some other debris from the crash, which looked more like props in a movie, they were a few feet from the edge of a steep precipice. The wind whipped at them feverishly. If they weren't careful, those gusts would toss them over the side just like the main body of the plane.

Why had he put himself in this situation? *Why* had he listened when Cox insisted they could beat the storm? They should've stayed in Tahoe as they'd initially discussed. Instead, Maxim had succumbed to the pressure of Governor Livingston's phone call. But only because he'd *wanted* to make the party. He couldn't slow down, couldn't stop working. That would give the emptiness in his life a chance to catch up with him.

"What are we going to do?" Adelaide called.

The irony of being caught in this situation with the one person he disliked more than any other hit him, and he began to laugh.

"What's so funny?" she asked. "We're stranded on the side of a cliff in one of the worst storms to hit the Sierras in a decade. We're going to die up here, and you're laughing?"

He felt no obligation to explain. "I've finally pushed fate too far," he muttered instead.

He doubted she'd heard his reply, but she must've understood a little of what he was thinking because she shouted, "Who do you figure will win the primary if we're...not there?"

There was only one person with any real prospects. Luke Silici, who worked for the governor's office, had been making noises about running for the senate, until Adelaide stepped up and surprised everyone. Then, feeling she'd get more party support than he would, he'd backed off at the last minute. "Luke Silici will enter in your absence. The die-hard conservatives won't have a prayer of producing someone who can beat him. Not this late in the game. That's why they pressured *you* to run against me. You were their best shot. Not that I believe you could've taken me."

She shouldn't have had a chance. He was the incumbent. But Adelaide had her husband's tremendous popularity on her side, the sympathy factor, the support of key Republicans who possessed the power to swing a large number of votes, and the success of her multimillion-dollar energy conservation company, which established her business acumen. She'd even stolen the Salazar endorsement.

He expected her to come back at him, listing those assets as proof that retaining his seat was far from a given—and welcomed the argument that would start. This was his first opportunity to privately confront the stunning widow who'd pulled her support from him the moment he began to oppose legislation her husband had favored. If they were about to die, he could say whatever he wanted, knowing he wouldn't be quoted in the *Sacramento Bee* the following morning.

But Ms. Fairfax didn't return fire. She merely said, "They didn't have to pressure me."

Those six words put him in his place and removed the distraction he'd so eagerly embraced.

"We have to find shelter or we'll wish we'd gone over with the plane," she said and made a move to get up.

"Not so fast." He yanked her down by her expensive wool coat and rolled onto his hands and knees. That was when he realized—as inappropriately as he was dressed for winter survival in a fifteen-hundred-dollar business suit—her apparel included a skirt. Although her legs had proved quite a diversion when he was boarding the plane, the panty hose and high heels that showed them off so well would give her little protection from the elements.

How could this have happened? He was freezing his ass off, staring at nothing but snow, and still couldn't believe he was stranded in a blizzard instead of on his way toward the fundraiser, where he'd hoped to convince the majority of his party, once and for all, that Adelaide Fairfax didn't have what it took to win against the Democrats come November.

"What are you doing?" she asked as he surveyed the mountain.

They had to continue shouting. "I'm trying to figure out where we should go in order to increase our chances of survival."

"Are you w-worried about an—an avalanche?"

Her teeth chattered as she spoke. Her coordination would start to suffer next. Mild hypothermia began with uncontrolled shivering, impaired coordination and blue lips. It could progress quickly to more serious problems and eventually death. Anyone who'd seen a survival movie knew that.

Death seemed to wait at the end of every avenue. He was astonished that they'd both escaped this far. Cox hadn't been so lucky.

"That's exactly what I'm worried about," he said, speaking more loudly.

"Are we in an—an avalanche area?"

Evidently, she wasn't much of a ski buff. "Any steep mountain covered with snow can avalanche. But they occur most often when new snow falls onto cement pack."

"Like it's doing now."

The wryness in her voice encouraged him. He hoped it meant she was tougher than she seemed. She'd certainly done well navigating the predominantly male world of business. But the way she'd reacted in that plane had him worried. "You got it, ace. The wet, heavy snow sitting on top of the hardened ice slides right off, especially when it's steep."

"Great. So if we d-don't want to go hurtling to the b-bottom of the canyon, what should we do?"

"Move carefully and get on stable ground."

"Say that again?"

"We need to find a safe place to build a shelter!"

"Out of *what*?"

"The only thing we've got—snow." Fortunately, he'd been an Eagle Scout and knew about snow caves. He'd had to build a total of three in his lifetime, on various campouts. Of course, those had been for fun, for practice. And it'd been twenty-seven years since he'd built the last one.

She cupped her hands around her mouth. "What about the p-plane? Maybe we can f-find some emergency supplies in the wreckage."

She was right. Legally, the pilot would've had to carry certain articles. But it wasn't as if the plane or the pilot came from Alaska. California was known for its predominately mild weather. Had the members of the state legislature concerned themselves with winter in the high Sierras when they considered emergency gear legislation?

Maxim hadn't seen any such bill since he'd been in office. He could only pray that they had.

"Regulations would demand some sort of supplies, but who

knows how well the owner or pilot complied. Or if those supplies went over with the main body of the plane." It was very
likely they had. The pilot himself had gone over, hadn't he?

Maxim didn't want to think about that. Christmas was next
week. What kind of holiday would Cox's family have? And
what about the two of them? *Any?* Probably not. But he didn't
believe it was advisable to extinguish all hope. Adelaide was
losing body heat faster than he was; it wouldn't help to dis-
courage her. "We'll look, but first we'll get warm and wait
out the storm."

"Sounds g-good."

Not as "g-good" as waking up to discover this was just a
nightmare, that he could still look forward to seeing his daughters next week when school ended. But at least he wasn't alone.
He'd found it ironic to be stranded with Fairfax's young widow.
Now he was grateful for her company. Because the only thing
worse than being stuck out here with her was being stuck out
here alone.

THREE

Maxim had no idea how long it took them to dig the cave. He couldn't see his Rolex, couldn't see much of anything. He wasn't even sure they were tunneling in a safe spot. They hadn't had the time, the visibility or the mobility to look around. They'd found what appeared to be a level spot and started digging. It was either that or continue to brave the cold without any shelter, which wasn't a viable option. If they didn't warm their extremities soon, they'd lose them to frostbite.

At least the physical nature of the work kept them somewhat warm. They covered their hands with the sleeves of their coats and took turns using a metal piece from the plane to scoop snow.

Adelaide had fallen silent almost as soon as they'd begun. Maxim knew her legs and feet must be even more frozen than his, but there wasn't anything he could do about it. Not until they had some way to block the wind.

"I wish we had supplies to build a fire," he said. It was a lame comment, but he wanted her to interact with him.

His efforts to draw her out didn't help. She said nothing. He only knew she was still alive because he had to let her take over with the shovel every now and then or he'd begin to sweat, heightening the danger of acute hypothermia. She needed to keep moving more than he did, anyway.

She attempted to further their progress, but her movements grew slower and more uncoordinated as the minutes ticked by. He was losing her.

The panic that struck at that thought didn't correspond to the way he felt about her in regular life. In the campaign, he'd forced himself to stick to the issues, but it hadn't been easy in the midst of her more personal attacks. Especially because her husband had done some unconscionable things and no one knew it, except Maxim and Harvey Sillinger, his campaign manager. Harvey was angrier than a junkyard dog that he wasn't allowed to expose what he'd learned. But Mark Fairfax was dead. The only person who'd be hurt by his duplicity was the wife he'd left behind.

Destroy the squeaky-clean image of her late husband, and you wipe away her power. This is a fight, man! Go for the jugular! She's running on the popularity of a man who pretended to have integrity but didn't. Harvey made this argument almost daily. Maybe they could remove the threat Adelaide posed by leaking a few carefully chosen details. But it would also destroy the positive memories she had of her husband, and Maxim refused to stoop that low. He knew what Mark's death had cost her. At the time of his funeral, he and the Fairfaxes had been political allies.

"Keep digging!" he snapped, hoping impatience would have some effect since persuasion hadn't. "Now! Hurry up!"

The added intensity seemed to work. At first. After the next few scoops, however, she grew completely unresponsive no matter how much he shouted.

"Shit!" he yelled to no one in particular. They were out of time.

Maxim gauged the depth of the hole. It wasn't as deep as he would've liked. They couldn't be too close to the walls or ceiling, or the snow would melt, and he couldn't have that. They had to stay as dry as possible. But staying dry would be a moot point if Adelaide couldn't make it long enough to take advantage of the shelter.

Stripping off his raincoat to cover the floor of the cave, he set their makeshift shovel near the opening so they could dig their way out if they got blocked in. He was supposed to leave a hole, but the metal plug was the best he could do under the circumstances.

If Adelaide had considered the possibility of being buried alive, she didn't mention it. She backed inside when he told her to and didn't resist when he began stripping off her clothes.

"Stay with me." Going by touch alone, he fumbled with the buttons on her suit. "I'll get you warm. Do you understand? Are you aware of what I'm telling you? Hang on."

The shallowness of her breathing alarmed him. He could barely feel it against his cheek. And what he felt wasn't as warm as it should've been. He was afraid her core temperature was dropping. He'd never felt a woman's skin that was so cold, so deathlike. Even Chloe had been warm when he'd found her...

"The outside temperature can fall to seventy below in a storm like this." He hoped his voice would give her something to concentrate on in the dark. "This cave should make it a whole hundred degrees warmer." He carefully removed her wet skirt. "That sounds practically tropical, doesn't it?"

Shivering, she held her arms close to her almost naked body. "N-no."

It wasn't the answer he'd been hoping to hear, but it proved she was coherent. "Talk to me, Adelaide. You can't go to sleep. You know that, right?"

He didn't think she'd respond again, but more words came... after a long delay. "That's all I w-want to d-do."

"If you sleep, you die," he said. "And we've got to get back home. We have an election battle to wage—against each other."

"S-somehow…the n-nomination doesn't…m-matter…any-more."

"I'll remember you said that once we're both safe and warm."

Thanks to the narrow confines of the cave, Maxim had trouble taking off his suit jacket. His button-down shirt wasn't any easier because his numb fingers couldn't seem to loosen his tie.

"W-what…are you…doing?" she asked.

"Only what I have to."

At last, he untied the damn knot. He wrapped his tie around his wrist, in case he saw some use for it later, and started to peel off the rubber boots that protected his Italian leather shoes.

"M-Maxim?"

"I think that's the first time you've ever used my first name," he said.

"Are you g-getting naked?"

"Yes. As fast as I can."

"Okay."

He laughed. "Somehow that wasn't what I expected you to say."

He took off her sensible pumps, which seemed anything but sensible in this situation, and slipped his socks, which were dry thanks to the overboots, on her feet. Then he put the overboots on over them, to insure they stayed dry, and pulled his leather shoes back on his own feet.

"Does that help?" he asked.

She didn't answer.

"Adelaide?"

"I'm f-fine. We'll be fine."

"That's the attitude," he said, but he sensed it was more of a capitulation than anything else. She didn't want him to bother her anymore. She preferred to be left alone. So she could drift into unconsciousness?

"You can't sleep," he reminded her and wondered what to do about her bra. Leave it on or take it off? It didn't seem wet, but if he was going to die, there were worse ways to go than pressed against the soft body of a woman.

In the end, he couldn't justify taking that liberty.

Leaving the bra on, he drew her into his arms.

"Oh! That feels g-good."

Her comment made him wish he'd removed her bra. Then it would've felt that much better. Having her even partially undressed was enough to bring his libido roaring to life. It'd been too damn long since he'd been with a woman, and he wanted to live while he could. What else would they do for the next several hours? They couldn't sleep—and nothing else had as much potential for distraction.

But the same vigilant conscience that wouldn't allow him to remove her bra wouldn't allow him to do anything else, either. Not when he suspected she wasn't thinking clearly.

When she wedged one slim leg between his thighs, he knew he wasn't thinking clearly, either. This was Adelaide Fairfax, his nemesis. She'd been stealing his endorsements and financial backers right and left, and hammering away at his Achilles' heel—his voting record on taxation issues—since September. Yet the feel of her against him provoked a sudden recklessness that made him want to roll her beneath him and make love to her more desperately and feverishly than he'd ever made love to a woman. The anger and resentment he'd felt toward her for the past four months only made that desire more potent. His grudging admiration of her beauty and equally grudging respect for her poise created a powerful drive to possess—and it happened more quickly than a match dropped in gasoline could burst into flame.

They were definitely making use of their clothing but they weren't actually wearing much of it. While Maxim's water-resistant coat protected them from the snow beneath, his suit jacket and Adelaide's wool coat covered them like blankets.

She had on only her bra, panties and nylons; he was still wearing his boxers. But Adelaide wouldn't have cared if they were completely naked. It didn't matter that he was her enemy. He was warm. And he even smelled good.

She pressed her frozen nose into his neck and breathed in the scent of soap. Maxim Donahue was built like a Giorgio Armani model—long, lean and spare. He dressed like one, too, in expensive tailor-made suits he wore as easily and comfortably as other men wore sweat suits.

His pulse beat against her lips, rhythmic and steady. She'd just count the pounding of his heart until help arrived. Then she'd be whisked away and would never have to be alone with him again.

But a rescue team wouldn't get anywhere close to them until after the storm. And she had no idea how long that would be.

Her feet were still so numb she couldn't feel them.

"Adelaide?"

She didn't move. "What?"

"You're not falling asleep, are you?"

"Of course not." But she didn't see how she could avoid it. She didn't have the strength to lift her eyelids.

FOUR

"Hey." Maxim spoke into Adelaide's hair, next to her ear, but she didn't move. "You still with me?" he said, more loudly.

When her head lolled on his arm, he grew alarmed enough to shake her. "What are you doing? Wake up!"

No answer.

With a curse, he leaned on his elbow. A moment before, he'd caught his own mind wandering, blanking out as if preparing for sleep. It'd happened so fast he almost wondered if he was the one who'd slipped away and was now hallucinating. "Listen, we're not...giving up, okay?"

She mumbled a few words. They weren't coherent, but at least they proved she was alive.

Thank God!

Closing his eyes, he let go of the breath he'd been holding. "If they find us...like this...they might...take a picture and... and put it on the front page of *The Bee*. Can you...imagine the caption?"

He hoped his comment would cause a reaction, and it did. "They'd better *not*!"

"They could. We have to remain conscious, make sure they don't."

"We'll…be…conscious."

Not if they didn't do something to stay awake. Less than sixty seconds later, he felt the tension seep out of her body.

"Adelaide, come on." Come on *what*? Where was he going with this thought? It took a moment, but at last he remembered. "We have to…to keep dalking."

"Keep…what?"

He was having trouble enunciating. He had to capture each word, chase it around in his head, then drag it to his mouth.

"T-talking." There, he'd said it. But the effort was wasted. His warning brought no response.

"Adelaide, fight…please." The sexual desire he'd felt earlier was completely gone. Now he wished for that spike of testosterone, for the flare of physical strength it had given him. In its place sat a hard knot of dread, but it was muted like everything else seemed to be. It certainly wasn't enough to overcome the sluggishness bogging him down. And with the storm still raging, they had a long wait ahead.

"Shall…we sing…some Christmas carol?"

No answer.

"Jingle bells, jingle bells, jingle all the way—" He stopped. That was all he could remember, which was ridiculous. He wasn't any kind of Scrooge. He liked Christmas. But apparently he hadn't paid much attention to the lyrics of even the more popular songs in quite some time. Probably because he didn't usually sing, didn't have what he would consider a voice. So he settled for something more repetitive and less vocally demanding. "Ninety-nine bottles of beer on the wall, ninety-nine bottles of beer, take one down, pass it around, ninety-eight bottles of beer on the wall."

His words ran together as if he was drunk. He tried to sing more clearly, hoping Adelaide would join in, but she didn't.

Only the flutter of her heartbeat, which he could feel when he pressed his lips to her throat, gave him hope—until that heartbeat became erratic, weak.

Feeling her heart wind down finally triggered the release of some much-needed adrenaline. Suddenly, he could think. Almost as important, he had the energy to move.

"Adelaide?" He kissed her throat, her jawline, her cold lips. "Hey, you're naked…with…the enemy."

Forgetting the scruples that had kept him circumspect and discreet, he unfastened her bra and slid his hand up to cup her breast. He didn't care about right and wrong anymore. He cared only about saving her life. To do that, he needed to rouse her to some level of awareness. "Can you feel me touching you?"

She moved, which encouraged him.

"Do you like it?" Parting her lips with his tongue, he kissed her while his fingers sought the more sensitive parts of her body. He wasn't having fun. He was too frightened. But he was putting everything he had into trying to interest her—or at least anger her. As far as he was concerned, either reaction would work. He simply needed to evoke an emotional response. Even a small rush of adrenaline could keep her lucid.

"Mark?"

He went still. She was out of it, all right. She thought he was her late husband.

He opened his mouth to correct her. But he feared despair would set in if he did. She was trapped on the side of a mountain, in the middle of a terrible blizzard, with little chance of survival. With him, a man she hated. But only when she knew who he was.

"Yeah, it's me." He cringed at the lie but didn't regret telling it when it worked better than he would've guessed. For the first time since the crash, he sensed some fight, some real strength in Adelaide. She was weeping now, but she clung to him, kissing him so passionately he began to experience a flicker of the desire that had crashed over him when he'd first encountered her barely clad body.

God, what am I doing?

He was saving her life, he told himself and, at her urging, slid his hand down her flat stomach to take off her panty hose.

It wasn't Mark, and Adelaide knew it. But that didn't mean she had to accept it.

Shutting out the reality, she concentrated on Maxim's mouth, his muscular chest, the thickness of his hair—and told herself it was the husband she'd lost. Sure, his kiss seemed a little different than she remembered, but it was so good she didn't mind. He showed more emotion, and the groan that rumbled from deep in his throat let her know he wanted her. The way he handled himself—handled her—was slightly more commanding. She liked it better. *Because it's been so long.*

"I love you," she whispered through tears she couldn't seem to suppress.

He stopped moving. She imagined him staring down at her, even though neither of them could see. "Is something wrong?" she asked.

"Adelaide—"

She pressed a finger to his lips. She didn't want him to ruin it. She had her husband with her. That was all that mattered. Maybe he'd disappear in a few minutes, leave her as alone as she'd been before. But at least she'd have this final memory—a better parting than the one she'd agonized over for so long—to carry her through whatever came next.

"Tell me you love me," she whispered, craving those words more than any others.

He hesitated.

"Mark?"

"You know it's true." Although he'd spoken a little too gruffly to make it entirely believable, there was no mistaking the sincerity in the words that followed. "You're the most beautiful woman I've ever laid eyes on, Adelaide Fairfax."

She chose to focus on that instead. *You're the most beautiful woman I've ever laid eyes on*... Wrapping her fingers around the proof of his arousal, she couldn't help smiling at his sudden intake of breath. The passion that had begun to wane in their marriage was back. Her doubts, her insecurities, they were stupid. Wasted energy, just as he'd always said. "Feels like you're ready."

"I'm ready. But—"

"Shh." She regretted ever breaking the silence. She'd only wanted to clear the air between them, hated that he'd died before she could apologize for the accusations that had sent him storming from their home. "Just make love to me. Tell me I'm all you ever wanted. Tell me that never changed."

"You're taking my very soul," he murmured.

"Don't fight it." She meant that teasingly, but he seemed to take her response at face value. His hands and mouth found her again, drawing a greedy response from every single nerve— until she was so sensitized she quivered at his lightest touch. She wanted to be with him completely, craved the old sense of connection they'd known when they were first married. But he resisted her attempts to take their lovemaking that final step.

"What are you doing?" she asked, confused by his hesitancy. "I want to feel you inside me. *One more time.*"

"Adelaide, I can't. I'm not Mark. You know that, don't you? I'm—"

"Shh!" Couldn't he take what she was willing to give him and spare her the harsh reality? It was her last night on earth; this was all she asked of it. "I don't want to hear what you're saying."

"It's the truth. I can't do this unless..." He seemed to struggle to find the right words. "I have to know you're okay with it, that I'm not taking advantage of you."

"We're taking advantage of each other," she said and arched into him, seeking the fantasy that had enveloped her only moments before.

Stubbornly, he clung to his resistance. "You're sure?"

She let her kiss answer for her, let it coax him to succumb, to forget that she was pretending he was someone else. And it worked. His restraint snapped. She felt it go.

Mumbling words she couldn't quite make out—*heaven help me* or something like that—he rolled her beneath him.

FIVE

They didn't die that night. But when Maxim opened his eyes the next morning, he was almost disappointed to be breathing. They were still stranded, still freezing, and still without much hope. He'd also made love to his election opponent while allowing her to fantasize that he was her dead husband. How sick was that?

Even sicker was the fact that he'd enjoyed it.

What had he been thinking? Certainly not of waking up with her in the morning.

But it didn't matter. So what if they'd made love? The experience had been so passionate and intense, so all-consuming, it had kept them *alive*. Best to leave it at that.

Adelaide was beginning to stir. He felt his body react when her breast brushed his arm. Her softness brought memories of their earlier intimacy and a surprising desire for more. But he was in no hurry for her to achieve full awareness...

He'd tried to tell her he wasn't Mark, and she'd responded as if she understood. But who could say what was really registering and what wasn't?

He pressed a thumb and finger to his eyes. Then something

else occurred to him. He could no longer hear the wind. Had the storm abated?

Maybe the worst was over. Maybe the rescue crews were on their way. If so, it wouldn't be long before they were both taken home, and then they could forget what had happened here.

Fresh air rushed in when he removed the piece of metal he'd wedged into the corner. As light streamed in with it, he felt a desperate urge to escape the confines of the cave—and the physical reminder of the line he'd crossed last night. But a groan told him Adelaide was awake. He glanced over to see her watching him warily.

"Tell me we didn't," she muttered.

Now that he could see her, it wasn't difficult to spot the dried blood on her right temple. She'd been hit by something and had probably suffered a concussion. That explained a lot about her behavior, making him especially glad he'd identified himself properly before taking their lovemaking all the way.

"Now you're asking me for more lies?"

"Can't we consider it an extension?"

He would've smiled at the wryness of her response, but he was still worried that he might've gone too far last night. He wasn't exactly sure *how* it'd all happened. The passion was suddenly there. It had brought them together. Was it entirely his fault that they'd made love? He didn't think so. He remembered trying to stop himself, but she'd been pleading with him to continue.

Still, that bump on her head made him nervous... "Works for me," he said, "as long as you understand the reality."

"Which is..."

"You need me to explain it?"

"I thought you were Mark."

"No, you *wanted* to think I was Mark, and I let you. There's a difference."

"So you were doing me a favor."

"That's a good way to look at it," he said with false cheer.

She rolled her eyes. "You're so self-sacrificing."

"As a public servant, I aim to please."

"Do you do those kinds of favors for all your constituents?"

"Now you're going to attack my reputation?"

She seemed to realize that she was being purposely contentious. "It's freezing," she said with a sigh. "Any chance we can seal the hole until we hear a helicopter?"

"You're kidding, right? We have to get out, do whatever we can to make it easy for the Civil Air Patrol to find us."

"Do you always have to be so big on reality?"

This time he did smile. "Put on your coat and crawl out so I can get mine."

She didn't answer. Neither did she move. "I can't believe it," she mumbled, and he knew she was busy replaying the "favor" he'd done her. He'd told her he *loved* her! But that was when he thought they'd never see daylight again.

"If it helps, we had no choice," he said. "If we hadn't gotten so…involved, we probably wouldn't be alive right now." Their activities had certainly warmed *him*.

"I didn't realize what I was doing."

He focused on widening the hole. "That scares me, and you know why. Are you going to keep it up?"

"No." She burrowed under the coats. "You might push me off a cliff if I do."

"I won't kill you after going through *that* just to save you." He grinned to himself.

"You're all heart."

When the hole was finally big enough to crawl through, he tossed the piece of metal he'd been using outside. "Are we going to stay in here and stress over the fact that we—" he wanted to say "had sex" to make it as impersonal as possible, but what they'd done wasn't impersonal at all "—made love? Or can we forget about it, like we should, and move on?"

"You're willing to forget about it?" She popped her head out from under the clothes, seeming more embarrassed than angry. Maxim could understand why that might be the case. But he couldn't hold the request she'd made last night against her. He'd read about the disorientation that often resulted from a knock on the head, not to mention the effects of hypothermia. Without those two elements, he doubted she would've been able to pretend. Playing the role of Mark had been a stretch for him, even in the physical sense. Her husband hadn't been much bigger than she was.

"I'm willing to forget about it," he said. "Are you getting out or not?"

"There's just one more thing."

He was sure he'd regret asking, but she'd piqued his curiosity. "And that is...?"

"What about birth control?"

"What about it?" He hadn't used any. It'd been so long since he'd had to worry about it that he didn't even own a condom, let alone carry one around in his wallet, which was in his briefcase on the plane, anyway. "Birth control hardly seemed important when I thought we were going to die."

"And now that we might live?"

It was taking on a whole new significance. "What are the chances?"

"Considering...everything, they could be pretty good."

Just what he wanted to hear. Not only had he made love to Adelaide Fairfax while letting her pretend he was Mark, he might've gotten her pregnant.

Shit... That was the absolute last thing he wanted. He loved his two children, but they were grown. And he and Adelaide weren't even friends.

Swallowing a sigh, he refrained from sharing those thoughts. He knew it was better not to show her how upset he'd be if their encounter resulted in a pregnancy. "I see."

"So…you didn't get fixed after you were finished having kids?" she asked.

There'd been no need. His wife had had her tubes tied during the cesarean section performed at Callie's birth. "No."

Adelaide's face fell. But a moment later, she set her jaw, and he knew he was looking at the shrewd businesswoman who'd taken Fairfax Solar public. "Then I'll make you a deal."

Surprised by her sudden calm, he raised an eyebrow. "What's that?"

"You tell no one what happened up here…"

He liked it so far. "And…"

"And if I'm pregnant, you let me keep the baby and pretend it isn't yours."

He wasn't sure he'd be able to do that, not after being a parent and knowing what it was like. But there were other considerations he felt more comfortable voicing. "You're running for office. How will you explain a pregnancy when you're not married?"

"Maybe Mark made a deposit in a sperm bank before he died," she said with a shrug.

"Is it true?"

"No."

I love you. She'd been crying when she said that. Her emotion had reminded him of what he'd felt before his own marriage disintegrated, made him want to experience again that same level of intensity. "You regret not having children when you had the chance?"

"I never had the chance. Mark was infertile."

Maxim had always assumed it was her, that she'd been too wrapped up in her career to want a child. "You could've adopted."

"We were looking into it."

And then her husband had died.

"Anyway, I wouldn't have asked for this, wouldn't have

planned it," she went on. "But if it's already happened because of last night—"

"Last night won't amount to anything," he interrupted.

"You don't know that."

"Let's wait until we're sure we have something to worry about before we start making difficult decisions. Right now, we need to concentrate on getting off this damn mountain."

"Help will arrive soon." She shoved her blond, shoulder-length hair out of her face and, for a moment, he was transfixed by her blue eyes. Even in this cave, he could make out their startling color. "With the storm over, Yosemite park rangers or...or CAP rescuers will be able to track the plane's emergency locator transmitter beacon," she said.

He wished he could be as confident. "*If* the signal went off."

"It went off. The ELT is activated automatically on impact."

"Not if it was cushioned by too much snow. And even if it went off, we're in some pretty rugged mountains, Adelaide."

Her full lips, which she'd used so artfully last night, twisted in distaste. "Don't call me that."

Offended by her tone, as well as her refusal to let him address her by her first name, he studied her—and tried to tell himself he didn't like what he saw. That what had taken place last night hadn't changed the way he felt.

"You can try to distance yourself all you want, but it won't change what happened. Anyway, as I was saying, the signal could easily bounce from ridge to ridge, making it difficult to track. Or maybe the fire burned so hot it destroyed the box containing the equipment. Even if that's not the case, the ELT is so far down the mountain, who knows what they'll think when they find it."

She curled up. "Surely they'll search above it."

"Maybe they will, if they have time before the next big storm. Regardless, we can't sit back and wait. We have to search for supplies, light some flares, make a fire, do anything and everything possible to survive another night, if it comes to that."

She didn't react to his mention of another night. "Is there any chance Mr. Cox is still alive?"

"None." He scowled to tell her he didn't want to be reminded of the pilot, but she didn't give up.

"You're sure?"

"I'm positive. But you can see for yourself. We have to hike down there. If anything's left of the plane, we might find some food. Eating and drinking will help us keep our body temperatures in the safe zone."

"Fine." She rubbed a hand over her face. "Where are my clothes?"

"They're wet. That's why I took them off."

Their eyes met, making him wonder if she was reliving the same memories he was.

"If you want me to thank you for that, I don't think I can," she said.

"I'm not asking for your thanks. Just answer one question."

"What's that?"

"Are men so interchangeable?"

A muscle flexed in her jaw. "I don't know what you mean."

"It seemed easy for you to accept a replacement."

"Well, it wasn't. It required a great deal of effort to block out your true identity. But I managed. Otherwise, I wouldn't have enjoyed it," she said, but she pulled her gaze away as if she feared he might read a different response in her eyes. Then she dragged her coat around her shoulders and crawled out—and he tried not to look at the bare bottom she accidentally flashed him as she wriggled through the opening.

SIX

Adelaide's hands and feet were freezing, despite the sun. And her coat wasn't meant to be worn without a layer of clothing beneath. After three hours of struggling to get down the sheer cliff to where they thought they saw the shadow of the fuselage, she wished she'd braved putting on her wet bra and underwear. The rough wool fabric chafed, and since Maxim was leading the way, his hand often went up her coat to help her down. The descent was steep enough that she didn't complain about him touching her bare thighs—she wanted to feel secure during the climb—but she knew what he had to be seeing whenever he glanced up.

"This is humiliating," she grumbled.

"At least we're alive," he said.

"That's easy for you to say. I'm not staring at *your* ass every time I look up."

He laughed so freely it made him seem younger—and even handsomer, which was really something, since he was already one of the best-looking men she'd ever met. The media agreed; reporters often compared his charisma and appearance to John

F. Kennedy, Jr.'s. Tall, dark and handsome, Maxim also came from money and was considered a real "catch."

"You don't have anything to say to that?" she asked when it became apparent he wasn't planning to continue the conversation.

He studied their options for farther descent. "I'm not stupid."

"What's that supposed to mean?"

"It means nothing I say is going to help. I can't say I don't mind seeing your bare ass or you'll think I'm getting some sort of sexual gratification out of it. And I can't say I do mind without making you even more self-conscious."

"It leaves me with no dignity."

He maneuvered onto a rock outcropping a few feet lower in elevation and turned back for her. "You had too much of that to begin with." His hand went up her coat again, and he gripped her thigh while she secured her footing.

"How can anyone have too much dignity?" she asked once she'd reached the ledge he was on. It was so cold that their breath appeared in small, foggy puffs.

"You manage it quite well."

She tilted up her chin. "You think I'm too stiff?"

"Not stiff, exactly. Unapproachable."

"Some people would say that about you."

"Those people don't know me."

"I could say the same."

"That's because no one knows you."

"I have friends," she argued.

He peered below. "Friends or acquaintances?"

"Friends! Franklin Salazar is my friend. I just received his endorsement, didn't I?"

"Franklin isn't your friend. I wouldn't even call him an acquaintance. He just liked your, ah, assets. Tough for a guy to compete with that."

"You're saying I got his endorsement because of my *figure*?"

He climbed down farther. "I'd be more specific, but you might slap me."

"He endorsed me because he knows I'll fix the damage you've caused since taking over," she snapped.

"You're kidding, right? It's taken me this long to clean up the mess your husband made."

She'd been waiting for his help, but now she didn't move. "Don't you dare talk about Mark! He's not here to defend himself."

He sighed. "Fine. Mark was perfect. It's just the rest of us bastards who have flaws." He blew on his hands. "Are you coming or not?"

"No."

"What's the matter?"

"I need my bra." He had all their clothes rolled up and fastened with his tie, which he'd hung around his neck and tossed over his shoulder so he could carry them as a bundle. She wasn't sure why he'd bothered bringing them along. She expected to be rescued before they had the chance to dry out. "Give me my panties, too," she added as an afterthought.

Lines of impatience appeared on his forehead. "Will you quit worrying about things that aren't important? I'm not so impressed with what you've got that I can't forget about it, okay? Your clothes are soaked."

The "I'm not so impressed with what you've got" stung more than it should have. "You didn't have any complaints last night."

"It was *dark* last night. It didn't matter whether it was you or anyone else in that cave."

Surprised by the harshness of his response, Adelaide blinked at him.

He seemed to soften but didn't apologize. Dropping to his knees, he found her bra and her lacy red Santa panties, her one concession to Christmas, and handed them to her.

She put them on while he retied the rest of their clothes. Her things were as wet as he'd said but she was already so cold and numb that she could barely tell the difference.

"Let's go." He stretched out an arm toward her, but she refused to lean on him any longer. He didn't owe her anything. Just because they were stranded together didn't mean they had to be friends.

Waving him away, she said, "Go ahead and see if you can find the plane. Or, better yet, find some help. I'll get there when I can."

He shook his head. "We should stay together."

"The blizzard's over. We'll be fine. Just tell them where they can find me if you reach them first."

"Adelaide—"

"Don't call me that," she said again. Every time he did she heard his voice from last night: *You're the most beautiful woman I've ever laid eyes on.* Even though she'd known it wasn't really Mark who'd whispered to her in the night, the use of her name had made those words personal. She'd believed they were spoken in sincerity. But that couldn't be true. Maxim didn't appreciate anything about her. The whole experience, every bit of it, had been staged for the benefit of survival.

"Well, regardless of what you prefer I call you, I'm not leaving you behind," he said. "So you have two choices. You can let me help you so we can travel faster—which is critical since the weather can change within minutes. Or you can climb down on your own and I'll wait a few yards ahead before continuing."

"Maybe I'll be the one waiting for you." Without giving him a chance to stop her, she started down from her side of the ledge.

It didn't turn out to be a good decision. All that white snow was blinding, and the canyon yawning so far beneath made her dizzy. But she felt for the safest toeholds she could find and kept moving. She didn't need Maxim Donahue; she didn't need anyone. Ever since her husband and parents had died, she'd learned how to soldier on alone.

"Adelaide, stop!" Maxim warned.

She ignored him, ignored everything except the tricky climb.

Staying where he was, he leaned over the ledge. "Look, if you want an apology, I'll apologize."

She wished he'd go down his own way and leave her the hell alone.

"I'm sorry, okay?" he called. "Will you hold still until I can reach you? You're scaring the shit out of me!"

That wasn't true, either. He only cared about himself. She would've told him so, except she was breathing too hard to speak. Clinging to the icy mountain took a lot of effort, more than she'd expected.

Spotting what appeared to be a fairly secure route, a path of bare rocks jutting out of the ice and snow, she paused for a moment to catch her breath. If she could get to the next plateau, she'd have a chance to rest and recover. Maybe she would prove that she was capable enough and Maxim would go on without her. Then she could sit and wait, or climb down at a more comfortable speed. Right now she felt the pressure to move quickly and efficiently, to show him she didn't need his help. But her fingers and toes were numb, and the wind kept whipping her hair into her eyes.

"Not that one! There's nowhere to go from there," he shouted.

She recoiled and glanced up to see him staring down at her with an intensity that told her he didn't think she'd make it.

"You're right...you—you might want to go the other way." She laughed as she clung to the mountain.

The wind howled through the canyon below. "You can do it," he said. "Just be careful. Those boots are too big for you."

She should've given them back. He was going to need them.

A dusting of snow fell on her as he moved. "One handhold at a time, okay?"

"I've got it," she breathed but she doubted he could hear. She

was talking to herself. She had to make a small leap and hope
she could reach the ledge. It was the only way to progress; she
couldn't stay where she was. Her strength was running out.

Concentrate. Almost there... With a deep breath, she jumped.

She might've made it. Her fingers touched the edge of the
rock, but before she could grab hold and pull herself up, a gust
of wind made her coat balloon like an umbrella, throwing her
off balance just enough that she grasped nothing but air.

Maxim had never felt more helpless in his life. As Adelaide
fell, she didn't scream. She didn't thrash around. She just slipped
down the mountain and out of sight.

God, she even died with dignity.

He clenched his fists, hoping and waiting for some sign that
he was wrong, that she was still alive. But he heard nothing
except the words he'd spoken earlier, rattling clumsily in his
head: *I'm not so impressed with what you've got that I can't forget
about it... It could've been anyone in that cave.*

Turning his face toward the rocks, he squeezed his eyes shut.
He'd caused this. She'd given her heart and soul last night because she'd been pretending he was Mark, and he'd thrown
them right back in her teeth. But only because he couldn't justify what he'd felt as easily as she could. He'd had to acknowledge who it was moaning in his ear, and the eagerness of his
reaction made him wonder if he'd ever hated her as much as
he wished.

Forcing back the terror that made him colder inside than out,
he scrambled down to the place where she'd fallen.

It was a difficult climb, but once he'd traveled ten feet or
so, he could see beyond the bank of snow that had hidden her
from view. She hadn't fallen all the way to the bottom; she was
lying on an outcropping of rocks.

But she wasn't moving. She looked small and pale, as white as the surrounding snow, especially with her dark coat torn open to reveal the smooth skin he'd touched last night.

He spotted red almost immediately. Was that her underwear? Or was it blood?

The thought that it might be blood created a hard lump in Maxim's stomach, a lump that got heavier the closer he came to her. She was scratched up; he could see that easily enough. But…he watched for movement, any hint of life—and saw her hand twitch.

She might be badly hurt, but she wasn't dead. The minute he reached her, she opened her pretty blue eyes and said, "Did you come…for your boots?"

SEVEN

Adelaide felt like an idiot for causing Maxim and herself so much additional trouble. She'd let sensitivity and pride urge her to act rashly and now she had scraped knees and an abrasion on her stomach to show for her icy slide down the mountain. Worse than that, she'd hurt her leg and could only limp, which meant she had to rely on him even more.

He didn't complain. He didn't say much of anything. He was too determined to get them to where they were going. Every hundred yards or so, he'd leave her in a safe spot, scout out what he planned to do next, then come back for her. She argued with him several times, insisting he take his boots and go. He could move so much faster without her and send the rescuers back, she told him. But he refused.

She was glad he hadn't relented when they finally found the plane. Although the fire and the crash had done significant damage, it wasn't as bad as she'd assumed it would be. The tail had been sheared off, leaving a jagged hole that exposed part of the interior, the nose was smashed and the charred walls and upholstery smelled terrible.

But there was some good news. They could climb inside to

avoid the worst of the wind. They had the comfort of knowing that if there was a working emergency beacon, they were now much closer to it. And they could take Mr. Cox home with them and make sure he received a proper burial.

Not that Adelaide wanted to spend much time in close proximity to his remains. Maxim must've felt the same because he pulled the frozen corpse out and moved it some distance away.

The absence of that morbid reminder of what had almost happened to them—what could still happen—filled Adelaide with relief. Until she saw Maxim return wearing the pilot's snow boots and carrying his parka.

"Take off that wet coat and put this one on instead," he said, tossing it to her.

She slid over so it wouldn't brush against her as it landed, drawing a frown from him.

"We have to be practical or we won't make it." The gruffness of his voice told her he wasn't any happier about appropriating Cox's clothes for his own use. She couldn't fault him for doing it, but neither could she follow his suggestion. The idea of borrowing from the dead made her ill.

"He'd want you to have it," Maxim said.

"Why would he?" she asked. "He didn't even know me."

"As a pilot, he was responsible for your safety. And it's not as if he'll miss it."

She shook her head. She knew she was being impractical, but she couldn't help it. Her hand recoiled every time she tried to reach out. "No."

He studied her but didn't insist. A moment later, he started rummaging around, gathering up items that might prove useful.

Because the plane had landed upside down, Adelaide sat on one of the overhead compartments and removed Maxim's rubber boots so she could warm her toes. Her leg throbbed from her fall and her stomach growled with hunger, but if anything else hurt, she couldn't feel it. She was too cold.

"We're in luck," he said. "There's a lot of stuff here that didn't burn."

She thought they could use a little *more* luck, like a helicopter hovering overhead, but there was nothing to gain by being negative. So she kept her mouth shut.

Maxim made a few other comments as he searched the various compartments that would still open; Adelaide sat there quietly.

Finally, he stood as tall as he could in the cramped hull and waited until he had her full attention. "What're you thinking about?"

She eyed the parka. *Mr. Cox lying in the snow without his coat.* "I'm thinking this is some Christmas."

"How were you planning to spend the holidays?"

Adelaide hadn't decided. Since Mark's death she generally volunteered at a homeless shelter on Christmas morning, to remind herself that she should be grateful for what she had. Then she went to her former in-laws' for dinner. But visiting the Fairfaxes wasn't the same without Mark. His older brother had remarried and had an obnoxious stepson who loved to bait her on political issues. Mark's mother's health was deteriorating, so she was getting cranky and inflexible and spent most of the dinner berating her stepgrandson. And Mark's father remained as uncommunicative as ever. These days, Adelaide felt like a stranger when she went there. Until she got stranded and couldn't see anybody even if she wanted to, she'd actually been thinking she might work as if it were any other day. She'd told herself she'd get more done without all the interruptions. "With Mark's family, I guess."

"You're still close?"

"It's only been two and a half years." *Only?* Those two and a half years had seemed like an eternity. But that response saved her from having to answer more directly. They'd never been close; they were simply all she had. "What about you?" she asked.

"My kids are expecting me to be home."

"Do you have dinner at your place?"

"Yeah." He surprised her with a disarming smile. "I'm hoping I've got a few more years before either of them marry and Christmas becomes a negotiation."

Adelaide could picture the domesticity of the scene—the roaring fire, the eggnog served in wineglasses, the laughter over dinner—and had to suppress a twinge of jealousy. The Donahues no longer had Chloe, which was heartbreaking. But they still had one another. "Who does the cooking?"

"I've hired someone to help."

"A woman?"

He glanced at her. "Yeah, a woman. Does it matter?"

She wasn't sure why it seemed important to clarify that. "I've just…had trouble finding the right person to help me with the same kind of thing," she said, but she didn't really need anyone to cook or clean. She wasn't home long enough to get her house dirtier than what the maid service could manage each Saturday. The dry cleaner handled most of the laundry. And it didn't make sense to hire a cook for one person who was gone most of the time and had a microwave available when she wasn't. She'd just thought it would be nice to have someone waiting for her at the end of the day.

She'd once interviewed a few applicants, but it seemed far too pathetic to pay for a warm smile, a "welcome home" and a TV companion. So she usually stayed at her office until she was too tired to do anything except listen to the news before bed.

"A friend recommended her to me," he explained.

"She doesn't mind working on Christmas?"

"Look what I found!" He held up a first-aid kit.

"That's great," she said, but she didn't see how a few bandages would make much difference to them. Either they'd be rescued before they froze to death—or they wouldn't.

He rooted around some more while she continued to ponder the woman who cooked his Christmas dinner.

"So…does she?" she asked when the conversation lapsed.

He was on his stomach, riffling through a compartment that was so smashed he couldn't get much out. "Does she what?"

"Mind working on Christmas Day."

"I guess not. She doesn't have to. It's her choice."

"Doesn't she have family of her own?"

"She's never been married."

Adelaide's feet were beginning to tingle and burn. They hurt—but she hoped the return of sensation was a good sign. "Does she eat with you, too?"

"Yeah. Then we exchange gifts and she goes to visit some distant relatives."

Adelaide drew her knees to her chest. There was something about this cook woman that bothered her, but she couldn't put her finger on why. "So you get her a gift?"

"Of course. Wouldn't you?" He groaned as he strained to pull out a blanket.

"How old is she?"

"Maybe if I had a hatchet..."

"How old is she?" Adelaide repeated.

"At least twenty-five."

"So she's not matronly Alice from *The Brady Bunch*."

He laughed. "Definitely not."

Definitely not? "What'd you get her this year?"

"I'm not sure. I think my daughter picked out a nice purse."

"Nice" meant expensive, at least in Maxim Donahue's vocabulary. Adelaide had never seen him wear anything that wasn't the best money could buy. She wondered what this young housekeeper would think of receiving a Gucci or Dolce bag. "Sounds like she does a fine job."

He didn't answer. He'd found a box of matches and was trying to light one. "Damn, they're ruined."

No fire. No heat. No help.

Adelaide pressed the heels of her hands to her eyes and brought the conversation back to Christmas dinner. "What time do you usually eat?"

"Midafternoon. You?"

She ignored the question. "That means she stays with you most of the day."

He straightened as much as possible in the upside-down aisle of the shattered plane. "Why are you so interested in my housekeeper?"

Adelaide pulled her coat tighter. "It just seems…like an odd situation."

"It's not odd. She cooks and I pay her."

"And she spends most of her Christmas with you, even though she's only twenty-five!"

He angled his head to look at her through the crack between two suspended seats. "Okay, now I see where you're going. But don't get too excited, Candidate Fairfax. You'll have nothing to report to the press when we get back, because I'm not having an affair with the hired help."

"I'm not digging for dirt!"

"Then why would you care if my housekeeper is young, attractive and unmarried?"

Adelaide forgot about her prickling feet. "You didn't tell me she was attractive."

"Well, she is."

"*How* attractive?"

Victory lit his eyes. "My housekeeper, Rosa, is nearly three hundred pounds, at least fifty-five years old and stays with us because she's supposed to. She's live-in help. Except for the relatives I mentioned, the rest of her family remained in Chile when she immigrated—legally—thirty-five years ago."

Adelaide rocked back. "You set me up! What a jerk!"

A wicked grin curved his lips. "You knew it was me last night and you enjoyed it, anyway, didn't you?"

"I don't know what you're talking about," she grumbled.

"In the cave," he said. "I'm saying there were moments you enjoyed our lovemaking even knowing I wasn't Mark. You—"

"Stop it." She scowled. "You're deluded."

He lowered his voice. "Am I?"

"Of course." She met his eyes because she wanted him to believe her; she wanted to believe what she was saying, too. Crediting all that passion to fantasy made everything so much… simpler. But she was having too many flashbacks. His hands cupping her face with palms too large to be Mark's. His mouth on her breast, warming her just when she thought she'd never be warm again. The sounds he'd made, the words he'd whispered. It was all unique to him.

"Would it hurt so much to admit it?" he asked.

She didn't answer.

"I knew it was *you*," he added.

"But it could've been anyone, remember?"

An expression of chagrin wiped the subtly coaxing smile from his face. "Could've been, but wasn't."

"I thought we decided to forget about last night, pretend it never happened."

"Some of us are better at pretending than others," he muttered. He was trying to hang a blanket across the opening to keep out the snow and cold.

"Was there a lot of blood?" she asked as she watched him.

"I don't know what you're talking about."

"Mr. Cox."

The blanket he'd anchored on one end fell, forcing him to start over. "No."

"What killed him?"

He sighed but shifted to the other side. "A head injury, I think. I didn't want to look too closely."

She could understand that. He was wearing the man's boots. "Right."

"We have a total of four blankets. Well, three," he corrected, "if you don't include this one."

"That's better than none," she said, but she couldn't manage any enthusiasm. She had yet to hear the swoop of a helicopter, which meant the Civil Air Patrol or whoever was out there searching for them, probably wouldn't make it today. Temperatures were falling as it grew dark. And the wind was picking up.

Remembering the hopelessness they'd faced immediately following the crash, she shivered. In an hour or so they'd lose what little sunlight they had.

"What time is it?" she asked.

He checked his watch. "Almost four."

They'd been in subzero weather for nearly twenty-four hours. "How're your feet?"

"I don't know," he said with a shrug. "I can't feel them. What about yours?"

"They burn." She chafed them, hoping to relieve the pain. "Did you ever hear about that little boy, back in the eighties, who survived in these mountains for five days? He did it alone. Both his parents died on impact."

"I'd rather not remember that, thanks."

"He made it out. They found him."

"He lost his legs."

"He's now a successful businessman."

"So you were being optimistic in bringing it up?"

No, she was considering how she'd deal with something so traumatic, if she could deal with it. "Here, let me help—"

He lifted a hand. "Stay where you are and keep covered."

"But it's snowing again." Which would make the crash site that much harder to spot, even if rescuers could get a helicopter in the sky.

"Other than hunkering down in here, there's nothing we can do—at least not until morning." He finally managed to block most of the opening, which cut down on the wind. "We'll be okay," he said over his shoulder as he finished.

She nodded, but that wasn't enough for him. Squeezing through the narrow passage, he crouched in front of her and raised her chin so she had to meet his eyes. "We'll be okay...

Adelaide." The way he said her name made it a challenge. He wanted to see if she'd object to his use of it, but she didn't. It still brought memories she'd rather forget, but he'd done too much for her; she had no right to complain about anything.

"Okay."

A day's beard growth—something she'd never seen on him before—covered his lower jaw, and his hair fell across his forehead in windblown tufts. She liked him this way. In a suit, he was too suave, too perfect, too...formidable. Or maybe it was just that she preferred a more rugged form of masculinity because she dealt with men in suits every day.

"Great."

"I— Let's take inventory, see what we have." She pulled out of his grasp.

He didn't immediately move. She could feel his gaze lingering on her but pretended not to, and he eventually turned to his cache. "We've got a sleeping bag, some wool blankets, a pair of snowshoes, two boxes of matches—which are no good because they got wet—half a dozen colored smoke bombs—which we can't light because we don't have matches—and rations."

"Rations?" Adelaide didn't think she'd ever been so hungry.

"Looks like military stuff."

"So it's freeze-dried?"

"Some of it." He opened a brown cardboard box the size of a large shoe box. "We've got bottled water, Cup-a-Soup, hot-chocolate mix, biscuits, cooked rice, granola bars, crackers and cheese, chewing gum, chicken pâté, orange-drink powder, a tin of tuna fish, fruit snacks, pork and beans and some condiments."

"That's a lot to fit in a box that size."

"They're not the largest portions I've ever seen." He slanted it so she could take a peek inside. "But we should have enough."

Maybe. That depended on how long they had to survive out here.

EIGHT

They'd eaten the pork and beans for dinner and then drank some water, but now that the sun had gone down, they sat in the pitch-black, chewing gum and talking to keep their spirits up. Adelaide was across the aisle from him in the sleeping bag. He was wrapped in the blankets. But it was getting so incredibly cold he knew they'd soon have to huddle together. He would've suggested it already. They'd both be more comfortable if they gave in and made the most of what they had in each other. But he was afraid she'd assume he was using their situation as an excuse to touch her again, probably because he wanted to touch her again and shut out the desperation of their situation, the same way they had last night.

"Do you miss her?" It was Adelaide who broke the silence that had fallen since Maxim had said he didn't think this storm would be as bad as the last one. The rising wind seemed to contradict him, but he felt it was more important to remain positive than to acknowledge reality.

"Who?" His mind was on his girls and whether or not they'd been notified that he hadn't reached L.A. Megan and Callie

were in school at San Diego State, but they'd be home next
week, just in time for Christmas.

"Chloe," she said.

Her mention of his late wife drew him back to the conversation. "Why do you want to know?"

"I guess I'm wondering whether you're as impervious as
you seem."

Impervious wasn't the right word. But this wasn't a subject
he had any desire to discuss, so he tried to dodge it by answering her question with one of his own. "What do you think?"

"It's hard to tell. You don't reveal much emotion. Unless
you're angry. I can always tell when you're angry."

He hadn't realized she watched him closely enough to be
aware of his personal habits. He'd made an art out of pretending
he didn't notice her. For the most part, he even tried to convince *himself* of that. What she called "anger" was actually frustration, because he felt envious of a man he didn't even respect.

"How can you tell?"

"There's a muscle in your jaw that tightens, and your eyes
glitter with hate," she said.

Not hate—determination. She was wrong again. But at least
he wasn't as transparent as he sometimes feared. "When have
I been angry around you?"

"You're always angry when you're around me," she said with
a laugh.

Apparently, she had no idea how hard he worked not to be-
tray the fact that he was attracted to her. When they were in a
room together, he had difficulty looking anywhere else. It was
as if he could feel every breath she took, no matter how many
people were crowded between them. It wasn't until she'd decided to run against him that he'd begun to dislike her. When
she jumped into the race, he'd been almost as relieved as he'd
been worried.

"I think you're mistaking preoccupation for anger." He tried to sound as indifferent as possible.

"Maybe."

He couldn't tell if she believed him or not.

"Are you going to answer my question?" she asked.

"About Chloe?"

"Yes."

"I miss her for the sake of my children." He hoped that would suffice. When it came to his late wife, his emotions were too confused to analyze. Her perpetually negative outlook had made him unhappy. But they'd had children before their marriage completely fell apart so he'd decided to stick it out in spite of her instability and neediness. And then she'd been diagnosed with cancer and somehow he'd felt responsible, as if wishing to be rid of her had made it come to pass. Trying to turn pity and compassion into love hadn't succeeded. He'd fallen short, been unable to do it, even for his children. Sometimes he still felt as though he wore a scarlet letter on his chest—a C for callous.

"You weren't in love with her."

"My decision to stay with her had nothing to do with my political aspirations, if that's what you're driving at."

"You stayed because of Megan and Callie?"

He doubted she'd believe him, but it was the truth. "Yes."

"That's how you made carrying on after her death look so easy."

Guilt washed over him. He hadn't been capable of mourning Chloe the way he'd wanted to, the way a husband should mourn the loss of his wife, especially one who'd died in such sad circumstances. He'd never even hinted that she was a burden. And yet he couldn't deny that there were moments when he recalled how much she'd changed after the birth of their second child, how difficult she'd become, and was glad to have her gone. She must have known he was merely tolerating her or she wouldn't have taken her own life.

What did that say about him?

"Just because we didn't share the same closeness you and Mark did doesn't mean it was easy to watch her suffer. When I learned what she was facing, I would've traded places with her if I could."

She didn't respond right away. When she spoke, she didn't question what he'd said, as he expected. She made an admission. "Mark and I were having problems when he died, too."

The frank honesty of those words surprised him. Did she know about Mark? Did she suspect? "What kind of problems?"

"I'm not sure exactly. He got so wrapped up in politics he grew almost...secretive." She gave an awkward laugh. "I was beginning to wonder if he was seeing another woman."

It wasn't another woman that'd taken Mark away, but Maxim had no plans to divulge what he knew, especially to Adelaide. He remained silent.

"I felt he was forgetting everything we'd promised each other, you know? Everything we'd once been to each other. We'd started off so strong, had so much fun together."

Being aware of the truth made it awkward to talk about Mark, but it didn't stop the jealousy that sprang up out of nowhere. "He was probably just busy, stressed," Maxim muttered. "You know how it is in politics."

"You think so?" she asked as if she valued his opinion.

He knew what she wanted to hear. "Of course," he said but winced at the lie. Only a fool would cheat on a woman like Adelaide, but Mark had been a fool, and more.

As it grew noticeably colder, Maxim thought about getting in that sleeping bag with her. He wanted to keep her warm, but it felt as though they were the only two people on earth, and that made barriers of propriety hard to maintain. It was difficult to worry about tomorrow when he wasn't sure he'd make it through today.

He talked about the election, what the governor must think

now that they'd gone missing, what they'd be doing if they'd stayed in Tahoe, what his girls were taking in school. He was trying to keep their minds off the cold, but it wasn't long before she interrupted.

"Are...are you g-going to stay over there all n-night?"

Her teeth were starting to chatter. He couldn't let her lose too much body heat before joining her in that bag, but he was afraid his body would give away the fact that the intimacy they'd shared before hadn't been *strictly* a matter of necessity. He'd wanted to make love to Adelaide Fairfax for a long time. He'd even dreamed about it on occasion—like after that chamber mixer they'd both attended in Roseville a couple of weeks ago.

"I'll come over in a minute," he said.

"Okay."

He waited for his arousal to disappear, but every time it did, the thought of joining her brought it back.

"Maxim?"

He was leaning forward, resting his head in his hands. "Yeah?"

"W-what about now?"

He knew that asking required her to sacrifice her pride. She'd rather pretend she didn't need him. For some reason, she tried not to need anybody.

Busy contemplating what to do, he didn't respond, which prompted her to ask, "Hey, are you still there?"

At the panic in her voice, he closed his eyes. "Of course I'm here," he said and took her hand. "I'm not going anywhere."

"Oh. Right." He expected her to let go, but she didn't. She wound her fingers through his. "But...you d-don't want to sh-share this bag with me?"

What the hell, he decided. Why worry about an erection? If he wasn't hard already, he would be the second he touched her.

"Sure." Silently cursing his unmistakable reaction to her, he felt his way over. With the dampness that seemed to permeate everything, their clothes hadn't had a chance to dry. He was still in his boxers and she was in her underwear, but he stripped off his coat and Cox's boots and climbed in. Then he used the blankets to cover the bag.

At first, Adelaide was timid about curling up against Maxim. They remained stiff, lying next to each other without speaking or moving. But as the minutes passed, she snuggled closer, eventually wrapping her arms around him. She could feel his erection pressing boldly against her abdomen—everything about Maxim Donahue was bold—but she didn't react to his arousal. And he kept his hands to himself, letting her take what she wanted from his body without asking for anything in return.

Adelaide tried to be appeased by that, but she quickly realized one-sided cuddling wasn't very satisfying. "Do you think you could act a little less...unwilling to be here?" she whispered.

He complied by shifting so she could lie on his shoulder, and she grew warm. She expected him to relax and drift off to sleep, but he didn't. His erection remained firm and ready, an ever-present reminder of what they'd shared last night. Soon she caught herself changing positions so she could feel the pressure of it.

"Adelaide?" He spoke her name gruffly.

"Yes?"

"Any chance you could hold still?"

"Sure," she said, embarrassed. But her embarrassment lasted only as long as her restraint. Reckless abandon seemed to be taking over. It started with a burning sensation low in her belly and was spreading through her veins, making her heart beat faster and faster, urging her to get on top of him...

"They'll be here in the morning." His voice sounded strangled, and she could feel the muscles in his arms and shoulders bunch as she straddled him.

"What if they're not?" she whispered, moving to make the

contact even more erotic. She knew what he wanted, and she was willing to give it to him. Why was he so reluctant? It wouldn't be their first time…

"They will be," he insisted.

"This could be our last night on earth."

She thought he understood her point when his hands slid lower, curved possessively around her buttocks. But then he said, "I can't pretend to be Mark again. If I make love to you, it'll be because you want *me*, not him."

So that was the problem.

Suddenly, all the desire that'd been pounding through her drained away. Not because she expected Maxim to be someone he wasn't. She hadn't been thinking about Mark. She'd been eagerly exploring a body that was nothing like her late husband's. She'd forgotten all about him.

But that was exactly what was bothering her. She couldn't believe it was possible to forget him so easily, especially with his worst enemy.

Sliding off Maxim, she turned away, trying to figure out how she could be so disloyal to the one man she'd promised to love forever.

NINE

He'd done the right thing, Maxim told himself. Their love-making would have no meaning if she was merely pretending again, and he wanted her too badly for a meaningless encounter. But that didn't stop the disappointment that rolled through him when she moved off him.

It's better this way. Why, he couldn't say from one second to the next, not with her rear pressed into his lap, which seemed to interfere with his thinking. But he tried to believe he'd made the ethical choice. The night would pass. They'd get home. And then he'd be glad he exercised some restraint.

Meanwhile the minutes dragged by like hours and he couldn't relax, couldn't sleep. He kept replaying those few moments after she'd asked him to hold her. She'd been so eager to touch him, so eager for him to touch her. She'd even climbed on top of him! Why had he forced her to reconsider?

Because he was trying to be fair. Because he'd wanted her to offer herself without any coaxing...

Closing his eyes, he struggled to shut out the appealing scent of her hair, but it filled his nostrils every time he drew a breath. Had she gone to sleep? He was pretty sure she had. She hadn't moved in a long time, ever since she'd turned her back to him.

Confident that she wouldn't know the difference, he allowed himself to curve more fully around her. He wanted to touch her breast but didn't go that far. He merely kissed her bare shoulder.

"I'm sorry," he murmured, but he wasn't sure why he was apologizing. For being unable to accept less than everything she had to give? For knowing that the man she loved with such devotion was a liar? For his outspoken criticism of Mark, which had put her on that plane in the first place?

Maybe he was apologizing for it all.

Pale tendrils of light threaded their way through the windows of the Cessna's carcass. It was morning. It had been for some time, but Adelaide remained still. She didn't want to wake Maxim. She preferred to luxuriate in the secure feeling of his arm anchoring her to him and the memory of him kissing her shoulder last night.

I'm sorry. Why had he felt the need to apologize? He hadn't done anything more to her than she'd done to him. They'd both been slinging insults over the past several months. Besides, the race didn't seem to matter anymore.

So what had motivated those softly uttered words? They were so...uncharacteristic of him. He was tough, demanding, uncaring, ambitious—wasn't he?

Definitely. But if that was all he was, why would he care whether or not she pretended he was someone else? Was it pride?

She'd chosen to think so, until his apology had made her reevaluate. She hadn't been able to categorize it under any of the bad qualities she'd assigned to him. She was convinced he wouldn't have said what he had if he'd realized she was awake.

So who was Maxim Donahue? Was he really as bad as she believed him to be?

Moving carefully, she maneuvered herself to face him. He didn't wake; he just stirred, then drew her against him as if they were regular and familiar lovers.

She laid her ear on his chest and listened to his heartbeat, praying that the steady rhythm would soon be drowned out by the rotary blades of a rescue copter. But she was afraid rescuers wouldn't be able to spot them. Judging by the obscure quality of the light, the latest snowfall had nearly buried the plane. Was the emergency transmitter working? Was the storm over?

It was crucial that they get up and do everything possible to make their position more visible. But if rescuers arrived today, these might be the last few minutes she'd ever spend in such intimacy with Maxim Donahue.

She didn't want to trade them away too soon...

"You okay?" he asked.

Apparently, her movement had awakened him, after all.

She tilted her head back to see his face. The shadow on his cheeks had darkened with another day's beard, making him look less like the man she'd spent the past months disliking and more like the man she was coming to know in a whole new way. "We made it through another night," she said.

"I told you we would. How's your leg?"

It'd been sore since she injured it, but preparing the wrecked plane as a shelter hadn't required much effort from her. Although she was fine for now, she was pretty sure her injury would complain more loudly when they got out and started digging. "I'll live. Well, maybe," she added with a laugh. "How'd you sleep?"

"I've had more restful nights. You ready to get up?"

She didn't answer. Instead, she held his face between her hands and stared into his eyes as she ran a thumb over his lips. "Did you mean it?" she breathed.

A certain wariness entered his expression. "Mean what?"

"That I'm the most beautiful woman you've ever laid eyes on?"

He said nothing.

"Or was that part of the act?"

He looked away. "What does it matter?"

"It matters."

When his gaze returned to hers, she no longer needed verbal confirmation. She could see it in his eyes. The always-in-control, forever-aloof Maxim Donahue had lifted the mask he normally wore to let her see the passion that simmered behind his cool exterior. And that sent an intoxicating flood of warmth and desire flowing through her.

Moving slowly, so he could stop her if he wanted, she pressed her lips to his.

They were warm and dry at first, but then they parted and his tongue met hers.

Someone moaned. She was almost positive it was her. But he moaned, too, the moment his hands found her breasts. He pulled off her bra so he could caress her, and she closed her eyes as his mouth left hers to trail small kisses down her throat.

Maxim couldn't hear for the pounding of his heart. Until the crash, he hadn't been with a woman since Chloe—and their lovemaking had lost its luster years before she was diagnosed. He felt younger than he'd felt in a very long time, more excited than he could ever remember. Somehow, nothing seemed to matter except being with Adelaide.

"You feel...amazing," he murmured.

She was breathing too hard to answer; the rapid rise and fall of her chest told him that. But she wasn't unresponsive. Her hands clutched his hair, guiding his mouth to her breast, and he groaned again when he realized she tasted as good as she felt.

He shoved her panties to her knees so he could eventually move lower. But he wasn't quite ready for that. Lightly pinning her down, he explored more leisurely what he'd rushed through the other night.

"What is it you want?" he whispered when she began to writhe against him, gasping. "Tell me, Adelaide, and I'll give it to you."

"You know…what I want."

He was hoping to hear his name. "Tell me, or I'll stop." He held his hand still, as if he'd make good on the threat, and she took his mouth in a fierce kiss.

"I want you, okay? I want *you*," she said against his lips.

"Now?" he teased.

She gulped for breath. "Now!"

Somehow, in the tightness of that sleeping bag, he managed to get rid of his boxers. He had no idea when or where they went. The same was true of her panties. Then he and Adelaide were touching and tasting each other in a frenzy like he'd never experienced.

The next few minutes didn't last as long as he would've liked. They were too desperate for each other. But never in his life had he enjoyed five minutes more.

Adelaide didn't say what he'd been longing to hear, not even when he had her trembling on the brink of climax—but it wasn't much later that they heard the helicopter.

Adelaide sat in the backseat of the chopper across from Maxim. She had a blanket wrapped around her and was staring out the window at the swirling snow. The pilot and his partner had said they'd found them just when they were about to turn back. Apparently, the ELT had gone off but had stopped working after only a few minutes, and the severity of the storm system hadn't allowed them to search more than three hours yesterday, two this morning. If the Cessna hadn't fallen into such a wide crevice, the helicopter wouldn't have had room to land or time to wait for them to climb down into the clearing. The rescuers hadn't even been able to recover Cox. It was too risky to go after him until the current storm had passed.

That news hadn't made Adelaide happy. She'd argued that they should take Cox to his family right now. But once it started to snow, she seemed to realize the helicopter pilot was right and let the subject go. The truth was, they were damn lucky—lucky to be alive, lucky to have gotten out when they did, lucky to be home in time for Christmas.

Maxim hoped his girls hadn't assumed the worst. He hated the thought of what they must have suffered, believing he was dead. They'd already lost their mother.

The wind tossed the helicopter like a cheap toy. Feeling airsick, Maxim glanced over to see how Adelaide was coping with the bumpy flight and noticed how tightly she clasped her hands in her lap. She didn't speak, didn't complain, but she was clearly nervous. After what they'd been through, he didn't blame her. He was anxious, too.

Briefly, he considered trying to comfort her by squeezing her arm but refrained. She wouldn't even look at him. Now that they'd been rescued, neither of them knew what to think of the time they'd spent together—or the physical intimacy between them. The fact that they hadn't used birth control seemed far more important now than it had before, however. Was Adelaide carrying his baby? Was she worried that she might be? What would they do if she was?

Closing his eyes to shut out the blinding white of the snow, which made him dizzy, he told himself there was no use worrying until he knew for sure, and tried to put it out of his mind.

"We'll be down in ten minutes," the pilot announced, speaking through the earphones he'd given each of them.

"Sounds good to me," Maxim responded and the guy in the passenger seat sent him a thumbs-up.

Adelaide didn't comment. But she thanked the pilot once they landed. She shook Maxim's hand and politely thanked him, too—as if they were still professional acquaintances. Then a paramedic helped her across the tarmac to an ambulance.

There was a second ambulance waiting for Maxim. Although he would've preferred to ride along with Adelaide, it made sense for him to have his own transportation. As opponents, they shouldn't share an ambulance or anything else.

They should never have been on that plane together.

But, except for what had happened to the pilot, Maxim couldn't bring himself to regret it.

TEN

Harvey Sillinger slapped a file folder on Maxim's desk. "Now you've got to do it," he said, his eyes burning with exhilaration.

Maxim scowled at the intrusion. This was his first day back at work since the crash. He wasn't sure he was ready to deal with his campaign manager's intense personality. Christmas was in three days—his daughters would be arriving tomorrow. He'd wanted to spend a few quiet hours at campaign headquarters clearing off his desk before the new year. He'd thought he'd be able to do that when he walked in at eight and found Harvey so absorbed in a telephone conversation that he barely grunted hello. They'd already spoken several times since the rescue, had nothing pressing to discuss, and Harvey was the only one in the office. Maxim's other employees and volunteers were off for the holidays.

It should've been a low-key, catch-up morning, but nothing about his campaign manager was ever low-key. A longtime political veteran, Harvey lived to one-up his opponents. That was initially why Maxim had hired him. He'd wanted a heavy hitter and had planned to do all he could to retain his senate seat. Maybe he'd even wanted to prove something to Adelaide. But he was learning that Harvey had no sense of when he'd gone too far.

"What are you talking about?" Maxim asked.

Harvey motioned toward the file next to the mini Christmas tree some volunteer had placed on his desk. "I have the e-mails," he stated with obvious satisfaction.

Maxim could guess where this was going, but he'd already told his campaign manager that he didn't want to follow up on what they'd uncovered about Mark Fairfax. He was even more reluctant to hurt Adelaide now than he'd been before—for reasons he refused to disclose to Harvey and preferred not to think about himself. "Tell me this has nothing to do with Mark Fairfax."

"You're kidding, right?" Short and stocky but bursting with frenetic energy, Harvey leaned closer and lowered his voice. "I have correspondence here that proves Fairfax was having a very sordid affair when he died—" he paused for effect "—*with a male intern.*"

"Oh, God," Maxim muttered and dragged a hand over his face.

Harvey thumped the file, nearly knocking the Christmas tree to the floor. "Fairfax sent these messages to a boy of eighteen," he said as he caught it. "They're so explicit there's no way anyone can argue about what was going on." He chuckled. "Read them yourself. He had one hell of a dirty mind. It'll be a shock to everyone."

Especially Adelaide. "Why are you still at this?" Maxim asked, rising to his feet. "I told you I didn't want to know any more about Fairfax. We're running this campaign, *my* campaign, on the issues."

Harvey stiffened, glaring at him. "A political campaign is never about the issues. You know that. At least you did when

I came on. It's a sales job, pure and simple. And I'm the best salesman in the business."

"Then sell—but forget Fairfax."

"You're saying personal integrity isn't an issue?"

"The man's dead!" Maxim said. "The only person this will hurt is the wife he left behind!"

"You mean the wife who's trying to take your job?" Harvey yelled. "Who just stole the Salazar endorsement? You hired me to win this campaign and now you're tying my hands? I don't get it! You're the one who came to me with the tip on Fairfax. You're the one who wanted me to see if there was anything to it."

Maxim had received a voice-mail message from an anonymous caller who'd accused Fairfax of a lot of things, including bribery and a vague charge of sexual misconduct. Maxim had been interested in finding out whether or not he'd taken bribe money from some of the developers in the state. He knew it would reveal why Mark had changed positions and thrown his support behind certain projects. But he'd never expected the crazy accusation of sexual misconduct to take them where it had. A homosexual affair with a boy of eighteen? "I wanted to prove he was corrupt, but—"

"But we found something even more damning!"

"More sensational isn't necessarily more damning."

"Everyone takes bribes these days. Not everyone plays hide the salami with teenage boys."

"Stop it." Maxim scowled, but Harvey wouldn't back off.

"He solicited sex from the young men who volunteered to work for him. That's big news, Maxim, and people need to know."

The "need to know" line warned Maxim that Harvey was out of control. "The man's dead," he reiterated. "No one needs to know anything about—" he gestured at the file "—*this.*"

Harvey began to stalk around the room. "I can't believe it!

I thought you were reluctant because you didn't want to be perceived as desperate, grasping at straws, lowering yourself by accusing a dead man."

Maxim had said all that and more, but keeping what Mark did a secret had always been about Adelaide, not the campaign.

"I thought you wanted me to pull back because we didn't have enough proof," Harvey went on. "So I get you proof, *unimpeachable* proof. This puts Fairfax and his widow right in our crosshairs. And you're not *happy* about it? What am I missing here?"

Maxim shoved the file away and managed to knock the Christmas tree off the desk himself. "No, I'm not happy. I want you to shred every last e-mail and wipe away whatever's on your computer. And don't you *dare* breathe a word of this to anyone." This time he leaned forward. "I mean it, Harvey."

Apparently realizing that he wouldn't relent, Harvey stopped pacing. "I'm only doing my job."

"Your job is to help me win."

"Without this, you'll lose. You're giving her every advantage!"

Maxim threw up his hands. "Then so be it!"

Shaking his head, Harvey kicked the miniature Christmas tree to the other side of the room. "I'm out of here. Why sully my reputation with a loss that we could easily avoid?"

Clenching his jaw in an attempt to control his temper, Maxim carefully modulated his voice. "Harvey, it's Christmastime. Don't you have family somewhere? Can't you just... take a few days off?"

Harvey propped his hands on his hips. "Do you think you might change your mind if I do?"

Maxim imagined Adelaide hearing about her late husband's gay affair and knew changing his mind was out of the question. "No."

"Then why bother?"

"We might be able to strategize other ways to succeed."

"No. I don't pull punches, even if my opponent is a woman. I'm not that sexist," he said with a sneer. "And I can't stay if you won't use the advantage I'm giving you."

Maxim shoved a hand through his hair. Harvey was giving him an ultimatum? "Innocent people will be hurt, Harvey."

"The blame for that lies with Fairfax, not me." He reached for the file he'd dropped on Maxim's desk but Maxim snatched it up before he could touch it.

"No way are you taking this."

With a curse, Harvey turned on his heel and marched out.

"You'd better keep what you've found on Fairfax to yourself," Maxim called after him, but Harvey made no commitment one way or the other. He collected his briefcase and slammed his office door as he left.

Maxim sank into his chair. Would he read about Mark Fairfax and the intern in the paper tomorrow? Harvey had to have some way—favorable to himself, of course—of explaining why he was no longer heading up the Donahue campaign.

So where did that leave Adelaide?

Adelaide spent Monday morning shopping, which was what she'd done during the weekend, too. She was filling Sub-for-Santa orders for a local charity. She still had some difficulty getting around on her injured leg, but at least it was merely bruised and not broken. Shopping gave her something to do. After being stranded in the mountains with Maxim, she didn't feel like going right back to work. She'd decided to take two weeks to focus on the holidays, to allow her mind a rest from the campaign and the confusion she felt now that she knew Maxim better. Before the crash, winning that senate seat had meant everything to her. It'd given her a reason to go on. Now she wasn't even sure she wanted to stay in the race. But with so many people counting on her, she couldn't withdraw and lay off all her employees, especially at Christmas. Besides, she didn't know what she'd do with herself if she didn't spend the next months campaigning. She'd already bowed out of her solar business, put Rhonda Cummings, who'd worked with her for years, in charge, and Rhonda was doing a fine job.

Maybe she'd continue—but at a less frantic pace. If she didn't win the primary in June, she wouldn't be disappointed. She actually preferred Maxim to win. Now that she knew him and liked him, it was easier to forgive the comments he'd made about Mark's lackluster performance. He'd misjudged Mark. He didn't know him that well.

So would she go back to the solar business? That seemed the logical choice, but the idea didn't excite her and certainly wouldn't make Rhonda happy.

Maybe it was time to do some traveling. She'd always wanted to see Europe, Australia, Alaska. She'd pictured Mark at her side, but maybe Ruby, her former neighbor and closest friend, would want to go.

No, Ruby had just opened a dress boutique downtown. She couldn't leave it.

Once again, Adelaide seemed to find herself in no-man's-land...

Her cell phone rang as she was standing in line to buy a video game system. Setting her bags on the floor so she could reach her purse, she fished out her phone and checked caller ID.

She didn't recognize the number but answered, anyway. "Hello?"

"Adelaide?"

Maxim. She would've known his voice anywhere. "Yes?"

"How are you?"

"Better. You?" She tightened her grip on the phone. Crazy as it was, she'd missed him. He hadn't contacted her since they'd been home.

"I'm okay, I guess. Listen, do you have plans for tonight?"

She might've thought he was asking her out. She'd been yearning to hear from him. But the reluctance in his voice made her leery of assuming too much. She sensed that he didn't want to be making this call. "Is this where you try to convince me to drop out of the race?" she teased.

The question seemed to take him by surprise, as if it hadn't occurred to him. "Are you open to that?"

"Probably not."

He sighed. "Too bad."

"So this isn't about the primary."

"No."

Then he was worrying that she might be pregnant. She'd bought an over-the-counter test that boasted almost immediate detection, but she hadn't been able to bring herself to use it. It was more comfortable to live in denial, at least until she'd adjusted to the possibility.

But maybe there was a reason he needed to know now. Maybe he was going to ask the tall blonde he sometimes brought to political events to marry him...

Adelaide cringed at the jealousy that thought evoked. The fantasies she'd had of Maxim during the week she'd been home told her she'd developed a crush on him, but she trusted it wasn't more than that. "I'm free. Where would you like to meet?"

"Would you mind if I came over after dinner?"

After dinner. He wasn't trying to parlay this into any type of date. She interpreted that to mean he regretted what had happened between them and hoped she wasn't pregnant.

She felt her shoulders slump. "No. I-I wouldn't mind." They had to face reality sometime, didn't they?

There was a brief pause. "Will we be able to speak privately?"

How would he react if she was pregnant? *Let's wait until we're sure we have something to worry about before we start making difficult decisions* gave her no indication. He knew she'd want to keep the baby; she'd already told him as much. Would he pressure her to get an abortion instead?

She swallowed hard. "We'll be alone."

"Great. I'll see you tonight."

He was gone without a goodbye.

"It's your turn," someone said, nudging her from behind. She was holding up the line.

Gathering her sacks, she paid for the game system and headed down the center of the mall and out to her car. Her leg was aching too much to do any more walking—and she'd lost interest in shopping. She had to take that pregnancy test. It wasn't fair to keep Maxim in suspense if he needed to know, and she could use the intervening hours to cope, whatever the results.

If she wasn't pregnant, she'd put the plane crash behind her. And if she was, there'd be no forgetting the crash because it would change her entire future.

ELEVEN

Adelaide stared at the unopened pregnancy test she'd just put on her bathroom counter. She'd actually bought three more on her way home. They were sitting in the sack at her feet, held in reserve to ensure an accurate reading. Over the past week, she might've gone through the motions of getting ready for Christmas, but the possibility of a baby had been constantly at the back of her mind. Although she'd dreamed of becoming a mother, she'd put that hope out of her life when she'd learned Mark was infertile. She'd asked him, over and over again, if they could eventually adopt, but he'd been opposed to it. He'd said there was too much risk involved, that they had a good life and he didn't want to spoil it.

She'd talked him into it in the end, but she'd gotten the feeling he'd only relented to placate her, to ease some of the tension that'd crept into their marriage. And by then it was too late. A month later she was attending his funeral.

Oddly, she didn't feel the gut-wrenching loss that normally accompanied any thought of her late husband. Did that mean she was learning to live without him? Or was it the hope of having a child that buoyed her spirits?

If she was pregnant, it would be more than a little ironic that it had happened with Maxim...

"Get this over with," she said aloud.

The face that looked back at her from the mirror was flushed with excitement, even fear. But it wasn't until she reached for the box that she knew for sure which way she wanted the test to go.

"Please, God, let me be pregnant," she murmured. At forty-one, she didn't think she'd have many more chances.

Maxim hated the thought of what he had to do, but he didn't see any alternative. He had no doubt that Harvey was going public. There wasn't any way to stop him. He wouldn't have as much to gain but, for Harvey, the notoriety of destroying Fairfax's reputation and ruining Adelaide's chances to win the primary would be enough. He'd see it as an opportunity to build his own reputation as unrelenting and successful at all costs. Maxim had to tell Adelaide before she found out from the media.

But...how?

He had no idea. She'd blame him, and she had every right to. If he hadn't passed that anonymous tip on to his campaign manager, Harvey would be as much in the dark as the rest of the world.

He'd thought about the situation all day, but he still didn't feel prepared as he drove to her house, which was located in Carmichael, along the American River.

Adelaide owned a big rambler with a sizeable yard and a gorgeous view. Although it was in a neighborhood of other expensive homes, the mature landscaping gave the property a sense of seclusion. He knew because he'd been there before. When Mark was alive, he and Adelaide had hosted a political fundraiser.

Now that he stood on the doorstep next to a huge poinsettia, staring at a Christmas wreath, Maxim found it difficult to make himself knock. But he knew he had no choice.

She answered wearing a snug-fitting pair of jeans, fur-lined boots and a classic beige sweater. Her blue eyes seemed even bigger with her hair pulled back.

Seeing her again reminded him how attractive she was, but he'd only forgotten it in the anxiety of the past few hours. Before that, before talking to Harvey this morning, he'd pictured her almost every time he closed his eyes. It'd been all he could do not to call her.

"Hey." He gave her a smile he didn't feel.

"Hi." Opening the door wider, she let him in.

The inside of Adelaide's house hadn't changed. As soon as he stepped over the threshold, Maxim wished he'd picked a different place to meet. He could remember speaking to Mark in this very room, could see their wedding picture hanging on the wall.

He hated how much Adelaide idolized her late husband. He knew it would make the next few minutes all the more painful.

He hated it for other reasons, too…

"Can I get you a drink?" she asked.

"No, thanks." He couldn't pretend this was a social visit. Always a believer in doing the hard things first, he planned to jump right in, but she spoke before he could begin.

"Is this about the blonde you sometimes bring to political events?" she asked.

The blonde? He thought back, trying to figure out who she meant. Then he remembered. She must be talking about Liz, a woman he'd met at the gym. They'd dated occasionally, before Liz had gotten engaged to her personal trainer. But it had never been serious. She wasn't nearly as intelligent, capable or attractive as Adelaide. He'd known that from the beginning, had always been more attracted to the woman across the room than the one on his arm. "No."

She seemed to relax a little, which surprised him. She'd been worried about Liz?

"Oh. Well…" She motioned to the nearby sofa. "At least sit down."

Because she'd very likely be throwing him out in the next few seconds, he decided to remain standing. He wished he could touch her, maybe take her in his arms as he broke the news. But that would only make what he was about to say worse.

"That's okay," he said. "Listen, I'm sorry to bother you so close to Christmas. You probably have a million things to do, but…"

For some reason, he couldn't get the words past his lips. He didn't want her to hear that her husband had cheated on her with another woman, let alone a man. No, a *boy*.

His mind raced, trying to find some other way to break the news, but she interrupted him by touching his arm.

"Does this have anything to do with the fact that…that we didn't use any birth control when…well, you know."

He froze. What was she talking about? He'd assumed she would've done a pregnancy test by now and that he would've heard if their time together had resulted in a pregnancy. There'd been no communication between them in over a week. "I thought—I mean, you're not, are you?"

Her chest rose. "Actually—" she offered him a smile so hopeful it made him catch his breath "—I am."

Maxim felt as if someone had just punched him in the gut. "What'd you say?"

Concern and insecurity entered her eyes, eyes that were normally clear and decisive. "Are you sure you don't want to sit down?"

"No. You're pregnant. Isn't that what you just told me?"

She seemed close to tears, but didn't cry. She nodded.

Unsure how to respond, he considered what he'd come to say and knew he couldn't tell her now. He was going to have

a baby with this woman. And, oddly enough, he wasn't as unhappy about it as he'd told himself he'd be. A baby gave him
hope that, even with everything working against them, they
might be able to create a relationship. He wanted that, wanted
her. He just wanted her to love him in return—with all the
passion she'd felt for Mark—and wasn't sure that was possible.

The silence stretched out as he weighed his options.

"Are you terribly upset?" she asked.

She was watching him intently. If he cared about her as much
as he was beginning to believe, the way he handled the next
few minutes would be very important. "No, I'm not upset."

Her smile grew more genuine. "Really?"

"Really." But he wasn't even remotely willing to let her claim
the baby was Mark's. Would she try to insist? "What would
you like to do about it?" he asked.

"I want to keep the baby."

"I realize that." He was wondering what she wanted to do
about *him*. "Where do I come into the picture?"

He watched her throat work as she swallowed. "I don't want
you to—to feel forced or...or trapped. I understand that this
occurred because of...extenuating circumstances. If you'd prefer not to be part of the child's life, I'll handle it on my own.
I don't need any help." One of her hands moved to cover her
abdomen, an instinctively protective gesture.

That didn't reveal how she felt about him. But the fact that
she wanted this baby, *his* baby, made him inexplicably happy,
although he couldn't imagine why. He wasn't a young man
anymore; he'd turn forty-four in April. He'd thought he was
beyond all this. And yet...it felt like a second chance—for both
of them. "There's no way I'd ever support you telling anyone
that my baby is Mark's," he said.

"We could say I was artificially inseminated and I don't know
who the father is. That would provide the most protection for
your career—no breaking news story that you impregnated the

enemy." She laughed but it didn't sound as indifferent as she'd probably meant it to.

"Do you really think I'm that shallow?" he asked.

She didn't respond.

"We're talking about a baby, Adelaide. *Our* baby. My career doesn't come before that."

"That's how you feel?"

Could this really be happening? With Adelaide? "That's how I feel."

"So what do you propose, er, suggest?" she asked.

He stepped closer to see if she'd back off, but she didn't. "I suggest we keep our options open."

Her eyes drifted shut as he ran a finger over the contours of one cheek. "What kind of options are we talking about?" she breathed. "Dating?"

Maxim's pulse began to speed up. He'd never expected this, not from Adelaide, but she seemed...interested in his touch. Even here in the relative warmth of the valley with no snow or danger around them. Even in the house she'd shared with Mark. "Lovers, at least," he said.

Her eyes opened. "What about marriage?"

He pulled her against him. "I'd want that to be a possibility. What about you?"

"It could definitely be a possibility," she murmured.

"Good." Now was when he should tell her. But she was so open to him. For the first time since he'd met her, the remote Adelaide Fairfax was willing to trust him and accept him—as the father of her baby, maybe more.

"I missed you this past week," he admitted.

"I missed you, too," she replied and stood on tiptoe to kiss him.

Tell her! his mind raged. But she felt so good in his arms, he couldn't. Instead of letting go, instead of breaking the bad news, he deepened the kiss.

"I'm glad you're not upset about the baby," she whispered against his lips.

He wasn't upset as long as she wanted *him*, too. He knew she wouldn't once she learned what he was responsible for digging up about Mark. But somehow he'd stop her from finding out. He'd get hold of Harvey, do whatever he had to in order to prevent it from going public—even if it meant paying the bastard off. The longer he kissed Adelaide, the more convinced he became that he'd do anything to keep her.

"Make love to me," she whispered.

A flicker of guilt made him hesitate. That was a line he shouldn't cross. Not until he'd contacted Harvey and made some sort of arrangement, not until he could feel reasonably secure that she wouldn't be devastated tomorrow.

"I'd like to, but—" he searched for an acceptable excuse "—I'll come back. I've got some things to do."

She guided his hand to her breast. "Are you sure it can't wait?"

Suddenly he couldn't think of *anything* important enough to keep them apart. He'd fix the situation so she wouldn't be hurt, which meant he could stay and make love to her as many times as she wanted him to.

"I guess I can do it later." He could still see Mark watching them from that damn portrait so he swept her into his arms and carried her into one of the guest rooms. No way would he make love to her in Mark's bed.

As their clothes came off, he stared down at her and realized that she was exactly the woman he wanted—the woman he'd wanted for years.

"At last," he said and smiled when she responded so greedily to his touch.

TWELVE

Maxim watched Adelaide in those first minutes after he awoke. He wanted to have breakfast, spend the entire day with her, but he had to talk to Harvey as soon as possible.

"Hey," she whispered sleepily when he kissed her neck.

"I've gotta go," he told her.

"So soon?"

He laughed at the reluctance in her voice. He'd stayed far too long already and was afraid he'd be too late to stop Harvey. "Yeah, but I'll see you later." He got out of bed, then hesitated. His girls were coming home today, which meant he'd be tied up with them. "Actually, Megan and Callie are flying in for Christmas, so…"

"So you need to spend some time with them. Of course." She stretched as she turned to face him. "Have fun."

He wondered what his two daughters would think of Adelaide, but couldn't imagine that they wouldn't like her. He was eager to introduce them, to include her in his family. Would they be willing to accept her? "Any chance you can join us for dinner tomorrow night?" he asked.

"Isn't tomorrow Christmas Eve?"

"Yeah."

She propped herself up on the pillows. "Are you sure that's a good idea?"

"Positive." He wasn't as confident as he sounded. He'd dated since Chloe but not a lot, and he'd never brought a woman home to meet his children. But...he was hopeful they'd be open-minded.

"Okay."

"But just so you know, the baby's a secret. For a while."

"Of course. There's no hurry to tell anyone. I won't even start to show for three or four months." Her eyebrows drew together as she sobered. "But...are you really ready for another woman in your life, Maxim? Are they?"

He smoothed the hair out of her face. "We're all ready, as long as it's you."

She gave him a sexy smile. "I'll be there."

"I'm glad." He bent to kiss her again. "Maybe they'll go to bed early, and we can see if Santa has a little something for you."

Laughing, she fought to avoid him as he chafed her neck with his unshaved chin. "Go home," she complained. "I need sleep. You wore me out last night."

"Call me when you get up," he said and left.

He tried to reach Harvey as soon as he walked out of Adelaide's house, but Harvey wasn't answering. Maxim called him several times before he left for the airport at noon and tried again while he was on his way home with the girls. He knew he couldn't talk freely with them in the car, but he could set up a meeting.

"Shit!" he muttered after his sixth failed attempt.

"What's wrong, Dad?" Callie asked.

Frowning, he hit the off button on his Bluetooth. He hadn't meant to curse aloud. "Nothing." With a smile on his face to cover his growing unease, he encouraged them to talk about their classes, their grades, their friends and the boys they were dating. It wasn't until they got home and Megan and Callie went to unpack that he had a few minutes alone. He used the time to call Harvey again.

Harvey's voice mail picked up. "Harvey, get in touch with me, damn it," Maxim said. "I have a proposal for you. I think it's something you'll want to hear." He started to hang up but brought the phone back to his ear. "I don't care what time of day or night it is," he added, then disconnected.

"Dad?"

Maxim glanced up to find Megan standing on the stairs. With her auburn hair and greenish eyes, she looked like her mother, but Callie, his younger daughter, resembled him. It made him wonder who his new baby would look like—him or the fair-skinned Adelaide? "What?"

"Where's the wrapping paper?"

"I don't know. Did you check with Rosa?" His live-in house-keeper was in the kitchen, cooking one of the girls' favorite meals.

"She thinks we're out." She gave him the smile that told him he was about to do her a favor. "Any chance you'll go get some more? Or maybe a few gift bags? I'd do it myself, but I'm dying to take a shower and Megan's busy primping. She said Ryan's coming by to see her."

"I thought she told me she and Ryan hardly talk anymore," he said.

"I guess they talk enough that she's already told him she's home."

Maxim liked Ryan and didn't want to miss seeing him. But someone had to get the wrapping paper. And maybe Harvey would call while he had some time alone. "Sure," he said. "Be right back."

On the day before Christmas the weather dropped to forty-three degrees, bitter cold by Sacramento standards, but the extra chill didn't bother Adelaide. She spent the morning warm and snug in her house, visiting parenting sites on the Internet. She couldn't believe she was pregnant. Just when she'd been feeling most alone, just when she'd given up the hope of ever having a family, she was expecting.

It was almost too good to be true. But a baby meant she had so many decisions to make. Since their crash in the Sierras, her enthusiasm for winning the nomination and then a seat in the state senate had begun to wane; now it was entirely gone. She wondered if she could keep the people who worked for her on the payroll and have them campaign for Maxim instead.

Maxim... He hadn't liked Mark and he didn't pretend otherwise; that wasn't easy to accept. They'd have to discuss it eventually. But for two people beginning a new relationship, they were dealing with enough challenges. They had the baby coming, the public response to what they'd done, the surprise and possible resistance of Maxim's children. Best to adjust a little at a time.

Imagining what would happen when word of her condition reached the media, Adelaide cringed. It would be embarrassing. There was no escaping that. But she doubted it would hurt Maxim's career—especially if she threw her support behind him.

Propping her chin on one hand, she smiled dreamily as she remembered the way he'd reacted to news of the baby. Her life was heading down a path she would've considered impossible just ten days earlier, but the baby she was carrying changed everything.

Would they eventually marry? It wasn't as if she couldn't love Maxim. She was afraid she already did.

Who would've thought—

The ringing of the phone startled her out of her reverie. Reaching for the cordless handset on her desk, she saw M. Donahue on caller ID and smiled as she answered. "Hello?"

"Hey, gorgeous. I've got good news."

"What is it?"

"They were able to recover Mr. Cox's body yesterday. He'll be home for Christmas."

Adelaide wished Cox had made it out alive, but it was a relief to know his family would at least be able to say their goodbyes and lay him to rest. "How'd you find out?"

"The helicopter pilot called me."

"Why didn't he call me? I left him several messages."

"It was only by chance that he returned my calls first. I told him I'd notify you."

"Oh. Do you know when the funeral is?"

"He's originally from Bakersfield, so they're taking his body there and having a small, private ceremony next Monday."

"I'd like to attend, but if it's meant to be private, maybe I should just send my condolences to his family."

"That's what I plan to do. I can give you the address. Are you still coming tonight?"

Forcing aside the sadness she felt about Mr. Cox, she leaned her head against the back of her seat. They hadn't seen each other since he'd left her house yesterday morning. He'd been with his daughters since then, but he'd called several times. "If you still want me there," she said.

"I do. I want to celebrate Christmas with you. And I want you to meet Megan and Callie."

She'd met his children before. She and Maxim had run in the same circles for so long she'd even met his parents. But only in formal situations. Not in this capacity—not as the woman pregnant with his child. "Are you sure they wouldn't rather have you all to themselves? I don't want to intrude…"

"Megan's got an old boyfriend coming over. And Callie has two girlfriends joining us. You won't be intruding. Besides, I've told them to expect you."

"How did you explain our connection?"

"I said we got to know each other while we were stranded, and now we're friends."

"Were they surprised?"

"Of course. But they got over it quickly. Megan even said she thinks you're one of the prettiest women she's ever seen. She said I should've asked you out a long time ago, before you could get it in your mind to run against me."

She laughed. "Already a strategist."

"I wish I'd thought of that."

Closing her eyes, she pictured them all gathered around the Christmas tree. She'd imagined this scene once before, as an outsider looking in. Now she'd be part of it. Until this moment, she'd been afraid that tonight might not work out. She felt self-conscious about barging in on a family's celebration. She felt as if she'd been doing that for years—all the time she was growing up in the system after her parents had died in a house fire. "What should I bring?"

"You don't need to bring anything."

"What if I want to?" she insisted. "What would your girls enjoy?"

"Like most kids, they have a sweet tooth. You could bring a dessert, I guess."

Suddenly, it felt more like Christmas than any Christmas Adelaide had ever experienced. "I'm looking forward to it," she said and got off the phone so she could go to the grocery store. For the first time since Mark died, she felt like cooking.

Maxim sat in his living room alone. The area in front of the Christmas tree was now crowded with the gifts his daughters had wrapped. Megan and Callie were in the kitchen, laughing and talking with friends, their voices occasionally rising above the Christmas music playing throughout the house. He planned to go back in and join them. He needed to help Rosa finish cleaning up the brunch he'd made, but...something was bothering him, and he was pretty sure he knew what it was.

He'd gotten hold of Harvey Sillinger last night and been assured in no uncertain terms that there was nothing to worry about concerning Mark Fairfax. But Maxim couldn't put it out of his mind. Harvey's insistence that Maxim should've known him better than to assume the worst set off warning bells in Maxim's head. That statement was so off base it was almost absurd. He'd seen Harvey in action, knew he was ruthless. Usually, Harvey was proud of that trait. So why would he pretend to care about those he might hurt? And why would he suddenly be so amenable to keeping his mouth shut? Harvey hadn't been willing to commit himself to silence the day he'd stormed out of the office.

Something had changed in the past two days...

Rubbing his temples, Maxim went over the conversation they'd had last night.

"I can't believe you think I'd leak information you told me not to, Maxim," he'd said, defensive from the first moment Maxim had managed to reach him. "So what if we haven't known each other long? I did a good job while I was running your campaign. Anyone else would've been thrilled with what I accomplished."

This wasn't about what he'd accomplished, and Maxim had told him as much. Harvey was very dedicated. It was his tendency to forget who was boss that disturbed Maxim—that and the fact that he didn't seem to understand the meaning of the word *mercy*.

"I would've expected you to know me better than that," Harvey had gone on.

"I just want to be sure, Harvey. That's all," Maxim had said. "I just want to be sure."

"What happened to you while you were stranded in the mountains? That's what I want to know, because you certainly haven't been the same since you got back. You don't act like you even care whether you win the primary."

He cared. He loved his job and wanted to keep it, but he wouldn't do it by hurting Adelaide. "I nearly died, Harvey. Coming that close can give you a whole new perspective."

"From *my* perspective, you're losing your edge. But that's none of my business. You have nothing to worry about. Nothing from *me*, anyway."

The clarification had brought a stab of alarm. "What's that supposed to mean? You and I are the only ones who know about the intern, right?"

"Me, you and the intern," Harvey had said.

"The boy wouldn't have any reason to come forward. Why would he risk the embarrassment?"

"He probably wouldn't. So, like I said, you have nothing to worry about."

Sensing an undercurrent in the conversation, Maxim had decided to take that final step, to do all he could to guarantee that this situation wouldn't get away from him. "Is there any way to—" here, Maxim had chosen his words very carefully "—ensure your cooperation on this, Harvey?"

"What do you mean by that, Maxim? I'm an honest guy. I don't take payoffs."

"I'm not talking about a payoff. I'm talking about a *severance* package. To help you along until you find other employment."

"Oh, a *severance* package." After that, there'd been a long pause. "That might be just the thing," he'd said at length. "Especially if you can get it to me tonight."

"If that's how you want it," Maxim had said, and he'd met his former campaign manager at the office.

"This effectively ends our association, correct?" he'd said when he handed Harvey a thirty-thousand-dollar check.

"Sounds fair to me."

Just to be safe, Maxim had asked him to sign a paper saying he was satisfied with the terms of their separation, a paper he'd then locked inside his desk. Harvey had left immediately afterward, and Maxim hadn't heard from him since. As far as he knew, the issue was settled.

Then why did he feel so...*un*settled about it?

"Dad?" Megan called.

He dropped the hand he'd been using to massage his temple. "Yes?"

"Where are you? I want to show you the commercial I had to make for one of my classes."

Drawing a deep breath, he put his conversation with Harvey out of his mind. It was Christmas, and Adelaide was coming over. He had better things to think about than Mark's affair— and his own hand in discovering it.

"Coming," he called and went to the kitchen.

THIRTEEN

She was ready and, if she hurried, she'd be on time.

Grabbing the cheesecake she'd made, as well as the wine she'd bought, Adelaide headed for the door. She'd never been to Maxim's place, but she doubted she'd have any trouble finding it. She had GPS on her phone if she got lost. But just as she was stepping out of her house, she saw her friend Ruby pull into the driveway, going far too fast. She came to a screeching halt, and the Escalade jerked back and forth as she slammed the gearshift into Park and jumped out.

Something was wrong. They'd already exchanged gifts over the weekend and hadn't planned to see each other again until after Christmas. Ruby had said she'd be celebrating with her kids and her ex-husband, with whom she was thinking of reconciling. So...what was she doing here?

Adelaide waited on her doorstep as Ruby rushed toward her.

"Adelaide, oh, my God! I'm so sorry."

Sorry? Adelaide didn't know how to react. "For what?"

Confusion descended on Ruby's face and her steps slowed. "You mean...you don't know? It was just on the news. I heard it with my own ears."

The cheesecake and the wine were getting heavy, but Adelaide didn't dare move. "You're not making any sense."

Tears filled Ruby's eyes as she took the wine. Then they stood facing each other, both dressed in their Christmas finery, with Adelaide's heart beating like a jackhammer.

"It's about Mark," Ruby said.

Adelaide couldn't imagine what could be so terrible that Ruby would race over in such a panic. Mark was dead. She'd been dealing with that for two and a half years. Did news get any worse than goodbye *forever*? "What about him?" she asked.

Ruby motioned them inside. "I think you should sit down."

"I don't want to sit down," she said. "I have a dinner date, and I'm going to be—"

"He was having an affair, Adelaide, just as you suspected," Ruby cut in.

This stole Adelaide's breath. After so long, after finally convincing herself that she'd been acting crazy and paranoid and insecure when she'd accused Mark, she was learning that she'd been right from the beginning? "No…"

"Yes."

"With whom?"

"Let's go in," Ruby said and guided Adelaide back into the house.

Adelaide sat at the kitchen table while Ruby took the cheesecake and stowed it in the fridge, along with the wine. "I can't believe something like this would be on the *news*," she muttered. "I mean, I could see it if he was still in office, but—"

"It's pertinent," Ruby said. "You're essentially running in his place and on his reputation. So anything that blackens his name blackens yours."

"But…an *affair*? A lot of guys have extramarital affairs and it hasn't ruined their political careers."

Ruby frowned. "There's more to it."

"More?"

"Mark also took bribes from local developers."

"You've got to be kidding me!"

Ruby crouched in front of her. "I would never kid about something like this."

Adelaide stared at her helplessly. "He couldn't have. I mean… I would've known, wouldn't I?" She tried to think back. They'd always been well-off. Mark came from money, and she'd built the fledgling business they'd started when they got married into a multimillion-dollar enterprise. Would she have noticed if he had more money in his accounts than he should have? Probably not.

"I don't know," Ruby said, obviously miserable.

He wouldn't have needed the money. But the power might have tempted him. He would've liked doling out favors, being the big man who could make the difference. "How did this come to light?" she asked.

"Luke Silici."

The man who'd wanted to run against Maxim in the primary but backed off when she entered the race? *That* Luke Silici?

"There was a clip of him on the news, condemning Mark for lack of integrity," she was saying.

So he intended to join the race? He must be using this to open the door. But she'd already decided to drop out, hadn't she? Because of the pregnancy? He couldn't know that, of course, but even if he entered the race, there was no way he'd beat Maxim.

"It'll be okay," she said. Somehow, she'd figure it out, come to terms with it. There was a chance Silici had been misinformed. She'd do all she could to fight for Mark's reputation, to preserve her memories of him.

But Ruby wouldn't meet her eyes. "That's not all."

Adelaide remembered the hopes she'd had for this Christmas and felt them fade. "There's more than adultery and corruption?"

"Silici said he has copies of some of Mark's e-mails."

Adelaide let her breath go. "They *prove* he was taking bribe money?"

"I don't know what proof they have on the bribe issue. These apparently have to do with the affair."

Covering her face with both hands, Adelaide tried to calm down enough to think. It was going to be okay, wasn't it? She could live with whatever emerged—because it was in the past. It didn't change the present.

Squaring her shoulders, she lowered her hands. "Who was it? Virna? Or Susie?" She'd named Mark's two most attractive field reps, but Ruby shook her head.

"I wish I didn't have to tell you this…"

What could be left? Proof that he'd never loved her? "Tell me," she said. "If you saw it on the news, I'll find out, anyway."

Empathy softened Ruby's face. "It wasn't Virna or Susie or any of the other aides. It—it was an intern."

Adelaide felt a surge of righteous anger. Those interns were young, some of them just out of high school. "Which one?" she cried.

Ruby cringed. "Phoenix Day."

This was the last name Adelaide had expected to hear. She was so stunned she couldn't move. "There must be some mistake. Phoenix is a *boy*, the sweetest boy you could ever meet."

Ruby took her hands. "I know."

"You're saying— That can't be true," she whispered. "Mark wasn't gay. Mark…" Remembering his lack of interest the past couple of years they'd lived together, Adelaide fell silent. He'd told her he was too stressed to maintain much of a sex life, too pressured at work, too busy. Was it something else? Something more? An inappropriate attraction to *Phoenix*?

"The boy has agreed to come forward," Ruby was saying. "He's providing copies of the correspondence between him and Mark. At least, according to the news."

Adelaide didn't know how to respond, except to deny it, regardless of any proof anyone claimed to have. "This can't be true. It's a political move, a way to get me to bow out of the race."

"That's what I thought, too," Ruby said. "But…"

"But what?" Adelaide echoed.

"I don't think it's Luke who wants you out of the race. I think it's Maxim Donahue."

Adelaide opened her mouth to argue. Ruby had no idea of the baby or how the situation with Maxim had changed. But Ruby spoke before she could explain.

"It has to be," she insisted. "Silici said Maxim received an anonymous tip, that it was his campaign manager who ran down all the details."

Where was she?

The girls had their friends over. They were chatting happily as they munched on the appetizers Rosa had made, but Maxim had been too busy watching the clock to eat with them. Adelaide was late. She'd said she'd arrive at six, but it was nearly six-thirty. He figured he'd give her another fifteen minutes, so he didn't seem impatient, but when 6:45 p.m. rolled around she still wasn't there. Neither had she called him.

"Dad, didn't you say your friend would be here soon?"

Megan had finally noticed Adelaide's tardiness, perhaps because he'd grown so quiet.

"I'm sure she's on her way, but… I'll check."

Taking his cell phone, he stepped out of the room. But Adelaide didn't pick up. She didn't answer her house phone, either.

Where could she be? Planning to drive over there, he grabbed his keys from the counter and started for the door when he received a call. Assuming it would be her, he pulled his cell out of his pocket and punched the talk button without glancing at caller ID. "Hello?"

"Maxim, you are truly amazing!"

It definitely wasn't Adelaide. That voice belonged to his assistant, Peter Goodrich. Peter kept Maxim's capitol office running smoothly and interfaced with Jan Kenny, who ran Maxim's district office. He also volunteered on the campaign, so they spent a lot of time together. Maxim considered Peter his best hire. But he didn't want to talk to him on Christmas Eve. "Peter, are you drunk?"

"What? Of course not. You know I don't drink."

"You sound drunk." Tall and skinny, with a very deep voice, Peter was so circumspect that Maxim liked to tease him. But he was half-serious tonight. Peter sounded much more animated than usual.

"I'm just...surprised," Peter said.

"About what?" Maxim looked at his watch.

"You did it, man. There's no way she's gonna beat you now."

Slightly irritated because he didn't want to talk business while he was so preoccupied with other things, Maxim scratched his neck. "I don't know what you're talking about."

"I'm talking about Mark Fairfax. How did you know? I mean...what a shocker. I *never* would've guessed he was gay."

Until this moment, Maxim had only been paying partial attention. He'd been too busy watching the clock and keeping an eye on his driveway through the window, expecting Adelaide to pull in at any time. Now every bit of his energy and focus turned toward the conversation. "How do you know about Fairfax?"

"I guess it was on the news. I didn't see it, but someone called Martha and she called me."

Martha Sanchez worked for him, too. She handled all the scheduling for Maxim and the field reps. She wouldn't have felt as comfortable calling him at home, but she and Peter worked well together and had become close friends.

"I mean, it's true, isn't it?" Peter asked. "It's not a joke."

With a silent curse, Maxim crossed the room and sank onto the couch. Damn Harvey Sillinger! He'd taken the bribe money and he'd still gone after Adelaide.

"Maxim?"

"I'm here," he muttered.

"You seem upset."

He *was* upset. If word of Fairfax's affair had been on the news, Adelaide had heard about it, too. They were in politics, for crying out loud. They had people who were paid to watch and listen for any mention of their names in the media. If she hadn't seen it on the news herself, she'd probably received a call very similar to this one. *Son of a bitch.*

"Maxim? Isn't this good news?" Peter asked, uncertain now.

"No. It's not good news," he said and hung up.

FOURTEEN

It hadn't been easy to get Ruby to leave. But Ruby had kids. She couldn't miss Christmas. And although Ruby invited her, there was no way Adelaide wanted to join the party. She loved the children, but this was the first time the family would be celebrating the holidays together in three years. Adelaide refused to interfere with that. Besides, she'd rather be alone.

Bundled up in a wool coat, scarf and gloves, she sat on a bench in Capitol Park, gazing at the building that sheltered California's government. Called the People's Building, it was a domed piece of Greek Revival and Roman–Corinthian architecture resembling the Capitol Building in Washington, D.C. Tonight, the Christmas lights that adorned the building and the trees shone through the fog, making Adelaide feel as if she'd just stepped into the scene portrayed on the Christmas cards they sold in nearby gift shops.

Except she felt no warmth of spirit. She was cold inside, and as empty as the building appeared to be.

Mark had always loved it here, she thought. But not because of the beauty. It was the power that drew him.

Was it the same for Maxim?

Probably. He'd done just about everything he could to retain his seat, hadn't he? And that included making her believe he cared about her. She wasn't entirely sure it was an act, but even if he'd received the anonymous tip Ruby had mentioned and gone after Mark before they'd had the chance to get to know each other, did she really want another man obsessed with his own ambition? Could she deal with a second relationship like the one she'd had with Mark? He'd started putting so many things before her—among them, apparently, his interns.

She shuddered as she imagined what must have happened with Phoenix. Mark had hidden his interest in the boy so well. Or had she merely missed the signs? He'd certainly talked about Phoenix. He'd even had him over to the house. After learning that he didn't have a supportive family, she'd felt sorry for the boy. She certainly knew what being alone was like. But now she saw how effectively she'd been manipulated. It was Mark who'd told her about Phoenix's family. Who knew if it was even true? Had they been kissing and touching in another room while she was right there in the house?

Maybe. Her presence provided the perfect cover, should anyone ever raise any questions. She never would've suspected, hadn't watched them closely at all.

That must've made it pretty darn easy.

But Mark hadn't expected to die and have someone as tenacious and determined as Maxim take over his seat. Would this have come out if she hadn't entered the race? She doubted it. Why would Maxim have bothered with Mark otherwise? Ironically, it was her desire to stand up for her husband because of Maxim's lack of respect for him that'd brought the truth to light.

What did those e-mail messages say? Did she even want to know?

"You're *such* a liar," she told Mark. It wasn't only the fact that he'd broken their marriage vows that hurt. It was that she'd lost so much self-confidence wondering why she couldn't interest her own husband. "You bastard."

Her phone vibrated in her purse. It'd been going off all night. She would've cut the power, but Ruby had made her promise not to. She wanted to be able to check in. But it was Maxim again.

Adelaide wasn't ready to talk to him. Pressing the button that would shut down her phone, she got up and started to walk around the gardens.

An old man with white hair stood near an American Indian monument. He nodded as she passed him. "Merry Christmas," he said with a smile.

Adelaide wasn't home. Maxim had been to her place three different times.

Had she gone over to a friend's? Maybe. But he didn't know the people who were closest to her, wasn't sure who to call. He could understand why she might not want to spend the evening with him, but he was worried about her, worried enough that he'd taken to cruising the streets around her house, hoping to spot her car. It wasn't the best way to give his girls a good Christmas, but he was so preoccupied with this he couldn't go home. And they'd assured him they were fine, that they understood.

So where was Adelaide? She couldn't be in any stores or restaurants.

It was so late that even the businesses that stayed open on Christmas Eve were closed.

He remembered her mentioning Mark's parents and wondered if she'd gone to their home. Maybe they'd heard the news and called her.

After pulling to the side of the road, he used his phone to check information. Sure enough, the Fairfaxes were listed. But did he dare call them at midnight on Christmas Eve? He was the reason their son's reputation was ruined…

"This won't be easy," he muttered, but he dialed the number, anyway.

After several rings, he heard a woman's sleepy voice say, "Hello." Tempted to hang up, he hesitated. He didn't want to trouble these poor people, especially on Christmas. But he had to know if they'd heard from Adelaide.

"Mrs. Fairfax?"

The sleep cleared from her voice, changing to confusion. "Yes?"

"This is Maxim Donahue."

He could sense her unwillingness to believe him. "Is this some kind of crank call?" she asked.

"No, it's not. I'm looking for Adelaide. I was wondering if you've heard from her tonight."

"You're looking for— Do you know what time it is?" she snapped.

"Yes, ma'am."

"You have no business waking people in the middle of the night, no matter who you are. And after all you've said to discredit my son, why do you think I'd help you?"

Maxim wasn't sure if Mrs. Fairfax's words meant she knew the latest or not. Since Mark had changed and begun to go back on so many of his campaign promises, Maxim had been pretty vocal about his lack of admiration for him. She could be referring to that. "I disagree with just about everything your son did, Mrs. Fairfax. I won't pretend otherwise. But I'm worried about Adelaide. Will you please tell me if you've seen her or heard from her? If you know where she's at?"

"I have no idea. Why?"

Now he was certain they didn't know about Phoenix. She'd still be raging at him if she did. "I'm afraid you'll find out soon enough. I apologize for disturbing your sleep."

"Wait— What do you have to do with Adelaide?"

He told himself to hang up. But Mrs. Fairfax had answered his question. He figured he owed her the same respect. "I'm in love with her," he said and disconnected before she could rebound from the shock.

Christmas carols were the only songs she could find on the radio. Adelaide had heard enough of them for one year, but Christmas carols were better than silence, so she let them play. She'd gone to Midnight Mass at a beautiful church not far from the capitol building. She wasn't Catholic, but when she'd noticed the crowd gathering at the doors, she'd felt drawn to join them.

She was glad she had. The service had reminded her of the meaning of Christmas and given her a sense of peace. It had also reminded her of the baby she carried and the hope that having a child brought into her life. Did the past really matter? Not if she didn't let it, she decided.

But the minute she pulled into her driveway and saw Maxim there in his car, waiting for her, she tensed up again. She couldn't deal with the powerful emotions he evoked—in addition to the disappointment of learning what she had about Mark. She wanted to put Mark behind her and forget once and for all, and she was pretty sure that meant she couldn't have anything to do with politics.

That included Maxim.

After parking in her garage and cutting the engine, she sat in her car for a moment, but Maxim didn't approach. He got out of his vehicle and leaned against it, waiting. She could see the outline of his body in her rearview mirror.

What would she say to him? As humiliating as it was to admit, he'd been right about Mark. Mark wasn't the man she'd thought he was. But she couldn't blame Maxim for what Mark had done. Maxim's only sin was exposing him. Although that stung, she didn't have the right to be too angry. He'd been her election opponent before he'd been her lover, and any other opponent would've done the same thing.

The radio went silent when she pulled the door latch. She liked the new delay feature that let the music stay on after the engine was off, but the sudden silence felt ominous.

"Hey," he said as she came out of the garage.

"Hi."

He was wearing a heavy coat, a burgundy sweater and a pair of jeans. Just seeing him made her remember what it was like to be in his arms. She'd felt safer there than anywhere else. But she tried to convince herself that was only because he'd saved her life. What she felt was hero worship. Admiration for a handsome man. It wasn't love. She didn't want any part of love, not anymore.

He met her at the walkway leading to the house. "You okay?"

She pushed the button on her key chain that would close the garage door. "I'm fine."

"I've been worried."

"You shouldn't be here," she said. "You've got your girls at home."

"They're not the only ones who matter to me."

Ignoring that statement, she turned on her heel and marched to the house. "It's late and I'm really tired. Would you mind if we talked another time? It's been a...rough night."

"I know," he said. "I should give you some space. But...can I at least apologize?"

"For what? You wanted to win, and I was in the way. I understand."

"Adelaide—"

Raising a hand to stop him, she donned a polite mask. "Look, I don't blame you. If I were in your shoes, maybe I would've done the same thing. I mean, the object of any campaign is to win. Mark was... Mark was a cheat and a liar, and everything you've ever said about him is probably true."

"I don't care about that. I didn't come over here to rub your nose in what he's done."

"Why not? Enjoy it while it lasts. This was quite the political coup." She knew she was being harsher than she had a right to be. But she'd been wrong when they'd talked about the baby—she couldn't be open to any of the options he'd named. They required too much trust, and trust was something she didn't have anymore.

A muscle jumped in his jaw. "So you're blowing me off?"

"It won't work."

"What about the baby?"

"You get the senate seat. I get the baby." Stepping inside, she closed the door behind her.

Maxim was still standing on Adelaide's stoop when the porch light went off. He didn't know whether to bang on the door or leave. Memories of the time they'd spent in the mountains, especially of that second night when they'd said so much without saying a word, made him want to insist she come back and talk to him. But he couldn't force her to let him into her life if she didn't want him there. He'd been crazy to think she did. It was Mark she'd always loved, Mark she *still* loved, even though the stupid son of a bitch had been a complete fraud. Mark had never deserved her.

But maybe Maxim didn't deserve her, either.

Thinking of his girls waiting patiently for him at home, he released a long sigh and walked back to his car. He'd been so excited about having Megan and Callie meet Adelaide. Then Harvey had ruined it all.

The radio came on as soon as he started his car and Elvis Presley began singing, "I'll have a blue Christmas without you—"

Quickly changing the station, Maxim backed out of the driveway.

★ ★ ★

As she watched Maxim's headlights swing out into the street,
Adelaide felt like crying. But she choked back her tears. She'd
done the right thing. Despite all the years they'd been ac-
quainted, she didn't know Maxim, not really. Maybe he was
no better than Mark.

"Getting with me was just another way to protect his political aspirations," she said. But all the things she remembered
him saying to her when they were together seemed to dispute
that statement. *I can't pretend to be Mark again. If I make love to
you, it'll be because you want* me... *We're talking about a baby, Adelaide. Our baby. My career doesn't come before that... You're the most
beautiful woman I've ever laid eyes on...*

Had he meant any of it? It'd *felt* real. Unlike Mark, Maxim
didn't use flattery. He only said what he meant. That was why
she'd been upset enough to run against him. He'd told some
reporter that Mark had been worse for the district than if it
had gone unrepresented, that he'd been one of the most selfish
individuals on the planet.

And, as she'd just told him, he'd been right. Why was she
blaming him for being right?

The message light blinked on her answering machine. Seeing it, she realized she'd forgotten to turn her cell phone back
on after the church service. Ruby was probably going crazy
with worry.

Trying to put Maxim out of her mind, she crossed the room
and pressed the play button. Sure enough, her friend had called
a number of times. Adelaide was about to stop the playback
without listening to the rest. She was one touch of a button
away from erasing the whole thing when she heard the voice
of her former mother-in-law.

"Adelaide? Are you okay? What's going on? Maxim Donahue
just called here. Can you believe it? At midnight on Christmas
Eve? We don't even know him. I mean, we've met but never

really talked. He was looking for you. Only now I'm thinking he must've been drunk, because when I asked him why he
wanted to find you he said...he said he was *in love* with you.
And then he hung up. That's it. Isn't that crazy? He's the man
you're running against, isn't he? The one who never liked Mark?
Anyway, give us a call. We'd like to see you this Christmas.
You haven't swung by in a while."

Another message from Ruby came on right afterward. "Damn
it, Adelaide, this isn't fair. Why the hell won't you pick up?"

Adelaide scarcely heard it. As she hit the stop button, her
mother-in-law's message was still playing in her mind: *He said
he was in love with you.*

Was it true? Would Maxim really have come right out and
said that to Mark's *parents?*

Stunned, Adelaide slowly sank onto the sofa. Was she being
as smart as she assumed? Or was she letting Mark ruin what she
had with Maxim the same way he'd ruined the last few years
of their marriage?

Her hand shaking, she reached into her purse, got her phone
and turned it on. She'd missed eighteen calls from Maxim. Why
would he spend his whole Christmas Eve trying to reach her
if he didn't really care? He couldn't have been doing it simply
to neutralize the opposition. The scandal that had broken tonight would cripple her campaign; he wouldn't have to worry
about her even if she did keep running.

He said he was in love with you.

Her eyes welled up with tears as she dialed his number. She
didn't really expect him to answer. Not after what she'd said
to him at the door. But he did.

"Hello?"

"Maxim?"

"Yes?"

"I'm sorry. I—" Her voice broke but she battled through it.
"I think I'm just scared."

"I'm not like Mark, Adelaide," he said. "You can count on me."

Recalling the way he'd hauled her out of that Cessna and made her dig that snow cave, Adelaide smiled. He was right. She could count on him.

"Will you come back?" she asked hopefully.

"Are you kidding? I turned around the second I saw it was you. I'm already pulling into your driveway."

Tossing her phone aside, Adelaide hurried to the door—and rushed into his arms as he came up the walk.

"Thank God," she said. "I thought I'd lost you."

EPILOGUE

As Adelaide finished arranging the last of the presents under the tree, she could hardly believe an entire year had passed since she'd been stranded in the Sierras. So much had changed since then—she'd dropped out of the race, gotten married, had a baby. But she didn't regret those changes; they'd all been good. She didn't even regret that Maxim was still in politics. Not only had he won the primary, he'd retained his seat in the November election, but the way he handled his job was so different from Mark.

"What are you thinking about?"

She smiled as Maxim walked into the room carrying Connor, their three-month-old. "How close we came to walking away from each other last year."

"We didn't come *that* close," he said.

She arched her eyebrows at him and he grinned.

"I was in love. I wouldn't have let you get rid of me that easily."

Returning his smile, she adjusted the garland on the tree. "Do you think Harvey ever regrets what he did?"

"I would guess he does. He loved California politics. I'm sure he wasn't happy when there wasn't another politician in the state who'd work with him."

"You have to be able to trust your campaign manager," she said. "It was nice of Luke not to hire him. He could've justified doing it, you know."

"No, Luke's a good man. He didn't appreciate what Harvey did, even though Harvey returned my money." He held up his son and laughed when the baby gave him a goofy smile. "I've been encouraging Luke to run for the state assembly."

"That's a great idea." She reached for the baby. "Here, hand him to me and grab his car seat. We need to head to the airport to get the girls."

Maxim checked his watch. "You're kidding, right? We've got an hour."

The wait was making Adelaide crazy. "Maybe they'll get in early."

"And maybe we'll have to drive around that pickup circle a million times until they show up."

"Come on." She waved him toward the baby's car seat, which was sitting near the sofa. "I can't wait to see them. And I know they can't wait to see the baby."

"They just saw him at Thanksgiving."

"But he changes so fast. And they love having a little brother."

"They love having a mother again, too," he said softly. "Thank you for being so good to them."

Adelaide didn't even have to try. They enriched her life as much as Maxim or Connor. "I never dreamed I could ever be this happy," she said.

He raised her chin to kiss her. "And I never dreamed I could ever be this much in love. Merry Christmas, Mrs. Donahue."

Adelaide closed her eyes as their lips met. She had everything she could ever want, thanks to one snowy Christmas...

* * * * *

THE PERFECT HOLIDAY

SHERRYL WOODS

ONE

"Mom, it's snowing," Hannah shouted from the living room.

Savannah heard the pounding of her daughter's footsteps on the wood floors, then the eight-year-old skidded to a stop in front of her, eyes shining.

"Can I go outside? *Please?*" Hannah begged. "This is so cool. I've never seen snow before."

"I know," Savannah told her, amused despite herself. "We don't get a lot of snow in Florida."

"Wait till my friends back home hear we're going to have a white Christmas. It is *so* awesome. I am *sooo* glad we moved to Vermont."

Though she could understand her daughter's excited reaction to her first snowfall, from Savannah's perspective the snow was anything but a blessing. Since her arrival a couple of days ago, she'd discovered that the furnace at Holiday Retreat wasn't reliable. The wind had a nasty way of sneaking in through all sorts of unexpected cracks in the insulation, and the roof—well, the best she could say about that was that it hadn't fallen in on their heads…yet. With the weight of a foot of damp snow on it, who knew what could happen?

It had been three weeks since the call had come from the attorney informing her that she was a beneficiary of her aunt Mae's estate. The bittersweet news had come the day before Thanksgiving, and for the first time since her divorce the year before, Savannah had thought she finally had something for which to be thankful besides her feisty, incredible daughter. Now that she'd seen the inn, she was beginning to wonder if this wasn't just another of Fate's cruel jokes.

Holiday Retreat had been in the family for generations. Built in the early 1800s as a home for a wealthy ancestor, the huge, gracious house in the heart of Vermont ski country had become an inn when the family had fallen on hard times. Savannah could still remember coming here as a child and thinking it was like a Christmas fantasy, with the lights on the eaves and in the branches of the evergreens outside, a fire blazing in the living room and the aroma of banana-nut bread and cookies drifting from the kitchen. The tree, which they cut down themselves and decorated on Christmas Eve, always scraped the twelve-foot ceiling.

Aunt Mae—Savannah's great-aunt actually—had been in her prime then. A hearty fifty-something, she came from sturdy New England stock. She had bustled through the house making everyone in the family feel welcome, fixing elaborate meals effortlessly and singing carols boisterously, if a bit tunelessly. It was the one time of the year when there were no paying guests at the inn—just aunts and uncles and cousins all gathered for holiday festivities. To an only child like Savannah, the atmosphere had seemed magical.

If the house had been in a state of disrepair then and if the furniture had been shabby, she hadn't noticed it. Now it promised to be one of the world's worst money pits.

"Mom, did you hear me?" Hannah said again. "I said it's snowing."

"I heard," Savannah said glumly.

Hannah's blue eyes were alight with excitement. "Isn't it great?"

Savannah tried to work up some enthusiasm to match her daughter's, but all she could think about was the probability that too much snow would make the sagging roof plummet down on top of their heads as they slept. Still, she forced a smile.

"There's nothing like a white Christmas," she agreed.

"Can we get a tree and make hot chocolate and sing carols like you used to do when you were a kid?" Hannah pleaded. "Then it won't matter if we don't have any presents."

Savannah cringed at the realistic assessment of their financial plight. The divorce had left her with next to nothing. Her ex-husband hadn't yet been persuaded to send even the paltry child support payments required by the court. As for alimony, she had a hunch hell would freeze over before she saw a penny of that. Since their divorce had hinged on her objections to his workaholic tendencies, Rob clearly saw no reason she should benefit from the income derived from those tendencies.

Last night, after Hannah had gone to bed, Savannah had sat for hours with her checkbook, a pile of final bills from Florida and a list of the repairs needed before the inn could be opened to paying guests in the new year. Her conclusion had left her feeling more despondent than ever. It was going to take more than a glistening snowfall and a few carols to brighten her spirits.

No matter how hard she tried telling herself that they were better off than they had been, she still wasn't totally convinced. Maybe if they'd stayed in Florida, she would have found a better-paying job, something that wouldn't have left them scraping by after making house payments and buying groceries. At least they wouldn't have had to worry about the kind of exorbitant heating bill from last winter that she'd found in a kitchen drawer here. Maybe selling the heavily mortgaged house that had been her home with Rob had been another error in judgment. It had given her barely enough cash to make the trip and to make a start on the repairs the inn needed.

"Mom, what's wrong?" Hannah asked. "Are you afraid we made a mistake?"

Seeing the concern that filled her daughter's eyes and the worried crease in her forehead, Savannah shook off her fears. Hannah deserved better than the hand she'd been dealt up to now. For the first time since the divorce, she was acting like a kid again. Savannah refused to let her own worries steal that from her daughter.

"Absolutely not!" she said emphatically. "I think coming here was exactly the right thing to do. We're going to make it work. How many people get to live in a place that looks like a picture on a Christmas card?"

She gave her daughter a fierce hug. "How about some hot chocolate?"

"Then can we go out in the snow?" Hannah pleaded.

"Tell you what—why don't you bundle up in your new winter jacket and go outside for a few minutes so you can see what it feels like? I'll call you when the hot chocolate's ready."

Hannah shook her head. "No, Mom, I want you to come, too. Please."

Savannah thought of all she had to do, then dismissed it. It was only a few days till Christmas. Most of the contractors she'd spoken to said they couldn't come by till after the first of the year. Until she and Hannah made a trip into the small town at the foot of the mountain, she couldn't strip the old wallpaper or paint. Why not think of this as an unexpected gift of time?

"Okay, kiddo, let's do it," she said, grabbing her coat off a hook by the door. "Only for a few minutes, though. We're going to need some heavy boots, wool scarves and thick gloves before we spend much time outside. We don't want to start the new year with frostbite."

"Whatever," Hannah said, tugging her out the door, seemingly oblivious to the blast of icy air that greeted them and froze their breath.

There was an inch of damp, heavy snow on the ground and clinging to the towering evergreens already, and it was still falling steadily. With no chains or snow tires on the car, they'd be lucky if they got out of the driveway for a couple of days, Savannah concluded, sinking back into gloominess.

Then she caught the awed expression on Hannah's face as she tilted her head up and caught snowflakes on her tongue. She remembered doing the exact same thing the first time she'd visited Aunt Mae and seen snow. She'd been even younger than Hannah, and for several years the Christmas trips to Vermont had been the highlight of her life. She couldn't recall why they'd stopped coming as a family.

She'd come on her own several times after she was grown, but those visits had dwindled off when she'd met, then married, Rob. He was a Florida boy through and through and flatly refused to visit anyplace where the temperature dropped below the midfifties.

Now that Aunt Mae was gone, Savannah deeply regretted not having done more than write an occasional letter enclosing pictures of Hannah. Her aunt had never once judged her, though, and she'd been totally supportive when Savannah had told her about the breakup of her marriage. She'd sent one check explained away as a birthday gift and offered more, but Savannah had turned her down. She'd lied and said they were getting along okay, but she knew now that her aunt had seen through her. She had done in death what Savannah hadn't permitted her to do while she was living.

If other members of her family resented the gesture, Savannah didn't know about it. She'd lost touch with most of them years ago. She'd been estranged from her parents ever since she'd divorced a man of whom they enthusiastically approved. Aunt Mae had tried to broker a peace agreement between Savannah and her father, but he'd remained stubbornly silent and unyielding. He'd been convinced Savannah was a fool for divorcing a man who brought home a steady paycheck.

"Mom, I love it here!" Hannah announced, throwing her arms around Savannah. She was shivering even in her heavy coat. "I want to build a snowman. Can we?"

"I think we'll need a little more snow than this," Savannah told her. "Besides, I'm freezing. How about that hot chocolate?"

"I want to stay out here. I'm not cold," Hannah insisted.

"Then why are your teeth chattering?" Savannah teased. "Come on, baby. Even if you won't admit to freezing, I will. There will be more snow once we've warmed up. I'll teach you how to make snow angels."

"What are snow angels?" Hannah asked, her interest immediately piqued.

"You'll see. Aunt Mae taught me when I was a little girl. Now come inside and get warm."

Far more agreeable lately than she had been for months, Hannah finally acquiesced, following Savannah into the kitchen. Savannah studied her daughter's sparkling eyes, pink cheeks and tousled hair and knew she'd done the right thing, no matter what struggles might lie ahead.

Despite the sad state of the inn, they were going to have the fresh beginning they both deserved, she decided with a surge of determination. And it was going to start with the very best Christmas Hannah had ever had, even if she was going to have to do it on a shoestring. Some of her very best holiday memories had cost nothing.

As for the practicalities—the repairs, the marketing plan she needed to devise—they would just have to wait for the new year.

★ ★ ★

Mae Holiday had been one of the most eccentric people Trace Franklin had ever known. He had met her when he'd been dragged to Vermont for an idyllic summer getaway by one of the women he'd dated. That had been eight or nine years ago. Twice that number of women had passed through his life since then. Of them all, the one he hadn't dated—Mae—had been the most memorable.

She'd been the grandmother he'd never had, the mentor who tried her best to bring some balance into his life. Until the day she'd died at seventy-eight, it had frustrated her no end that she hadn't managed to convince him that romance was just as important as money.

Trace knew better. His parents had been madly in love, but it hadn't brought either one of them a blasted thing except heartache. Love had kept his mother with a man who never had two nickels to rub together, a man whose big killing was always "just around the corner."

While John Franklin had spun his dreams, his wife had cleaned houses, worked in fast-food chains and, finally, when it was almost too late to matter, gotten a steady job selling toys to families that could afford to give their kids elaborate back-yard swing sets and fancy computer games.

When Trace was fifteen, his mom had brought one of those games home to him, but by then he'd been way past playing childish games. He'd been working with single-minded focus on graduating from high school with honors and getting a scholarship to the best college in the state. He didn't want to play with toys. He wanted to own a whole blasted toy company.

And now he did. The irony, which Mae had seen right away, was that he still didn't have time to play. He wasn't even sure he knew how.

He was driving along the snow-covered roads of Vermont right now because of Mae. On his last visit to see her at the end of October, she had made a final request. She had known she was dying, had known it for fully a year before the cancer had finally taken her, but she hadn't said a word to Trace until that last visit when she had detailed her losing battle, reciting the facts with a stoicism and acceptance that had awed him.

"I want you to promise me something," she had said as they'd sat in front of the fire on his last night there. Despite the heat of the blaze, she'd been wrapped in blankets, and still she had shivered.

"Anything," Trace had responded, and meant it. Not only was Mae one of the earliest investors and biggest stockholders in Franklin Toys, she was his friend.

"I want you to spend Christmas here at Holiday Retreat."

It was only a couple of months away and it would require some juggling of his schedule, but there was no question that he would do it. "Of course I will," he said at once. "We'll have a wonderful time."

She had squeezed his hand. "I won't be here, Trace. You know that."

Even now, the memory of that moment brought the sharp sting of tears to his eyes. Her gaze had been unrelenting. From the beginning of her illness, she had refused to sugarcoat the truth to herself. Now that she was revealing it to others, she expected them to face it, as well. The cancer had spread too far and too fast before the doctors had had the first inkling there was anything wrong. She was dying and there was going to be no reprieve.

Trace had returned her unflinching gaze, heartbroken yet unable to face her death with less bravery than she was showing. "Why, Mae? Why would you want me here after you're gone?"

"Just do it for me," she whispered, her voice fading. "Promise."

"I promise," he'd said just as her eyes drifted closed. He'd been willing to do anything that would give her comfort. He owed her that much, and more.

Two weeks later Mae Holiday had died peacefully, a life-long friend—a man she had loved deeply but never married—by her side. Now Trace was on his way to Vermont to pay his respects...and to keep his promise.

TWO

There was smoke curling from the chimney at Holiday Retreat. Lights were blazing from the downstairs windows. Trace sat in his car and stared, trying to make sense of it. He'd expected to spend the Christmas holiday alone here, mourning Mae in private, reliving the happy times they'd spent together over the years they'd known each other.

And, he conceded with a rueful grimace, catching up on the mounds of paperwork he'd brought with him, along with his cell phone, laptop computer and fax machine.

What the dickens was going on? he wondered, thoroughly disgruntled by this turn of events. Mae had said nothing about anyone else being here. Nor had the attorney in the note that had accompanied a key to the inn. The note had merely advised that Mae had seen to having plenty of food and firewood on hand and that she hoped his visit would be a memorable one. If he had any problems, he was to contact Nate Daniels, the man Trace had heard of, but never met, the man who was the shadowy love of Mae's life.

Trace fingered the old-fashioned key in his pocket as he walked through the foot or so of recently accumulated snow.

He was halfway to the door when he spotted indentations, a hectic swirl of footsteps and something else. He looked more closely and saw…not one but two snow angels, the sort made by flopping down in new-fallen snow and moving outstretched arms to create wings.

At first the sight brought a smile, reminding him of innocent, long-ago days as a kid before the unpredictability of the family's day-to-day existence had registered with him. Winters back home had been relatively mild, so that rare snowfalls had been regarded with sheer delight. He hadn't owned a sled, but he'd had his share of snowball fights and made more than a few snow angels.

Then the full implication of the snow angels sank in, and pleasant memories gave way to edginess. Judging from the smaller size of one snow angel, there was a kid on the premises and that generally meant noisy chaos, the last thing he'd anticipated when he'd made the commitment to Mae to spend the Christmas holidays here. For a man who made his living by providing expensive hobbies and toys to children, Trace was amazingly uneasy when confronted with an individual child. For him, toys were a multimillion-dollar business, not entertainment. Unless he could persuade himself to use whatever child was around to conduct market research, this whole situation had just gone from bad to worse.

He was about to turn tail and run, but then he heard Mae's voice in his head as she'd extracted that promise from him. He'd never gone back on his word to her, ever. He wasn't about to start now.

Filled with a sense of dread, he made his way to the front door. He stood on the slick porch debating whether to ring the bell, rather than walking in on whomever was here. Then again, he had just as much right to be here as the unknown occupant did. More, perhaps. That remained to be seen.

He stuck the key in the lock, turned it and pushed open the

heavy door, noting as he did that it was in serious need of paint. It had once been bright red, as had all the shutters on the house. Now it was faded to a shade only slightly deeper than pink. Maybe he'd take care of that while he was here. It would be a fitting homage to Mae to see the doors and shutters restored to their scarlet holiday brilliance.

He was about to close the door when a girl—just about the size of the snow angel outside, he noted—skidded to a stop in front of him on one of the scooters his company made. It had been the hottest gift of the holiday season two years ago. It was not meant to be used indoors, though he could understand the temptation given the wide expanse of hardwood floors. And it wasn't as if those floors were in particularly great shape. They could do with sanding and a fresh coat of wax. Something else he could do while he was here…in Mae's memory.

First, though, he had to figure out who was this imp of a child regarding him with blatant curiosity, her golden hair scooped through the opening of a baseball cap, her T-shirt half in and half out of her jeans.

"Who are you and what are you doing here?" he demanded in the no-nonsense tone he used on executives who'd failed to deliver on their division's projections.

The kid didn't even flinch. "I'm Hannah and I live here. Who are you? And how come you have a key to my house?"

Trace's head began to throb. What the devil was Mae up to? "Are your parents here?"

"Just my mom. My dad divorced us. He lives in Florida. My mom's baking Christmas cookies." She cast an appealing smile at him. "Don't they smell great?"

Trace automatically sniffed the air. They did smell fantastic, just the way Mae's always had. He'd eaten fancier food than what was served at Holiday Retreat, but he'd never had any that tasted better or was prepared with more love. He wondered if

Hannah's mom shared Mae's talents in the kitchen, then sighed. That was hardly the point.

"Want me to get my mom?" Hannah inquired.

"I'll find her," Trace said, heading determinedly toward the kitchen. He'd taken only a step before he turned back. "By the way, that scooter is not an indoor toy."

The kid's smile never faltered. "Maybe not, but it works great in here." And off she went, completely unimpressed by his admonishment.

Trace sighed and went in search of her mother.

He wasn't sure what he expected, but it certainly wasn't the frail wisp of a woman who was bent over in an incredibly provocative pose, her head stuck halfway into the huge, professional-quality stainless-steel oven that had been Mae's pride and joy.

This room was where Mae had splurged, spending her money to design a kitchen that was both welcoming and efficient. Everything in it, from the refrigerator to the granite countertops, was top-of-the-line. When she had shown it to Trace a few years ago, she'd been as excited as a kid on Christmas morning. She told him it was how she'd spent her first dividends from her stock in Franklin Toys.

And now there was an interloper in here, he thought, feeling oddly possessive on Mae's behalf. Unless this woman could prove her right to be on the premises, Trace would have her packed up and out of here before nightfall, even if he had to call on local law enforcement to toss her out on her attractive backside.

Despite his impatience to accomplish that task, and rather than risk scaring her half to death while she was that close to incinerating herself, he waited, barely resisting the desire to haul her out of there immediately and demand an explanation for her presence.

Of course, he was also having some difficulty resisting the

urge to smooth his hand over that narrow curve of her denim-clad bottom. That, he concluded, was a very dangerous temptation. He admonished himself to forget it the same way he'd scolded Hannah only moments earlier. He hoped he paid more attention to the warning than she had, since there was likely a lot more at stake than scarred floorboards.

The woman finally retreated, holding a tray almost as big as she was. As she turned to set it on the granite countertop, she spotted him and let go of the tray with a yelp of surprise. Trace caught it in midair, then let out a curse of his own as the hot metal seared his fingers. He dropped the tray with a clatter. Cookies went flying. And the woman regarded him as if he were a living, breathing embodiment of Scrooge and he'd deliberately set out to ruin her Christmas.

"Look what you've done," she said, scowling at him as she bent to pick up the broken remains of sugar cookies decorated with pretty red and green designs. She waved a hatless Santa with half a beard under Trace's nose. "Just look at this."

She didn't seem one bit concerned with the fact that he'd burned himself trying to save her blasted cookies. He stepped past her and stuck his hands under cold running water. That finally got her attention.

"Oh, fudge, you burned yourself, didn't you?" she said. "What was I thinking? I'm sorry. Here, let me see."

She nudged up against him and grabbed his hand. Her touch was anything but soothing. In fact, now Trace was suddenly burning on the inside, too.

"Sit," she ordered before he could unscramble his thoughts. "There's a first-aid kit around here somewhere."

"Cabinet next to the stove," Trace told her, blowing on his fingers.

She stopped and stared. "How do you know that?"

"Mae was always getting distracted and having little accidents in the kitchen. She said it paid to keep the bandages close at hand."

Rather than fetching the first-aid supplies, the woman sank down onto a chair, her eyes promptly filling with unshed tears. "She did say that, didn't she?" she whispered. "I must have heard her say it a hundred times. And even before she remodeled in here, she kept aloe and antiseptic spray and bandages right by the stove."

Trace was startled by the depth of emotion in this stranger's voice. Her love for Mae was written all over her face. That much raw pain was more than he knew how to deal with; his own emotions were shaky enough. He stepped carefully around her and got his own ointment and bandages, using the time to collect himself and try to fill with renewed resolve the tiny chink she'd created in his desire to be rid of her.

When he was finished repairing the damage to his hand, he finally risked another look at her. The color had returned to her cheeks, but there was no mistaking the signs of a woman on the edge. He'd seen that same stressed expression often enough on his mother's face, the same tightness around the mouth, the wariness in her eyes.

"You okay?" he asked at last.

She nodded, still blinking back tears. "Sometimes it just catches me off guard, the fact that she's gone. I hadn't seen her in several years, but I always had such wonderful memories of being here, especially around the holidays."

That must have been a long time ago, Trace thought with a surprising surge of anger on Mae's behalf. He'd been here with Mae every year since that trip when they'd first met. He'd never been entirely sure how she'd cajoled him into coming, but year after year he'd found himself driving north from New York City, looking forward to spending time with the closest thing he had to family now that his folks were both dead.

Oddly, on none of those trips had he ever caught a glimpse

of the man in Mae's life. Only at the end had she explained why, that Nate had his own family responsibilities, duties that he had never once shirked through all the years they had loved each other. It had been an unconventional love—an impossible love—she had explained to Trace. The man's wife had suffered a nervous breakdown years before, when his children were little more than toddlers. Nate could never bring himself to divorce her during all the long, lonely years when he'd struggled as a single dad, watching his wife's mind deteriorate degree by degree. He had been the rock that held his family together...and the other half of Mae's soul. If she regretted anything about their long, secret affair, she never once complained of it to Trace. And it had certainly never soured her on the possibilities of romance.

It was little wonder, though, that Mae had sought out Trace's company around the holidays, he had realized as she told him the story. The loneliness at a season meant for sharing with family and friends must have been unbearable. Trace wondered if this woman even knew about that part of Mae's life.

"If you hadn't been here for years, why are you here now?" Trace asked, unable to hide the note of bitterness in his voice. "Did you come to pick over her belongings?"

She seemed startled by the hostility in the question—or maybe by the fact that he thought he had the right to ask it. "I'm here because my aunt left Holiday Retreat to me," she said eventually. "Not that it's any of your business, but I'm Savannah Holiday. Mae was my grandfather's sister. And you are? How did you get in here, anyway?" She sighed. "Hannah, I suppose. I've told her and told her about not opening the door to strangers."

It didn't seem to occur to Savannah Holiday that it had taken her a long time to get around to asking about his identity. In New York, the police would probably have been called the second he appeared in the kitchen doorway and the answers to all those questions could have been sorted out later.

"I'm Trace Franklin," he said. "A friend of Mae's." He retrieved the key from his pocket and plunked it on the table where it glinted in the sunlight. "And I got in with this, though I did see your daughter as I came in."

She stared at the key. "Where did you get that?"

"From your aunt."

"Why would she give you a key to Holiday Retreat?"

"Because she'd invited me here for the holidays." He was only now beginning to grasp just how diabolical that invitation had been. His finding the alluring Savannah Holiday and her daughter underfoot was clearly no accident, but Mae's last-ditch effort at matchmaking. He wondered if Savannah Holiday had figured out what her aunt was up to.

He regarded his unexpected housemate with a wry expression. "Merry Christmas!"

THREE

Compared to the man sitting across from her with his cool, flinty gaze and designer wardrobe, Savannah felt like a dowdy waif. She was pretty sure there was flour in her hair and, more than likely, red and green sprinkles on her nose. When it came to baking, she did it with more enthusiasm than tidiness or expertise. The results were equally unpredictable, though she'd been particularly proud of the batch of golden cookies that were currently lying in crumbles around her feet.

She regarded this interloper with caution, in part at least because his presence rattled her. She'd felt a little flicker of awareness the instant he'd entered the kitchen. At first she'd attributed it to surprise, but then she'd realized it was a whole lot more like the sensation she'd experienced the first time she'd met Rob. It was the caught-off-guard, heart-stopping reaction of a woman to a virile, attractive male...or a doe when confronted by a rifle-toting hunter. She was stunned to discover that she was even remotely susceptible to a man after the bitterness of her divorce, especially to a man wearing the clothes of a business executive to a country inn. It was something her uptight ex-husband would have done.

Because her reaction made her uneasy, she focused on the one topic guaranteed to take her mind off it. "You said Mae invited you here. You do know that my aunt died, right?" she asked.

"Yes."

His expression was almost as bleak as the one Savannah saw in the mirror every morning. "But you came anyway," she said, impressed despite the instinct that told her this man was anything but sentimental.

"It's what she wanted," he said simply. "I promised I would."

"And you always keep your promises?"

"I try," he said. "I don't make that many, and the ones I do make mean something."

"What about your family? Won't they miss you over the holidays?"

"In recent years Mae was the closest thing I had to family. What about *your* family?"

"Hannah's here. For all intents and purposes, she's all I have. My husband and I divorced a year ago." She hesitated, then added, "My parents and I aren't on speaking terms at the moment."

"I see."

She was grateful that he didn't bombard her with a lot of questions about that. "How did you know Mae? Forgive me, but you don't look as if you spend a lot of time in the country."

He laughed at that, and it transformed his face. The tight lines around his mouth eased. His dark eyes sparkled. "What gave me away?"

"The clothes, for starters. I'm amazed you stayed upright walking from the car to the house in those shoes. I don't think snow is kind to Italian leather. And I can't imagine that you'd be able to spend more than a few minutes outdoors before freezing in that shirt. Men around here tend toward flannel."

"But I think the real secret is what they wear under it," he said, barely containing what promised to be a wicked grin.

Savannah's thoughts automatically veered off in a very dangerous direction. She had the oddest desire to strip off his clothes to see if there were practical long johns underneath. She'd never thought that sort of men's underwear to be particularly sexy, but she imagined Trace Franklin could do amazing things for the look.

"You're blushing," he said, regarding her with amusement.

"Well, of course I am! I hardly know you, and here we are discussing underwear."

"It can be a fascinating topic, especially if we move from cotton to satin and lace."

She frowned at him. "You're deliberately trying to rattle me, aren't you?"

"Why would I do that?" he asked, trying for a serious expression. The twinkle in his gray eyes betrayed him.

"I can't imagine, especially when all I was trying to find out was what drew a city man like you to spend time in a country retreat." She studied him thoughtfully, then said, "There must have been a woman involved."

"Bingo. The woman who brought me here years ago was envisioning a quiet, romantic getaway with long hikes through the woods." He shrugged and gave her a beguilingly sheepish look. "Instead I spent the weekend holed up in Mae's study with my computer and fax machine taking care of a business crisis."

Savannah immediately felt a surprising empathy for the woman. "Now, *that* I can imagine. Your friend must have been disappointed."

"Dreadfully."

"What sort of business?"

"I own a company in New York," he said in such a dismissive way that it sparked her curiosity.

"Franklin," Savannah recalled thoughtfully. "Not Franklin Toys, by any chance?"

He seemed startled that she'd grasped it so quickly. "That's the one. How on earth did you figure that out?"

"There were some articles about that company on Mae's desk. Obviously she kept up with it."

"I imagine so," he said, his expression noncommittal.

"Because she knew you from your visits here?" Savannah persisted, sensing there was more.

He shrugged. "That was the start of her interest, I suppose."

She frowned at his evasiveness. "What aren't you saying?"

"What makes you think I'm leaving something out?"

"Instinct."

"Okay, then, here's the whole story in a nutshell. I suppose I owe you that, since I've shown up on your doorstep out of the blue," he said. "Your aunt was the one who encouraged me to start the company. I'd been with another toy manufacturer for a few years. I'd learned all I could, and I had a lot of ideas for ways to do it better. Mae was an early investor in Franklin Toys. Over the years she and I made a lot of money together, but I owe every bit of that success to her initial encouragement."

"I see," Savannah said slowly. "So that first trip here wasn't a waste of your time after all. Did your relationship with the woman last?"

"Only for as long as it took me to get her back to her apartment in New York that Sunday night," he said with no hint of regret. "My friendship with Mae lasted much longer."

"Then you came back here often?" she asked, feeling a vague sense of regret and guilt that he'd spent these last years with her aunt, when she should have been the one spending time here.

"As frequently as I could," he said. "Your aunt was a remarkable woman. I enjoyed my visits with her."

"Even if she did live essentially in the middle of nowhere," Savannah said, needing to remind herself that this man bore way too many resemblances to her ex-husband.

"Funny thing about that," he said, picking up one of the few sugar cookies they'd managed to salvage and breaking off a bite. "I got used to the peace and quiet. And the phone lines, fax and Internet connections work just fine."

"So even though you're here for the holidays, I suppose you brought all of your equipment along," she guessed.

"Of course."

Savannah shook her head. "I hope you watch your cholesterol. Anybody who's as much of a workaholic as you appear to be is clearly a heart attack waiting to happen."

"I'll try not to have one while I'm here," he promised solemnly.

"Thank you for that. I'm afraid I don't have the kind of insurance it would take to cover your medical expenses if you collapse and fall down the stairs."

He grinned. "I do."

"Well, then, I suppose you can stay," she said grudgingly, thinking of the extra work involved in having a guest in a house that was all but falling down around them.

He regarded her with a wry expression. "I had no intention of doing anything else."

"You'll have to pitch in and help," she said, deliberately ignoring his remark. "I'm afraid the inn isn't officially ready for guests again."

"I'm not a guest—not the way you mean, anyway. And I came expecting to take care of myself. The attorney said the refrigerator would be stocked, and I brought along plenty of food from the city."

"Caviar, I imagine," she said, feeling strangely testy at the thought of sharing the house with a man whose tastes, like Rob's, probably ran to the expensive and exotic. "Maybe some imported Stilton cheese? Smoked salmon? The finer things you absolutely couldn't live without?"

His grin spread. "Junk food, if you must know."

Once again, Savannah felt the full effects of that devastating smile. She hoped he wouldn't do it too often. It might make her forget that he was completely unsuitable for a woman who'd already been burned by a man who put his work before his family.

"What exactly do you consider junk food?" she asked.

"Potato chips. Popcorn." He leaned closer and lowered his voice to confide, "I also have a cooler filled with chocolate mocha almond ice cream. I'm addicted to the stuff."

Her eyes widened. Chocolate mocha almond was an indulgence she rarely allowed herself. Aside from the calories, the brand she loved was outrageously expensive. She'd developed a taste for it during her marriage, but had had to forgo it since the divorce. The store brands simply didn't live up to the gourmet ice cream. She had a hunch that cooler of Trace's was stocked with the best.

"Exactly how much ice cream did you bring?" she asked, hoping it sounded like a purely casual inquiry.

"Enough for you and Hannah…if you're good," he teased.

"When it comes to chocolate mocha almond, I can eat a lot," she warned him.

He surveyed her slowly, appreciatively, then shook his head. "Not as much as I can," he said. "And I brought enough for a week. I'll make you a deal. If you let me share in whatever you're fixing for Christmas dinner, I'll provide dessert."

"But that's three days away," Savannah protested.

He winked. "I know. Patience is a virtue."

"Another of Mae's favorite sayings," Savannah recalled as again a wave of nostalgia hit. "Are you sure I can't talk you into sharing sooner?"

He glanced at the piles of cookies on the table and the obvious remnants of hot chocolate in two mugs. "Are you absolutely certain you won't go into some sort of sugar-overload crisis?"

"Absolutely."

"Then I'll bring it in," he said.

"I'll help," Savannah said eagerly, grabbing a jacket off a hook by the door and following him outside.

The instant she spotted his fancy new four-wheel-drive sports utility vehicle out front, she was momentarily distracted from thoughts of ice cream. It could turn out that Trace Franklin was the answer to her prayers.

"I don't suppose you'd be willing to let me borrow your car?" she asked.

"First you want my ice cream, and now you're after my car," he said, shaking his head. "You ask a lot for someone I've barely met."

"I need to get to town to pick up paint and things to start on the work that's needed around here." She glanced toward her own car, a faded six-year-old sedan with questionable tires. "I doubt my car will make it down the mountain, much less back up on these icy roads."

His expression grew thoughtful. "Okay, here's my best offer. I'll trade you breakfast tomorrow for a trip into town."

Apparently the man's obsession with business never quit. "You really do like to negotiate, don't you?"

He shrugged. "Force of habit. I like creating win-win situations. Is it a deal?"

Savannah held out her hand. "Deal." She hesitated. "You could have dinner with Hannah and me this evening, if you like. It won't be fancy. I'm fixing spaghetti."

He seemed startled by the invitation. "It just so happens that I love spaghetti." His gaze narrowed suspiciously. "What do you want in return for that?"

"Ice cream for dessert?" she asked hopefully.

Rather than answering, he reached into the car, then turned back with something in hand and tossed it to her. Savannah caught it instinctively. It was a pint of ice cream. And she'd been right—it was the best.

"It's all yours," he said. "Consider it a gesture of good faith."

He retrieved a huge cooler, which obviously contained the

rest. Savannah eyed it enviously. "Is that thing really filled with more of this?"

"Packed solid," he told her. He studied her warily. "Am I going to have to put a lock on the freezer?"

"I would never steal your ice cream," she said with a hint of indignation, then grinned. "That doesn't mean I won't try to talk you out of it."

His gaze locked with hers and anticipation slid over her once again, making her senses come alive.

"This is really, really good ice cream," he said quietly. "It could take more than talk."

Savannah barely resisted the urge to fan herself. She was surprised steam wasn't rising around her. Oh, this man was dangerous, all right. She was obviously going to have to watch her step the whole time he was underfoot. Any man who prided himself on being a shark when it came to business was likely to be equally determined when it came to anything else he wanted.

Well, she'd just have to make sure he didn't decide he wanted her. One glance comparing her flour-streaked jeans to his tailored wool slacks put that notion to rest. They weren't in the same league at all.

She lifted her gaze to his, caught the desire darkening those gray eyes. Uh-oh, she thought. Apparently clothes didn't matter to Trace, because the look in his eyes was anything but neutral.

More worrisome, though, than that discovery was the realization that she wasn't nearly as upset by it as she probably ought to be. In fact, a little *zing* of anticipation had her blood heating up quite nicely. She could probably strip off her sheepskin-lined jacket and be quite comfortable in the twenty-degree temperature out here.

"You'll want to get all your stuff inside," she said, her tone suddenly brisk. "Who knows how many deals you might have missed while we've been talking?"

"The ones worth making can always wait," he said.

"Still, I'd hate to feel responsible for you missing out on something important. Besides, I promised Hannah that she and I would go cut down a Christmas tree this afternoon."

He regarded her as if she'd just mentioned a plan to cut down the entire forest.

"There's a perfectly good tree lot in town. I passed it on my way out here," he said. "Those trees are already cut. Less work. Less waste."

"Is that an expression of environmental concern?" she inquired. "Because the trees I'm talking about are grown specifically for the holidays. It's how some people make their living."

He looked skeptical. "Still seems like a lot of work."

"But this is a tradition," she countered.

He looked as if she'd used a foreign term.

"Didn't you have any holiday traditions when you were growing up?" she asked.

"Sure," he said at once. "Staying out from underfoot while Mom and Dad argued over how much money was being wasted on presents."

Savannah couldn't imagine a home in which the holidays had meant anything other than a joyful celebration. For all of the problems she and her parents were having now, they had given her years of memories of idyllic Christmases. Very little of that had had anything at all to do with the materialistic things. It had been about family togetherness, laughter...traditions. For some reason, she suddenly wanted to share just a little of that with this man to whom tradition meant so little. She'd never been able to get through to Rob, but maybe Trace Franklin wasn't a lost cause.

"Would you like to help us?" she asked impulsively.

He looked even more disconcerted by that invitation than he had been by her request that he join them for dinner. "I had planned to get some work done this afternoon," he said predictably.

"Surely the company founder can take a break for a couple of hours," she coaxed. "Most people do relax around the holidays. I doubt anyone will be too upset if they don't get a fax today or even tomorrow. Some people might actually be hoping to leave work early to finish their holiday shopping."

A vaguely guilty expression passed across his face, as if he'd already forgotten that Christmas was only a few days away.

"You're right," he said eventually. "The work can wait. In fact, maybe I'll call my secretary and tell her to let everyone leave early."

Savannah grinned at the unexpected evidence that Scrooge had a heart. "That's the spirit," she said. "I'll get my coat and hurry Hannah along. You'd better change into something warmer, too. My hunch is that this could take a long time. Hannah rushes through most things, but she's never made a quick decision about a Christmas tree in her life."

As Savannah left Trace to finish putting his groceries away, she was all too aware that his gaze followed her as she exited from the kitchen. And that she unconsciously put a little extra sway in her hips because of it.

Oh, so what? she thought as a guilty blush crept into her cheeks. If she could grant Hannah's not-so-secret Christmas fantasy of a pair of skis, then surely Fate wouldn't mind granting her the chance to flirt with a handsome man for a couple of days. After the holidays, what were the chances she'd ever see Trace again? Slim to none, more than likely. He was the perfect guy on which to practice a little harmless flirting. She had to get back into the dating game one of these days. Here was her chance to relearn the rules with a man who absolutely, positively was not her type, and better yet, a man who wouldn't be around long enough to break her heart.

Then she recalled that desire she'd read in Trace's eyes only moments before. *Harmless* was not the first word that came to mind. Okay, she concluded, *wicked* would be nice, too.

FOUR

Trace hauled all of his business equipment into Mae's den, but before he could plug any of it in he was so overcome with emotion that he sank into the chair behind her antique desk and drew in a deep breath. As he did, he was almost certain he could still smell the soft, old-fashioned floral scent she had worn.

The room looked as if she'd just left it moments earlier. A jar of her favorite gourmet jelly beans sat on the desk. He noted with amusement that most of the grape-flavored ones were gone. They had been her favorites, though she had claimed that she continued to buy assorted flavors precisely so she wouldn't get in a rut. She'd never realized that Trace had added a half-pound or so of the grape-flavored jelly beans each and every time he came to visit, secretly stirring them into the mix.

The inn's guest book was still beside the phone with reservations carefully noted. He turned to today's date and saw his own name written in her graceful, flowing script. He saw that Savannah's arrival had been noted for a date only a few days earlier in a script that seemed less steady.

Had she made those final arrangements for her niece's inheritance when she'd known the end was near? Had she cleverly schemed to bring him together with Savannah even as her health was failing? It would have been just like her to plot something for those she loved, something to make them less lonely once she was gone.

Ironically he didn't think Savannah had picked up on the scheme yet. He'd been the subject of so much matchmaking in recent years that he'd seen what Mae was up to the instant he'd realized he wasn't going to be alone at Holiday Retreat over the holidays. It was no accident that he and Savannah were here at the same time. Mae had wanted some of the seasonal magic to rub off on her heart-weary niece and a man she thought was missing out on romance.

So, why hadn't he run? He could have apologized for the intrusion and headed back to New York and the safety of his workaholic routine. It wasn't entirely duty to Mae that had kept him here but—mostly, he had to admit—the sweetly vulnerable Savannah herself. Though she wasn't complaining, it was obvious that her life hadn't been easy lately. Still, she'd maintained an air of determination and her sense of humor. She was too unsophisticated to be his type, but there was something about her—a fragility encased in steel—that drew him just the same. It reminded him of a young man who'd fled Tennessee years ago with little more than a dream and the determination to make it come true. And in many ways it reminded him of his mother, who'd had the strength to endure poverty and hardship. Only in recent years—after spending most of his youth condemning her for the choices she had made—had he come to realize just how strong she had been.

"Trace, are you ready yet?" Savannah asked quietly, startling him. "My goodness, you're not even changed. Is everything okay?"

He met her concerned gaze. "Sorry. I got distracted."

Savannah came closer and perched on the edge of the desk.

She regarded him with sympathy. "You feel her presence in here, don't you? I feel it most in the kitchen. It's like she's watching over my shoulder." A grin tugged at the corners of her mouth. "Making sure I don't burn the place down, more than likely."

"She wouldn't have left the inn to you if she didn't trust you to take care of it," he told her, knowing with everything in him that it was true. Mae had been sentimental, but she had also had a practical streak. Her New England heritage, no doubt. "This place meant everything to her. When Franklin Toys started doing really well, I suggested she retire. She had plenty of money to live comfortably for the rest of her life. Know what she told me?"

"That retirement was for people waiting to die," Savannah said. "She told me the same thing. She loved having her company, as she referred to the guests who came here year after year. She said they kept her young. What she missed was having family underfoot for the holidays."

"You and Hannah and I are here this year," Trace said, unable to keep a note of sorrow from his voice.

"Too late," Savannah said, a tear sliding down her cheek.

Trace thought of his suspicions about Mae's reason for bringing them together. Not that he intended to get too carried away trying to see that *all* of her wish came true, but celebrating this Christmas with her niece was the least he could do for the woman who'd believed in him.

"You said yourself that you think she's watching over you," he reminded Savannah. "What makes you think she's not here right this second, gloating over having gotten us up here to celebrate the holiday and her memory at the same time?"

Savannah's expression brightened. "You're absolutely right! Let's not disappoint her. We'll make this the most memorable holiday ever. We'll do everything just the way she used to do it, from the greens in the front hall to the candles on the mantel and in the windows."

"Perfect," he said enthusiastically. "Give me a minute to call my office and change, and I'll meet you and Hannah out front. We'll find the best tree on the tree farm."

"It has to be huge," Savannah warned.

He hesitated, phone receiver in hand. "How huge?"

"Really, really big." She held her arms wide. "And very, very tall."

"How were you and Hannah going to get such a huge tree back here by yourselves?"

"I was counting on help."

"Are you sure you didn't know I was coming?"

"Nope. Mr. Johnson has a truck. He also has a fondness for Mae's sugar cookies."

Trace winced. "The ones on the kitchen floor?"

"Those are the ones."

"Think he'll accept any other sort of bribe?" he asked, knowing that he was going to hate the alternative if Mr. Johnson declined to haul that tree.

"Nope. I think this tree is riding in your pristine, shiny SUV, shedding needles all the way," she said happily.

Trace groaned. "I was afraid of that."

She patted his hand, sending a jolt of awareness through him.

"I'll go get a blanket to lay in the back," she said soothingly. "Now, hurry, or you'll have Hannah to deal with. Trust me, she's worse than a nagging splinter when she's anxious to get someplace. Right now she's making a family of snow angels on the front lawn, but her enthusiasm for that will wear off shortly."

"I'll hurry," Trace promised, unable to tear his gaze away as she left the room. He sighed, then dialed his office.

Two minutes later, he'd told his stunned secretary to shut the company down until after the new year, changed into warmer clothes and was heading out the front door, only to be greeted by squeals of delight as Hannah upended her mother into a snowbank. Savannah was sputtering and scraping snow out of her mouth. There was a dangerous glint in her eyes as she regarded her traitorous daughter.

Oblivious to her mother's reaction, Hannah spotted Trace. Emboldened by her success with her mother, she raced in his direction. Trace braced for the hit. "Oh, no, you don't," he said, scooping her up when she would have tried to knock him on his backside. He held out a hand and helped Savannah up, even as Hannah tried to squirm free of his grip.

He looked into Savannah's dancing eyes. "What do you think? Should I drop her in that snowdrift over there?"

"No!" Hannah squealed. "Put me down. I'll be good. I promise."

Trace kept his gaze on Savannah's. "Your call."

"Hannah does keep her promises," she began thoughtfully. "Then again, that snow was really, really cold. She needs to know that."

"I know it. I know it," Hannah said. "Really, Mom. I swear."

Before he realized what she intended, Savannah scooped up a handful of snow and rubbed her daughter's face with it, dribbling a fair amount inside the collar of his coat while she was at it. Accident? he wondered. Probably not.

"Mom!" Hannah squealed, laughing.

Savannah clapped her gloved hands together to get rid of the excess snow and regarded Trace with a pleased expression. "I think it's okay to put her down now."

He lowered Hannah to her feet and caught her grin. "I hope you learned a lesson," he said, fighting to keep his own expression somber.

"Oh, yes," she retorted just as seriously. "I learned that my mom is very, very sneaky."

Trace nodded, shivering as the snow melted against his suddenly overheated skin. "I caught that, too. What do you think we should do about it?"

"Hey," Savannah protested, backing up a step. "Don't you two even *think* about ganging up on me."

"Never dream of it," Trace said, winking at Hannah.

She winked back, then giggled. "Never," she agreed.

Savannah looked from one to the other. "I'm going to regret this eventually, aren't I?"

"Could be," Trace said. He took a step closer, reached out and tucked a flyaway strand of hair back behind her ear. "But you'll never see it coming."

Her gaze locked with his, and suddenly the tables were turned. The desire to kiss her, to taste her, slammed through him with enough force to rock him on his heels. He hadn't seen that coming, either.

"We are never in a million years going to get this tree into the house," Trace said, eyeing the giant-size pine that Hannah had picked out. "What about that one over there?" He pointed to a nice, round, five-foot-tall tree. It was cute. It was manageable. Hannah was already shaking her head.

"No," daughter and mother replied in an emphatic chorus.

"I suppose it's also a tradition that the tree has to be too big to fit inside," he grumbled as he began to saw through the trunk. He'd worked for a lawn service one summer and had some skill at sawing down trees and branches, but nothing this size. He should have brought along a chainsaw.

"Exactly," Savannah said, grinning and apparently thoroughly enjoying his struggle with the tree.

"I think my mother had the right idea after all," he said. "A ceramic tree that lit up when she plugged it in."

"Oh, yuck," Hannah said. "That's so sad."

As he breathed in the scent of pine and fresh, crisp air, Trace was forced to agree with her. Despite his grumbling about the endless search for the perfect tree and his protests over the size of their choice, he hadn't felt this alive in years. Something that might have been the faint stirrings of holiday spirit spread through him. He couldn't remember the last time he'd felt like this.

"Stand back, you two. When this thing falls, you don't want to be in the way," he warned as he heard the crack of the wood and felt the tree begin to wobble. One hard shove and it would hit the ground. Before he could touch it, the tree began to topple…straight at him. It knocked him on his back in the deep snow. He found himself staring straight toward the sky through a tangle of fragrant branches.

"Uh-oh," he heard Hannah whisper.

Her mother choked back a giggle and peered through the branches. "Are you okay?"

"What the devil happened?" he asked, frowning up at her.

"I gave the tree a teeny little push to help it along. I guess I pushed the wrong way. You aren't hurt, are you?" The twinkle in her eyes suggested she wasn't all that worried.

Trace bit back his own laughter and scrambled out from beneath the tree. "You are in such trouble," he warned even as she began backing away, her nervous scramble hampered by the deep snow.

"You wouldn't," she said, regarding him warily.

"Oh, but I would," he responded quietly. "Nobody pulls off a sneak attack on me twice in one afternoon and gets away with it."

She tried to escape, but she was no match for his long legs. He caught up with her in a few steps, scooped her up and dropped her into the cushion of snow.

Hannah's laughter mingled with theirs. He whirled on her. "Okay, young lady, you're next. Don't you know better than to injure a man's pride?"

Hannah was quicker to scamper away, but Trace still caught

up with her, grabbed a handful of snow and rubbed her face with it. Just then he felt himself being pelted with snowballs from behind. In seconds all three of them were engaged in a full-fledged snowball fight.

"Oh, my," Savannah said a few minutes later, collapsing into the snow. "I haven't laughed that hard in ages."

"Me, either," Trace said, his gaze clashing with hers. In fact, he could barely recall ever laughing that hard.

Or wanting a woman as much as he wanted the virtual stranger lying beside him in the icy snow right this minute. With all the heat crackling between them, he was surprised they hadn't melted the snow right out from under them.

He started to reach out to touch her cheek, but recalling Hannah's presence, he drew back. "Do you know what I'd like to do right now?" he asked, his gaze locked with Savannah's.

She swallowed hard at the question and shook her head.

Trace realized that her thoughts had drifted down the same dangerous path as his own. "Not *that*," he protested, deliberately teasing her.

Her cheeks, already pink from the chill in the air, turned an even brighter shade. Another woman might have called his bluff, but she merely kept her gaze on him, apparently waiting to see just how deep a hole he intended to dig for himself.

"What *I'd* like to do," he said, "is go back to the house, build a nice warm fire in the fireplace, and…" He deliberately let the suspense build. He saw the pulse beating a little more rapidly in her neck. He permitted himself a hint of a smile, then said softly, "Take a nap."

She was still blinking in confusion when Hannah plopped down between them and said, "Grown-ups don't take naps."

"Sure we do," Trace told her. His gaze went back to Savannah. "In fact, sometimes when adults take naps, we have the very best dreams ever."

Savannah shot him a knowing look, then rose gracefully

to her feet. "Well, by all means, let's get home so you can get some sleep," she said testily.

She muttered something more, something obviously meant for Trace's ears, not Hannah's. He caught her hand and held her back until they were well out of Hannah's hearing.

"What was that?" he inquired.

She leveled a look straight at him. "I said, I hope you have nightmares."

"No dream with you in it could ever be a nightmare," he said, locking gazes with her once more. "Then again, you could take a nap with me."

"In your dreams," she retorted.

He winked at her. "Exactly."

She stopped in her tracks and scowled up at him. "Is this some sort of game with you?"

There was a hint of anger behind the question that threw Trace completely. "Game? I'm not sure what you mean."

"When you found me at the inn, did you decide I was Aunt Mae's gift to you or something? Because I am here to tell you that hell will freeze over before I fall into bed with you just because it's convenient."

With that, she whirled away and stalked off as gracefully as the deep snow permitted, leaving him to deal with the tree. He considered running after her, trying to explain, but maybe it was better to give her time to cool down.

So he struggled with the monster tree, finally getting a firm grip on the trunk, then dragging it through the snow. The trek took forever. By the time he reached the car, Savannah and Hannah were nowhere to be seen. Since the inn was less than a mile down the road, they'd probably decided to walk.

Trace wrestled with the tree and finally got it half in and half out of the SUV, cursing at the mess it was making of the car's interior. He tied it securely, then climbed into the vehicle and turned the heater up full blast.

He was still stinging from Savannah's tongue-lashing as he drove back to the inn. Granted, he'd only been teasing her, but she didn't know him well enough to understand that. He'd deserved every bit of scorn she'd heaped on him.

As he pulled up in front of the house, he noted that the lights were blazing and that smoke was curling from the chimney. Dusk was falling rapidly, and along with it, the temperature was dropping.

He lugged the tree onto the porch, then left it there to be dealt with after he warmed up with a cup of coffee or maybe some of that hot chocolate Savannah and her daughter were so fond of.

Inside, he stomped the snow off his boots and tossed his jacket over a chair, then headed for the kitchen where he could hear the low murmur of voices. He found Savannah at the stove stirring a pot of spaghetti sauce. The weathered older man to whom she was talking caught sight of Trace and gave him a wink.

"You must be Trace. Savannah here's been giving me an earful about you," he said. "'Course, it's not exactly the same high praise I was used to hearing from Mae."

Trace saw Savannah's back stiffen, but she didn't turn around. Obviously, the walk had done nothing to cool her temper. She was still royally ticked at him. The apology he owed her would have to wait, though. The man regarding him with such amusement had to be Mae's longtime lover.

"You must be Nate Daniels," Trace guessed at once. "I heard a lot about you over the years, as well, all of it good."

"Only because Mae never had a sharp word to say about anyone," Nate said. "Maybe that's because she brought out the best in people."

"I know she did in me," Trace said solemnly, his gaze on Savannah.

Nate looked from him to Savannah, then stood up and began pulling on his jacket. "Think I'll be going along now."

Savannah whirled around at that. "I thought you might like to stay for dinner."

"Not tonight," Nate said, shooting a commiserating look toward Trace. "I'll be around next time you're interested in having company. Meantime, you two need anything, you give me a call. I'll be happy to do what I can. You both meant a lot to Mae. I know she'd be happy that you're here together for the holidays."

Savannah regarded him with a disappointed expression. "Come by anytime," she said, her voice husky, her eyes shimmering with unshed tears. "I want to hear everything you can tell me about my aunt."

Nate clasped her hand in his. "Come on now, girl. Don't you be crying for your aunt. She's at peace."

"I know. I just wish I'd been here for her."

"She understood why you couldn't be here," Nate assured her. "And I was here. She wasn't alone."

"Thank you for that," Savannah said.

"No need to thank me. My place was by her side," he said simply. "I only wish I'd been able to give her more. Now let me get out from underfoot, so you folks can have your dinner." He regarded Trace with a stern expression. "And a nice long talk."

Trace accepted the admonishment without comment. "I'll walk you out," he offered.

Nate shook his head. "No need. I know the way. Seems to me like you have better things to do," he said, casting a pointed look at Savannah, who'd deliberately turned her back again.

"Yes," Trace agreed.

He waited until he heard the front door close before attempting his apology. "Savannah?"

"What?"

"I'm sorry if I offended you earlier."

"*If?*" she asked with a hint of disdain. She faced him, eyes flashing heatedly. "You all but propositioned me in front of my daughter!"

"I made sure that Hannah was out of earshot before I said a word," he reminded her, but she didn't seem the least bit pacified. She turned away and began stirring the spaghetti sauce with a vengeance. "Okay, I'm just plain sorry. I never meant to give the impression that I seriously thought you and I ought to be back here tumbling around in bed together."

"Oh, really?" she asked skeptically. "Then exactly what *did* you mean?"

"I was just teasing. Your cheeks get all flushed and your eyes sparkle when you get indignant. That was the only reaction I was going for. I was out of line."

She turned slowly and studied him. "Apology accepted. I probably overreacted, anyway. It's been a long time since I've flirted with a man."

"You'll get the hang of it again." He reached for her hand and tugged lightly until she was standing directly in front of him. "I only think it's fair to warn you, though."

"Warn me? About what?"

"Next time I might not be teasing."

She gulped visibly, then nodded. "I'll keep that in mind."

"Is it all right if I stay here, or would you rather I go?"

She seemed startled—perhaps even dismayed—by his offer to leave. "Aunt Mae invited you here. I'm certainly not going to kick you out."

"I know what Mae wanted," Trace said. "What do you want?"

She drew in a deep, shuddering breath, then stiffened her shoulders as she looked straight into his eyes. "I want you to stay."

The satisfaction that swept through Trace felt a lot like the exhilaration he felt when a difficult business negotiation ended well. "Then that's what I'll do," he told her solemnly.

She muttered something that he couldn't quite make out.

"What was that?" he asked.

A flush crept up the back of her neck. "I said, like I really had a choice."

"Of course you have a choice."

"Not if I want that tree to get put up tonight," she said, facing him with a renewed sparkle in her eyes.

Trace laughed despite himself. "I do love a woman who's always working an angle."

"Of course you do," Savannah said. "Makes you feel more at home, doesn't it? I'll bet you spend most of your time with female boardroom piranha types."

Trace chuckled at the all-too-accurate assessment. "True enough," he admitted. "But something tells me that's about to change."

FIVE

Savannah sent Trace in search of Hannah, while she got dinner on the table. She also needed the time to compose herself. She knew precisely why she had overreacted to Trace's teasing. It was because she had actually been tempted to take him up on his offer to slip away for a so-called *nap*. Even if they'd actually done no more than crawl into bed together and snuggle, it would have satisfied the yearning that had been building in her ever since he'd arrived earlier in the day.

Of course, she doubted a man like Trace would have settled for simply holding her in his arms. He would have wanted much more, and while she was tempted by that, she didn't want to wind up with her heart broken when he left in a few days. It was better that she'd made her position perfectly clear. If she was lucky, there would be no more temptations.

Next time I might not be teasing.

Trace's words suddenly came back to haunt her. How convenient that she had forgotten the warning.

At the sound of his laughter as he and Hannah came toward the kitchen, Savannah's pulse raced a little faster. The same wicked yearning that had gripped her earlier teased her senses now. She sighed. Resisting him was going to be a whole lot harder than she'd ever imagined. She'd just have to keep reminding herself that he was cut from the same cloth as her workaholic ex-husband.

"Mom, can we put the Christmas tree up tonight?" Hannah pleaded as they finished up bowls of ice cream after the best spaghetti Trace had eaten in years.

"According to tradition, we never put it up till Christmas Eve," Savannah told her, but she sounded regretful, as if this were one tradition she could be persuaded to change.

"Maybe it's time to start your own tradition," Trace suggested, earning a high five from Hannah. "Besides, the sooner the tree is in its stand and has some water, the better it will be, right? It'll last much longer, and it will fill the house with the scent of pine. Why not start enjoying it now?"

Hannah studied her mother, clearly trying to gauge her mood. "Please," she begged finally. "I'll go up in the attic and bring down all the decorations you said are up there. Trace will put it up and string up the lights. You won't have to do anything."

"Except keep the carols going on the CD player and the hot chocolate flowing," Trace corrected. "What do you say, Savannah?"

"I say that you two are a formidable team," she said, feigning an air of resignation that was belied by the spark of excitement in her eyes. "Go on. Bring in the tree."

"Do you know where you want it?" Trace asked. "Once it's up, I don't want to be hauling it all over the house."

She frowned at him. "It goes in front of the window in the living room. That's where it's always been."

"And you're happy with that?" he persisted.

"Why wouldn't I be?"

"Since you're starting new traditions and all, I just thought you might want to go for broke and pick a new location."

"I think the old one is just fine," she said. "That way, anyone driving up to the house will be able to see the lights on the tree."

Trace resigned himself to moving the sofa that normally sat in front of that window. "Where should I move the sofa?"

Savannah regarded him blankly. "The sofa?"

"The one in front of that window."

Her eyes suddenly lit with understanding. "So that's why you were so eager to have me put the tree somewhere else. You're going to be stuck moving furniture."

"Hey, I'm not complaining." He glanced at Hannah. "Did you hear me complain?"

"No," she said at once.

"I'll put that sofa just about anywhere you want it except the attic," he insisted.

Savannah regarded him with a wry expression. "I think on the wall facing the fireplace will do."

"Got it. Tree in front of the window. Sofa in front of the fireplace. And the easy chairs currently on that wall? Where should they go?"

A chuckle erupted from deep inside her, lighting up her face. "Maybe Hannah and I can rearrange the furniture while you get the tree in its stand."

"No way," Trace protested. "I'm providing the brawn here. Just give me instructions."

By the time Savannah finished with the instructions, he was pretty sure that not one single piece of furniture in the living room would be where it had started out. He figured he could live with that, as long as she didn't change her mind a million times.

"That's it?" he questioned. "You're sure?"

"As sure as I can be before I see what it looks like," she said.

Trace sighed. "I'll get started. You might want to hunt for some painkillers and a heating pad in the meantime."

"Very funny."

He leveled a look at her. "Who's joking?" he asked as he headed for the living room to rearrange the furniture.

By the time everything was in its newly designated place, including the tree, the room did have a cozier, more festive air about it. A fire crackled in the fireplace, and the fresh scent of pine filled the air.

Hannah had brought down stacks of boxes of decorations from the attic. They were now scattered over every surface, as she took each one from its tissue and examined it with wide-eyed delight.

"These must be really, really old, huh?" she asked him.

"They certainly look as if they're antiques," Trace said, noting the loving care with which she handled them. It must be nice to have family heirlooms to be brought out year after year, each with its own story. But now with Mae gone, who would share those stories with Hannah?

Savannah came in just then carrying a tray of steaming mugs filled with hot chocolate. Her eyes widened as she saw the decorations.

"Oh, my," she whispered. "I remember these. Mae used to tell us kids about them when she'd take them out of the boxes. We were never allowed to touch them because they were so old and fragile, but we each had our favorites."

She immediately picked up a blown-glass rocking horse, its paint beginning to wear away. "This was mine. This and the angel that goes on the top of the tree. Is that still here?"

"Over here," Hannah said excitedly, picking it up gingerly. "She's beautiful."

Dressed in white satin with red velvet trim, the angel had flaxen hair and golden wings. The delicate porcelain face had been rendered with a serene look totally appropriate for gazing down on the holiday festivities year after year. Even Trace, with his jaded, unsentimental view of the season, could see the beauty of it.

"We always drew straws to see who would get to put it on the top after all the other decorations were on the tree," Savannah said as she held the angel. "My dad or one of my uncles would lift up whoever won so we could reach the very top."

"Can I put it on this year?" Hannah asked. "Trace could lift me high enough."

"Maybe this year your mom ought to do it," Trace suggested, seeing the nostalgia in Savannah's eyes.

"No," Savannah said at once. "It was always one of the kids. Of course Hannah should do it—that's the tradition."

"Well, it'll be morning before we get to it unless we get started," Trace said. "There are a lot of lights here, and there must be hundreds of decorations. You two sit back and relax while I get the lights on. You can tell me when they're in the right place."

"Ah, my favorite job," Savannah teased, settling onto the sofa with Hannah beside her. "Supervisor."

Trace had a devil of a time untangling all the lights, making sure they worked and then getting them on the tree. It was the first time such a task had fallen to him, and he was beginning to see why his father had always grumbled about it. Trace would have settled for three or four strands strategically placed, but Savannah was having none of that.

"At least four more strands," she insisted. "I like a lot of lights."

"I'm not hearing any carols while I work," Trace chided. "What happened to the music? Isn't that your job?"

"Oops. I forgot. What will it be?" She shuffled through a stack of CDs. "Bing Crosby? Nat King Cole? Kenny G? The Mormon Tabernacle Choir? Vince Gill? The Vienna Boys Choir?"

"Your aunt certainly had eclectic taste," Trace commented.

"She loved Christmas music. She used to buy at least one new album every year. Obviously she kept up that tradition. So, what's your pleasure?"

"Surprise me," Trace said.

Despite the suggestion, Savannah didn't surprise him at all when she chose the old standards of Nat King Cole. As the singer's voice filled the room, Trace recalled the way his father had scoffed at the sentimentality of the holiday music. Trace had inadvertently carried that same disdain with him into adulthood. Now, though, with Savannah and Hannah singing along with the music, he began to enjoy the songs.

"Come on," Savannah encouraged. "Sing with us."

"No, thanks, I'd rather listen to you," he said as he wrapped the final strand of lights around the tree.

"But singing helps to get you into the holiday spirit. It doesn't matter if you're off-key," she told him.

"Sorry," he said, his voice a little tight. "I don't know the words."

She stared at him with obvious astonishment. "You never learned the words to all the old standard Christmas carols?"

"They weren't played much at our house. My father objected. He said it was just more crass commercialism. We were lucky he let us put up a tree. After a few years, he carried on so about that, that my mother settled for the little ceramic tree I told you about earlier."

"But you must have heard the carols when you were at your friends' houses," she persisted. "Or on the radio."

"I didn't pay much attention," he said defensively.

"How awful," she said, studying him with sympathy.

"Savannah, I got along okay without knowing the words to a bunch of songs that get played once a year."

She studied him seriously. "Can I ask you something?"

"Sure," he said, despite the wariness creeping over him.

"As a man who doesn't seem to have many happy memories of the holidays, how did you end up running a toy company?"

"Long story," he said.

"It's still early. We have time."

"I don't want to bore Hannah with all this. Besides, we've got a tree to decorate." He deliberately turned to Hannah. "Sweetie, are you ready to start hanging those decorations?" he asked, shutting down the topic of his career.

"Sure," Hannah said eagerly. "Mom, you've got to help."

Savannah cast one last curious look at him, before smiling and picking up several decorations.

By the time they were finally finished and all the boxes were empty, there wasn't a bare spot on the tree's branches.

"Ready for the lights?" Trace asked.

"Wait. Let me turn off the overhead lights," Savannah said. "It's better in the dark."

As soon as the main lights were off, Trace plugged in the tree's. The hundreds of lights shimmered, reflecting off the ornaments and filling the room with dazzling color. Even he was a bit in awe as he stared at it.

"It's beautiful," Hannah whispered.

"The very best tree ever," Savannah agreed.

Suddenly she was slipping her hand into Trace's. "Thank you," she said.

"Just following directions," he said.

"No. It's more than that. I think we all need a touch of magic in our lives this year, and you've made sure we have it."

"All I did—"

She cut off his protest. *"Thank you,"* she repeated emphatically, gazing up at him.

Trace thought he'd never seen anything so lovely in his life as he gazed into her sparkling eyes, which put the lights on the tree to shame. "You're welcome," he said softly, resisting the need to kiss her only because Hannah was in the room.

"I think I'll go to bed," Hannah announced with rare impeccable timing.

"Night, baby," Savannah said, sounding just a little breathless.

"Good night, Trace. Thanks for helping with the tree." Hannah stood on tiptoe to give him a peck on the cheek.

"Good night, angel."

"I'm glad you're here," she murmured sleepily as she headed for the stairs.

Trace looked into Savannah's eyes, aware suddenly that he was caught up in something he couldn't explain with his usual rational practicality. "I'm glad I'm here, too."

The most amazing sense of contentment stole through Savannah as she settled onto the sofa with Trace beside her. He was careful not to sit too close, but she could still feel the heat radiating from him, and she was drawn to it more than ever.

It had been an incredible evening. Even listening to Trace and Hannah bickering over where to place the ornaments on the tree had been wonderful. Hannah wouldn't have risked such a debate with her father. Things were always done Rob's way. It was a lesson Hannah had learned early, to keep peace in the family.

It was more than that, though. Maybe it was the cozy fire. Maybe it was the hot chocolate and salvaged chunks of sugar cookies.

Or maybe it was simply that for the first time in years, there was no real dissension as the holidays got under way. It had always been a battle to get her husband home from the office in time to help with the preparations. And unlike the bantering between Hannah and Trace, there had been a superior edge to her ex's tone that had always sent Hannah to her room in tears.

"Can I ask you something?" Savannah said, studying Trace intently.

He kept his guarded gaze directed toward the fire, but he nodded.

"Christmas is still a couple of days away. Why did you come up here early?"

"I told you."

"I know. You promised my aunt. But she's been gone for several weeks now. You could have waited till the last second and still fulfilled your promise."

He glanced at her, then looked back at the fire. "You'll think I'm crazy."

Savannah laughed. "I doubt that. Even in the brief time I've known you, I can tell you definitely have all your wits about you."

"Okay, then, here it is. I was planning to wait till Christmas Eve, rush up here, spend the night and rush right back to the city on Christmas Day."

"But you changed your mind. Why?"

"I woke up this morning with this weird feeling that I needed to be up here today." He met her gaze. "Normally I would have dismissed it and kept to my original plan..." His voice trailed off.

"But?" Savannah prodded, intrigued by the distinctly uncomfortable expression on his face. For a man who exuded confidence, it was a rare display of vulnerability.

"You know that cooler of chocolate mocha almond ice cream?"

"Very well. What does that have to do with anything?"

"It was delivered to my apartment this morning with a note that said I should get it up here before it melted."

Savannah stared at him. "Someone sent you that ice cream as a gift?"

His gaze held hers. "Not just *someone*. It was your aunt's handwriting."

"Oh, my," Savannah whispered. "How could that be?"

"I called the store and the delivery service. The arrangements had been made weeks ago." He shrugged ruefully. "I guess Mae was afraid I might not keep my promise without a little nudge from beyond the grave. Needless to say, I packed my bags and hit the road."

She studied him closely. "Are you teasing me?"

"Absolutely not," he said. "I have no sense of humor. Ask the people who work for me. Heck, it's even in most of the articles about Franklin Toys."

"That's absurd," Savannah said, dismissing the suggestion out of hand. "You've been joking and laughing with Hannah and me since you got here."

"I know," he said, his expression serious. "What do you make of that?"

"We're good for you," she said, her voice suddenly a little breathless. Could it really be that she had something to offer this man who had everything money could buy?

"Which, I suspect, is exactly what your aunt had in mind when she plotted this meeting."

Suddenly it all made sense to Savannah. The inheritance of Holiday Retreat at a time when she desperately needed a change in her life. The unexpected arrival of a handsome stranger on the inn's doorstep. Yes indeed, Aunt Mae had been scheming, all right. The realization horrified her.

"I am so sorry," she told Trace with total sincerity. "She shouldn't have dragged you up here with an ulterior motive. If you want to get back to the city and your friends for Christmas, I will certainly understand."

Her declaration seemed to amuse Trace for some reason. His eyes were glinting humorously when he reached out to caress her cheek. "Are you kicking me out, Savannah?"

"No, of course not. I just wanted you to understand that you're free to go if there's someplace you'd rather be, people you'd rather be spending the holiday with."

As an answer he leaned forward and touched his lips to hers in the lightest, tenderest of kisses. There was a whisper of heat, the promise of fire…and then he was on his feet.

"I'll see you in the morning," he said as he headed for the stairs.

"You're staying?" she asked.

"Of course I'm staying."

"Because it was what Mae wanted?" she asked, determined to clarify the reason.

"No, darlin'. Because it's what *I* want." He winked at her. "Besides, I promised to take you into town tomorrow."

With that he was gone, leaving Savannah staring after him. She touched a finger to her lips, where she could still feel his mouth against hers. "And you always keep your promises," she whispered to herself. It was such a little thing, but it meant more than Trace could possibly imagine.

She lifted her gaze to seek out a picture of Aunt Mae that sat on the mantel. "Thank you."

Just knowing that there was one man left who kept his promises restored her faith that the future would turn out all right.

SIX

The scent of fresh-brewed coffee drifted upstairs, pulling Trace out of a perfectly fascinating dream. For once it had nothing to do with mergers and acquisitions, but with a woman—Savannah, to be precise.

How could a woman with so little guile, so little sophistication, get under his skin the way she had? That kiss the night before—little more than a friendly peck by most standards— had packed more punch than any kiss he'd experienced in years. He'd left the room, not because he believed in hasty, uncomplicated exits, but because he wanted so much more. If he'd gone after what he'd wanted, more than likely he would have scared her to death. Then she would have kicked him out and he would have spent another lonely holiday season back in New York.

"I hope to hell you knew what you were doing, Mae," he muttered.

When the scent of sizzling bacon joined that of the coffee, Trace quickly showered and dressed in a pair of old jeans, a dress shirt and a heavy pullover sweater. That was about as casual as his attire ever got these days. He reminded himself if he was going to paint the front door and trim and sand the floors, he needed to buy something else to wear.

When he walked into the kitchen, Savannah regarded him with flushed cheeks and wisps of curls teasing her face. "Is that your idea of work clothes?" she asked. "Or do you intend to supervise today, the way I did last night?"

Trace noted that she, too, was wearing jeans, but her University of Florida sweatshirt had seen better days, as had her sneakers. She still looked fabulous. He still wanted her. A part of him had been hoping that last night's desire had been an aberration.

"Did I say I was working?" he inquired as he poured himself a cup of coffee, breathed in its rich scent, then took his first sip. "Good coffee, by the way."

She grinned. "Glad you like it, since it's yours. I figured you wouldn't approve of the instant I had on hand."

Trace shuddered. "Good guess." He met her gaze. "Exactly what sort of work are you planning to do today?"

"I want to pick up paint for the guest rooms, a tarp for the roof and..."

"Whoa! Why a tarp for the roof?"

"Because it's leaking."

"Why not get it fixed?"

"I would if I could get the contractor over here," she explained with exaggerated patience. "He said he can't come till after the first of the year."

"Then call another contractor."

She frowned at him. "Don't you think I thought of that?"

"I'll handle it," he said at once.

"What do you mean, you'll 'handle it'?"

"I'll get someone over here to repair the roof."

"Even if you are a business mogul, I doubt you'll be any more successful than I've been," she said. "Besides, there's at least a foot of snow up there. They won't even be able to look at it, much less start the repairs."

"Okay, you have a point," he conceded. "Though that would also seem to make the tarp a waste of time, too, unless you're planning to put it over the snow."

She frowned at him. "Okay, then, no tarp."

"What else do you want from the hardware store?"

"The paint and tools to scrape the wallpaper will do it. I don't want to spend any more till I know what the rest of the repairs are going to cost. And I have to set some money aside for new brochures and advertising. I need to start getting paying guests back in here as soon as possible. I've already missed the start of the ski season."

Trace thought he heard a hint of desperation in her voice that she was trying hard to hide. "Savannah, do you have the money to get this place up and running again?"

"I have enough," she said tightly.

"What about a loan? I could—"

"Absolutely not. I won't take money from you."

"Then let me talk to the bank."

"No, I am not going to start off my new life with a pile of debts. Things will get done when I can afford to do them."

Trace admired her pride and her independent streak, but as a practical matter he knew it was better for a business to present its best face from the outset so that word of mouth would spread. She might not take money from him, but she wasn't in a position to turn down a little practical assistance in the form of labor. She could hardly tell him not to pick up his own supplies. He'd just have to be a little sneaky about it. That meant getting in and out of the hardware store without her catching sight of his purchases.

"Fine," he said. "Holiday Retreat is yours."

There was one more thing he could do, too. It would require a few phone calls, routing his attorney away from his new girlfriend for a couple of hours, but he could pull it off by Christmas.

"Is Hannah coming into town with us?" he asked as he ate the scrambled eggs Savannah put in front of him.

"Of course. She's dying to take a look around. We stopped at the grocery store on our way up here, but that's all she's seen. I'll go get her. We can be ready to leave whenever you're finished with breakfast."

"Did you eat?"

"I had a piece of toast," she said.

Trace frowned at her. "I have enough eggs here for three people." He stood up, grabbed a plate from the cupboard, then divided up his eggs, added two slices of bacon and set it on the table. "Sit. You need the protein."

Savannah opened her mouth to protest, but his scowl achieved what his directive had not. She sat down and picked up her fork.

"You know, I have to get used to serving the guests around here without sitting down to eat with each and every one of them," she told him.

"I'm not a guest."

She nibbled thoughtfully on a piece of bacon. "Which means I probably shouldn't have cooked this for you," she said.

"Right. I told you I'd look out for myself."

"I'll remember that tomorrow morning."

He regarded her slyly. "Of course, it wouldn't hurt to get in a little practice in the kitchen. You wouldn't want the first real guests to starve, would you?"

She laughed. "I don't think there's any chance of that. I may not have had a lot of practice at cooking for a crowd, but Aunt Mae has a whole box filled with recipes she perfected over the years. I can read directions with the best of them."

"I seem to recall some sort of baked French toast Mae used to make," Trace said, his gaze on Savannah. "I don't suppose..."

To his surprise, Savannah's eyes lit up. "I remember that. She always made it Christmas morning."

"Then it's a tradition?" Trace asked hopefully.

"Yes, it's a tradition. And yes, I'll make it. And yes, you can have breakfast with Hannah and me on Christmas morning."

"Before or after we open presents?" Trace asked, only to see her shoulders stiffen slightly.

Hannah arrived in the kitchen just in time to hear the question. "We're not having presents this year, 'cause we're poor," she said with absolutely no hint of self-pity.

"We are *not* poor," Savannah said, obviously embarrassed by her daughter's comment. "It's just that the divorce and the renovations needed on this place have left us temporarily strapped for cash, so we're keeping Christmas simple."

"I see," Trace said slowly.

Simple might be good enough for Savannah, maybe even for Hannah, who seemed resigned to it, but not for him. For the first time in years, he had the desire to splurge on the holidays.

Oh, he always sent truckloads of toys to various homeless shelters in the city, but his personal gift list was small and mostly confined to business associates. He couldn't recall the last time he'd had anyone in his life to whom he'd wanted to offer even a small token of affection.

He made a mental note to make a few more calls the second he had some privacy.

"Why don't you guys grab your coats while I clean up in here?" he suggested. "I'll meet you at the car in a few minutes."

Savannah regarded him curiously, almost as if she suspected something was up because he'd let her description of their financial plight pass without comment.

"Go on. Warm up the car," he encouraged, tossing her the keys. "You cooked. I'll clean up. That's *my* tradition."

"I thought you didn't have any traditions," she replied.

"I'm starting a new one."

To his relief, she seemed to accept that.

"We'll be outside," she said. "Try not to break any dishes."

"Hey," he protested, "I know what I'm doing."

He loaded the dishwasher, turned it on, then grabbed his cell phone. It took less than ten minutes to set things in motion. That was one of the benefits of being rich. Trace rarely threw his weight or his money around. When he did, people were eager enough to do as he asked. He'd always been satisfied in a distant sort of way when he thought of the delight his toys would bring to kids on Christmas morning, but he'd never actually experienced that sense of awe and wonder that was pictured in his commercials. Maybe this year things would be different.

Satisfied that Christmas was under control, he grabbed his coat and joined Savannah and Hannah, who'd already retreated to the slowly warming interior of the car. Hannah shivered dramatically when he opened the door.

"I hate cold weather," she declared.

Trace regarded her in the rearview mirror. "You're living in the wrong place, then, kiddo. Weren't you the one who was out here half-buried in snowdrifts yesterday?"

"It's colder today," she insisted. "And now I've seen snow. Yesterday I hadn't."

"Does that mean you want to move back to Florida?" Savannah asked.

There was no mistaking the note of trepidation in her voice, Trace thought. He glanced over and saw the tight lines around her mouth.

"No," Hannah said at once. "Even if it is cold, I want to stay here."

Savannah's relief was almost palpable. "Why?" she asked.

"Because since we got here, you've started laughing again," Hannah said quietly. "You never laughed in Florida."

Savannah turned her head away, but not before Trace saw a tear sliding down her cheek. He wanted to reach for her, to hold her...to make her laugh.

Instead he glanced toward Hannah. "How about you and

me making a pact?" he said. "The one who makes your mom laugh the most today wins."

Hannah's eyes lit up. "Okay. What's the prize?"

"Hmm," Trace began thoughtfully. "If you win, I make us all hot-fudge sundaes for dessert tonight."

"Good prize," Hannah said enthusiastically. "What if *you* win?"

"Then you make me the biggest, mushiest Christmas card ever, something I can hang on my office wall."

"Deal," Hannah said, slapping his hand in a high five.

He glanced toward Savannah and saw that her lips were twitching. It wasn't a real laugh, but it was at least the beginning of a smile. He pointed it out to Hannah.

"I get the first point," he said.

"That's not a real laugh," Hannah scoffed. She leaned over, slipped her hand down her mother's back and tickled Savannah until she giggled aloud. "*That's* a real laugh," Hannah said triumphantly.

Savannah wriggled away, then scowled at both of them. "What do *I* get if I maintain a totally stoic facade all day long?"

"Never happen," Trace said.

"No way," Hannah agreed.

"Bet I can," Savannah retorted, her eyes twinkling.

"Okay, that does make it more interesting," Trace agreed. "If you win—and that's a really big *if*—you get Hannah's mushy card."

"What about you? What will you give me?"

Trace met her gaze evenly and felt his heart take a leap into overdrive. "Same as last night," he said softly.

He noted the flush that crept into her cheeks as she remembered that fleeting kiss they'd shared.

"You'll have to do better than that," she challenged.

His gaze remained steady. "Oh, I promise you, darlin', it will take your breath away."

★ ★ ★

The blasted heater in the car must have shot the temperature into the nineties, Savannah thought, barely resisting the urge to fan herself as Trace's words hung in the air.

Unlike the day before, when his seductive teasing had merely irritated her, today she was immediately all hot and bothered and wishing for more…maybe because she knew for a fact exactly what Trace's kiss could do to her. Worse, she wanted another of those kisses so badly, she was going to have to try really, really hard not to laugh for the remainder of the day. Given Hannah's determination to win that bet she'd made with Trace, Savannah was going to have a real struggle on her hands.

She could do it, though. She just had to remember her resolve… and keep a whole lot of distance between herself and those two coconspirators.

The second they reached the hardware store, Hannah begged to take a walk through town.

"Back here in thirty minutes," Savannah instructed, relieved to be rid of one of them. She looked at Trace. "I'll meet you back here in a half hour, too."

"You sure you don't need my help?" he asked, regarding her with a knowing grin.

"Nope. I'm sure someone will help me carry whatever I buy."

"Here's the spare key, then, in case you finish before I get back. You don't mind if I come in and pick up a few things myself, do you?" he asked.

"What sort of things?" she asked suspiciously. Trace didn't strike her as the type who had a lot of fix-it projects back home. Then again, didn't most men get a little giddy around wrenches and screwdrivers and power tools? Maybe he just wanted to soak up the atmosphere.

"This and that," he said vaguely. "I'll know when I see it."

"Fine. It's a big store. I'm sure you won't be in my way," she said.

They parted at the front door. Savannah headed straight for the paint supplies. She'd already thought about the colors she wanted for each of the guest rooms—rich, deep tones, accented by white trim. In no time at all, she'd picked out the appropriate paint chips and had the colors being mixed while she chose brushes, rollers, an edger for trimming and a paint pan.

Just as she headed through the store toward the wallpaper-removal materials, she thought she spotted Trace coming around the end of the paint aisle, but then he vanished from sight. She didn't see him again until she was unloading her purchases into the back of his SUV.

"Find everything you were looking for?" he asked, tucking his own mysterious packages beside hers.

"Yes. What about you?" she asked as he lifted something heavy into the car. "What on earth is that? It looks as if it weighs a ton."

"Just a tool," he said, immediately turning his attention to the street. "Any sign of Hannah yet? Maybe we should go meet her. We could grab some lunch while we're in town. There's a little restaurant on Main Street that Mae used to like."

"The Burger Shack," Savannah said at once. "Is it still in business?"

"It was last time I was here. I took Mae a burger, fries and a chocolate shake from there."

"I can almost taste their shakes," Savannah said. "They made 'em the old-fashioned way with milk and ice cream. They were so thick, a straw would stand straight up in them."

When she looked at Trace, his lips were curving into a grin.

"Sounds like that's a yes," he said.

"Absolutely," she said eagerly. "And here comes Hannah."

She noticed that her daughter was carrying a shopping bag and that her eyes were sparkling with excitement. "What did you buy?" Savannah asked.

"Mom, I can't tell. It's almost Christmas, remember?"

Savannah started to question where Hannah had gotten the money to buy a gift, then stopped herself. Rob had probably slipped her a little money before they'd left Florida. Knowing him, that had been his gift to her, and she was turning right around and spending it on Savannah. On Trace, too, more than likely. Her daughter had the most generous heart of anyone Savannah knew, something she clearly hadn't inherited from her father.

"And that's all you need to tell us," Trace said, making room in the back of the car for Hannah's purchases. "Your mom and I were just talking about lunch. You interested?"

"Only if you're talking about that burger place on Main Street. The smell coming out of there is awesome. And I saw lots of kids my age going in. It must be the cool place to go."

Trace grinned. "Then it sounds like it's unanimous."

"Guess what?" Hannah asked excitedly. She went on without waiting for a response. "I met this girl at the store. Her name's Jolie. Isn't that a great name? And she's my age. We'll be in the same class at school. She says the teacher is really great. Her name's Mrs. Peterson. She's been here, like, forever, but everyone loves her because she's so nice."

"Really?" Savannah said, since Hannah didn't seem to expect much of a response. She was already rushing on.

"And guess what else?" she said. "Jolie says there's going to be caroling in town tonight and that everyone will be there, so we should come, too." She regarded Savannah hopefully. "Can we, please?"

Savannah instinctively thought of how uncomfortable Trace had been when she'd asked him to sing carols at the house the night before. She glanced at him.

"I think it sounds like a wonderful idea," he said with apparent sincerity.

Hannah grinned at him. "Jolie says they give out song sheets, so you'll know all the words."

"Then I definitely say we do it," Trace said. "Savannah?"

Being out on a cold, snowy evening two days before Christmas singing carols with her daughter and Trace? Savannah couldn't imagine anything more romantic. That probably meant she ought to say no, but of course she wouldn't. Not if it meant disappointing Hannah.

Sure, as if that were the real reason, she mentally scolded herself. She was going to do it because there was no place on earth she'd rather be tonight.

"Yes," she said, noting the smile that spread across Hannah's face. It was almost as bright as the warmth stealing through her.

SEVEN

Savannah had the radio blasting as she got into a rhythm of applying paint to the walls of the first guest room. The beautiful deep shade of green brought the color of the ever-greens in the surrounding forest inside. When the white trim was added, it would be reminiscent of the way the scenery looked right now with snow clinging to the trees' branches. She envisioned a thick, warm comforter in shades of green and burgundy on the queen-size bed, with aromatic candles to match on the dresser.

Glancing out the window, she caught a glimpse of Hannah building her first snowman and chattering happily, no doubt to Trace, though Savannah couldn't figure out exactly where he was. He'd been up to something, though for the life of her she couldn't figure out what it was. The instant they'd arrived home after lunch, he'd disappeared into Mae's den. She hadn't seen him since.

Despite her declaration that she intended to handle the paint-ing task on her own, a part of her had been counting on his defiance of that. She'd expected him to show up by now, if only to critique her work, maybe try to coax a laugh out of her in his ongoing attempt to win that bet with Hannah. Instead, much as her ex-husband would have done, Trace had retreated to whatever work he considered more important.

Oh, well, this was her job, not his, she thought with a sigh. And a man she barely knew was hardly in a position to disappoint her.

Besides, the painting was going very well, she decided, as she stood back and surveyed the room. There was an elegance and warmth to the result. Once the finishing touches were in place—probably after she could hit the January white sales at the Boston department stores—it would be perfect.

Satisfied, she snapped the lid back on the can of paint and prepared to move on to another room, the one she thought of as the blue room, though at the moment it had faded wallpaper that needed to be stripped. It was already late afternoon, so she probably wouldn't get much of the stripping completed before they left for the caroling in town, but any progress on the messy task was better than none.

She was about to peel off her first chunk of paper when something that sounded a lot like a big-time power tool kicked on downstairs, followed by a muttered curse, then giggles and deep, booming laughter. Savannah went to the top of the stairs and looked down just in time to see Hannah and Trace cast a furtive look in her direction.

"Uh-oh, we're busted," Trace said.

"If she heard you cussing, she'll probably send us to our rooms," Hannah said, looking downcast.

Hands on hips, Savannah scowled at them. "What are you two doing?"

"Nothing bad, Mom. Honest." Hannah's expression was filled with sincerity.

"Trace?"

"She's right. It's just a little surprise," he said.

Savannah remained skeptical. "A surprise, or a shock?"

Hannah giggled. "Mom's not real good with surprises."

"Maybe because I've had so many bad ones," Savannah said. "By the way, I'm not hearing any reassuring explanations. Do I need to come down there?"

"No," they both said at once.

The quick chorus only roused her suspicions further. She started down the steps, only to have Trace take the bottom steps two at a time and meet her when she was less than half-way down. Putting both hands on her shoulders, he gazed into her eyes.

"Do you trust me?" he asked.

Now there was a sixty-four-thousand-dollar question. "I suppose," she said, hedging. Only Mae's faith in him was giving him her current benefit of the doubt.

"Well, you can," he said, clearly disappointed by the less than wholehearted response. "You need to go back to whatever you were doing and let Hannah and me finish up what we're doing."

She returned his gaze without blinking. "I was thinking of quitting for the day, maybe coming downstairs for a snack."

"I'll bring you a snack," he said at once. "Anything you want."

"An entire pint of your ice cream?"

"If that's what you want," he said at once.

"Okay, that's it. Something bad is going on down there, isn't it?" she said, trying to brush past him.

"Mom, please," Hannah wailed. "You'll spoil everything. It's not bad. I promise."

Savannah told herself that it was her daughter's plea, not the pleading expression in Trace's eyes that won her over. "You can't keep me up here forever, you know."

"Just another couple of hours," he said, looking relieved. "Still want that ice cream?"

"No, that was just a test."

He grinned. "I figured as much."

Savannah sighed. "I'm going back to strip wallpaper."

"Maybe you ought to take a break," he suggested. "Maybe take a long, leisurely bubble bath or something."

"Who has time for that?" Savannah grumbled. "This place isn't going to get fixed up by itself."

He tucked a finger under her chin. "When you start saying things like that, it's exactly the time when you need a break the most."

"This from a workaholic like you?" she scoffed.

"Actually that's something your aunt used to say to me every time I protested that I couldn't get away from the office to come visit. It got me up here every time," he said, an unmistakable hint of nostalgia in his voice. "And she was always right. I always felt better after a few days with her. I even got so I barely cracked open my briefcase the whole time I was here."

"Did she talk you into taking a bubble bath, too?" Savannah teased.

"Nope, but you probably could," he retorted, then added in an undertone, "especially if you were joining me."

Heat and desire shot through Savannah like a bolt of lightning. "Any bubble bath I take, I'll be taking alone," she told him, keeping her own voice muted.

"Too bad."

Before she made the fatal mistake of agreeing with him, she whirled around and went back upstairs. She started toward the room where she'd been about to work, then changed her mind and headed another floor up to her bathroom, where she poured some lavender-scented bubble bath into the tub and turned on the water, knowing that the sound would be enough to keep Trace's imagination stirred up. He wasn't the only one under this roof who had a wicked streak, she thought with satisfaction as she sank into the warm water. Hers had just been on hold for a while.

Unfortunately the memory of his suggestion that he join her and the sensual feel of the water against her skin combined to make the bath far less relaxing than she'd envisioned. In fact, she concluded as she stepped from the tub and wrapped herself in a thick terry-cloth towel, it really was too bad that she wouldn't find Trace waiting for her in her bed. Thank goodness they were going caroling in a couple of hours. It was definitely going to take a blast of icy air to cool off her wayward thoughts.

"Quiet," Trace admonished Hannah when they heard Savannah moving around upstairs. Since they were due to leave for the caroling in less than a half hour, he figured they had five minutes, maybe less, before she started down from the private quarters on the third floor. He squeezed Hannah's hand. "Not a word till she gets all the way down and sees what we've done."

They'd only made a dent in the work that was needed to put Holiday Retreat back into shape for guests, but the outside of the front door and the exterior trim were now a bright red, the brass fixtures glistened and the foyer and living room floors were polished to a mellow sheen. Hannah had even fashioned some greens and ribbon into a decoration that had been hung from the brass knocker. In his opinion, with just a little effort, they had made a vast difference in the appearance of the inn. It looked as it had on his first few visits, before Mae had let some of the maintenance slip.

Beside him, Hannah was practically bursting with excitement as they waited for her mother.

"I should open the door," she whispered. "Otherwise, how will she know about the paint and the decoration?"

Trace grinned at her. "Good point. Why don't you sneak out the back door, run around to the front and open it when I give the word that she's almost down the steps. I'll make sure it's unlocked."

Hannah took off, thundering across the floor in her eagerness.

"Don't forget your coat," Trace called after her just as he

heard Savannah's footsteps descending from the third floor to the second.

Since he didn't want Savannah to miss Hannah's grand entrance, he stepped into view as she started down the last flight and blocked her way. She paused halfway down, regarding him warily.

"I am not going back up," she told him.

"Never said you should."

"Then why are you standing in my way?"

"Am I in your way?" he asked, still not budging.

Savannah sighed heavily, just as Trace heard Hannah hit the porch running.

"You look lovely," he said in a voice meant to carry outside.

Her gaze narrowed. "Announcing it to the world?"

"Why not?" he said. "It's worth announcing."

At that instant he heard Hannah turn the doorknob. He stepped aside as the door burst open.

Clearly startled, Savannah looked straight at her daughter, then caught sight of the freshly painted door. Her eyes lit up.

"Oh, my," she said softly. "It's beautiful." She looked from Hannah to Trace. "Is that what you two were up to?"

"Only part of it, Mom," Hannah said. "Come down the rest of the way and look around some more."

As soon as Savannah stepped off the bottom stair, she glanced around, her expression puzzled.

"Down," Hannah said impatiently.

Savannah's gaze shifted to the floor with its brand-new shine. "What on earth?" There were tears in her eyes when she turned to Trace. "You did this? That's what I heard down here? I couldn't imagine the wood ever looking like this again. It's beautiful."

Hannah beamed at her. "I helped, Mom. Trace and I did it together."

"It's just a start," Trace said. "We only had time to do the foyer and the living room. We'll do the dining room tomorrow."

The tears in Savannah's eyes spilled down her cheeks. "I don't know how to thank you."

"You could start by not crying," Trace said mildly, stepping closer to brush the dampness from her cheeks. "We wanted to do something to help. Hannah made the decoration for the door. She's got a real knack for that sort of thing."

Savannah's gaze shifted to the greens. "Trace is right, sweetie. It's absolutely beautiful. Aunt Mae would be so pleased with all of this."

She turned to Trace. "I know you did it for her, but thank you."

It had started as something he wanted to do for Mae, but that wasn't how it had ended up. Trace realized he had done it to put that sparkle into Savannah's eyes, the sparkle that shimmered even through her tears.

"It was the least I could do," he said. "Now, do you want to admire our work some more, or shall we head into town for the caroling?"

"Let's go," Hannah said at once. "Mom can look at this forever when we come home."

Savannah laughed. "So much for savoring the moment."

"I made you laugh," Hannah gloated. "That's a whole bunch of points for me and hardly any for Trace. Those sundaes are mine!"

"Ah, well," Trace said with an exaggerated air of resignation. "I suppose the art already on my office wall will have to do."

Savannah was quiet on the ride into town. Too quiet, in Trace's opinion. When they'd finally found a parking place a few blocks from the town square and Savannah was exiting the car, he pulled her aside. "Everything okay?"

"Of course," she said brightly, though her smile was as phony as that too-chipper tone.

"Tell me," he persisted.

She sighed. "I was just thinking about all the Christmases I missed with Aunt Mae, years when I could have had this, instead of…well, instead of what we had."

"You can't go back and change things," Trace reminded her. "You can only learn from your mistakes and look ahead."

She regarded him intently. "Are there things about your life that you'd change, mistakes you regret?"

He hesitated over the answer. "I wish things had been easier for my mother," he said slowly. "But I was a boy. I had no control over that. She made her own choice to stay married to a dreamer who was very good at criticizing everything *she* did, but did nothing himself."

A half smile touched Savannah's lips. "You say that, but you sound as if you still believe that you should have fixed it somehow."

"I suppose I do believe that," he admitted. "But by the time I had the money to make a difference in her life, it was too late. She'd already died of pneumonia. She'd let a flu go untreated too long because my father thought she was making too much out of a little cold. Once she got to the hospital, there was nothing they could do. That was the beginning of the end for my dad. He was devastated. I finally saw that in his own way, he had felt my mother was everything to him. He died less than six months later."

"Oh, Trace, I'm so sorry," Savannah said.

He forced aside the guilt that the memory always brought. "Time to take my own advice. I can't change the past. I have to let it go. We all do." He managed a smile. "I think I hear a band warming up. It must be about time for the caroling to begin."

As if on cue, Hannah, who'd been hurrying ahead of them, bolted back. "Hurry up, you guys. The carols are starting. And I see Jolie. Can I go say hi to her?"

"Of course," Savannah said. "But then you come back to join us. Got it?"

"Got it," Hannah said, racing away from them.

Left alone with Savannah, Trace reached for her hand and tucked it through his arm. "This is nice," he said, looking into her shining eyes. "The stars are out. The air is crisp. I can smell the bonfire up ahead. It definitely feels as if Christmas is in the air. And there's a beautiful woman on my arm."

In the glow of the gas lamps on the street, Trace could see Savannah blush. If a simple compliment rattled her so, it must have been years since she'd heard any. Which made her ex-husband even more of a fool than Trace had imagined.

"You know, as much as I loved growing up in Florida," Savannah said, "this is the only place it's ever really felt like Christmas to me. Just look around. All the stores are decorated along Main Street. There's a tree in the center of the green that's all lit up, and snow underfoot. It's like a Currier and Ives Christmas card. What could be more perfect?"

She looked up into Trace's eyes, and he felt his heart slam to a stop.

"You," he said softly.

"What?"

"You're the only thing I can think of that's more perfect than all of this."

For the second time that evening, she was blinking back tears.

"Hey," he protested. "I didn't mean to make you cry again."

She gave him a watery smile. "It's just that no one's ever said anything so sweet to me before."

"Then you've been spending time with the wrong people," he said emphatically.

Suddenly she stood on tiptoe, and before he realized what she intended, she was pressing a kiss to his cheek. "Thank you. I'm really glad you're spending Christmas with us."

Trace could have let it go at that. It was a tender gesture, not an invitation, but the night was cold and that kiss promised heat. He captured her chin and gazed into her eyes, then slowly lowered his head until his mouth covered hers.

She tasted of mint and felt like satin. Then the anticipated heat began to work its way through his system, hinting of a simmering passion just waiting to be unleashed. He unzipped her jacket and slid his arms inside, pulling her close until their body heat mingled. She melted against him. They were a perfect fit, her curves soft and yielding, his body hard and demanding.

Trace could have been content to stay right here, doing nothing more than learning the shape and texture and taste of Savannah's mouth for hours on end, but sanity finally prevailed. This was a small town. Savannah was a newcomer. The last thing she needed was him stirring up gossip. Whatever happened between them—and there was little doubt that something would—he didn't want there to be regrets. Not of any kind.

With a sigh, he slowly released her. His gaze clung to hers as he slid the zipper of her jacket up, then tucked her scarf more securely around her neck.

"Trace, what...?" She swallowed hard. "What was that about?"

"New beginnings," he suggested. He drew in a deep breath of the cold air, then added, "And speaking of that, I had an idea I thought I'd run by you."

"If it's anything like that last one, the answer's yes," she replied, amusement threading through her voice.

"Don't agree until you've heard it," he said. "What about holding an open house at the inn tomorrow before midnight church services? The downstairs rooms can be ready by then, and it would get people talking about the place."

She was staring at him, her expression dazed. "Are you crazy? I can't be ready for an open house tomorrow night! Even if we could finish up with the downstairs rooms, what about food?

We'd need wine and eggnog. All of the good dishes would have to be washed, the table decorated. I can think of a million reasons why it would never work."

He waited through the tirade, then asked, "Is that it? Any other objections?"

"I think those are quite enough."

"Okay, your turn to listen to me. I can have a caterer here first thing in the morning. He's already on standby. He'll bring all the food, the drinks, the table decorations, linens, crystal and china. All you need to do is say yes and stay out of his way." He pulled his cell phone out of his pocket. "What's it going to be?"

She regarded him with obvious astonishment. "You've already done all that?"

"I put it into motion, checked to make sure the caterer I use for our big marketing events was available. I haven't given the go-ahead. That's up to you. I thought it might be the perfect way for you and Hannah to get to know your neighbors, a way to let them know that the inn is back in business."

She looked torn. "It's a wonderful idea, but I can't let you do it."

"Why?"

"Because…" Her voice faltered. She frowned at him. "I don't know why exactly. It's just too much. Besides, how would we let people know?"

He sensed that she was weakening and pressed his advantage. "I think we can count on Hannah and her friend to take care of that. Say the word, and we can send the two of them through this crowd. It'll be faster than an instant-message e-mail."

"What if no one comes?" she asked worriedly. "It is Christmas Eve, after all. People have plans. Then you would've gone to all that expense for nothing."

"I'm not worried about that. I'm sure people are curious. Some are probably anxious to know if you intend to reopen the inn. It's been a historic landmark in the town for years. I think they'll be more than eager to take a little side trip on their way to church." He waited while the wheels turned in her head. He could practically see the pros and cons warring in her brain, as her expression shifted from dismay to hope and back again.

"You're absolutely certain we can pull this off?" she said at last. "It won't be the biggest mistake either of us has ever made?"

"Darlin', when it comes to business, I try really hard never to make mistakes."

"Okay, then," she said decisively. "Make that call. Then let's find Hannah and Jolie and put them to work."

Trace confirmed the plans with the caterer, who was eager to do anything for the bonus Trace had promised him. After that, finding the girls wasn't all that difficult. They were right in front, singing at the top of their lungs. Trace pulled Hannah aside and told her the plan.

"That is so awesome!" she said. "Jolie will help."

She pulled her friend over, introduced her to Trace and Savannah, then told her the plan.

"Sure," Jolie said at once. "I'll tell my mom and dad to spread the word, too. They know everybody. And this will be way better than sitting around at home while my relatives say the same old things they say every year."

"Tell them I'll appreciate whatever they can do to let people know," Savannah told her.

The two girls were about to race off when Jolie turned back. "I was supposed to ask you if it would be okay for Hannah to spend the night at my house tonight. A couple of my other friends are coming over, and my mom said it would be okay. She's right over there, if you want to meet her."

Trace saw the indecision on Savannah's face, but he also saw the anticipation on Hannah's. "Let's go over and say hello," he suggested. "You can discuss it with Jolie's mother."

Five minutes later, Savannah had given her approval for Hannah to spend the night at Jolie's. Donna Jones had been reassuring about the slumber party and enthusiastic about the open house at Holiday Retreat.

"I can't wait to see it," she said. "And I know all my friends are dying to meet you. Mae Holiday was loved and respected, and everyone wants to let you know that. You'll have a huge crowd. An open house on Christmas Eve is a lovely thing to do for the community."

Savannah looked relieved by her genuine excitement. "I'll see you then. What time should I pick Hannah up tomorrow morning?"

"Oh, don't worry about that," Donna said. "You'll have enough to do. I'll bring her by around noon, unless you'd like her there earlier to help out."

"Noon will be perfect," Savannah said, just as the band began to play "Silent Night." She slipped her hand into Trace's and began to sing.

A sensation that felt a whole lot like contentment stole through Trace. Not that he was familiar with the concept. For all of his success, for all of the people who filled his life day in and day out, he'd never experienced a moment quite like this. Maybe there was something magical about the holidays after all.

Or maybe Mae had been even wiser than he'd realized. Maybe she'd known exactly how to grant wishes before they'd even been made.

EIGHT

The bright red front door closed softly behind Savannah, and she suddenly realized that she was all alone in the house with Trace. Her heart thundered in her chest as she met his gaze and saw the familiar heat slowly begin to stir.

As he had earlier, he reached for the toggle on her jacket zipper and slowly slid it down, his intense gaze never once straying from her face. His knuckles skimmed along the front of her sweater, barely touching it, yet provocative enough to have her breasts swelling, the peaks instantly sensitive.

"Tell me to stop now, if that's what you want," he said quietly.

"I…" Her voice quavered. She swallowed hard and kept her gaze level. "I don't want you to stop."

"Thank God," he murmured, his mouth covering hers.

Savannah hadn't expected the whirlwind of sensations that tore through her at his touch. Trace had kissed her before, each time more amazing than the last, but this was different somehow. Probably because of where it was destined to lead.

It had been so long since any man had wanted her, since she'd been open to feeling this reckless surge of desire. From the moment of her divorce, she had resolved never to let another man take away even one tiny bit of her control over her life or her body. In little more than a couple of days, Trace had made that resolve crumble. She'd wanted him almost from the moment he'd stepped into the kitchen on that first day.

The reaction then had been purely physical. Now it was so much more. She knew the kind of man he was, had seen for herself that the workaholic traits she despised covered a vulnerability spawned years ago. She knew he was kind and generous. Best of all, he'd had Aunt Mae's apparently unwavering faith. That stamp of approval alone would have been enough to convince Savannah that Trace was someone to be respected and admired...maybe even loved.

In one corner of her brain, she wanted to apply reason to all of the feelings he stirred in her, wanted to dissect them with logic, but the rest of her mind was clamoring for something else entirely. Majority wins, she thought, barely containing a giddy desire to laugh with sheer exhilaration.

And then Trace's tongue was teasing her lips, tasting her, and the last rational thought in her head fled. From that instant on, it was all about sensation, about dark, swirling heat and a racing heartbeat, about the brush of his hand over flesh, about the clean male scent of him and the way his eyes seemed to devour her as he gauged the effect of each lingering, provocative caress.

She felt a connection with this near-stranger that she hadn't felt in years with her ex-husband. It was as if Trace could read her mind, as if he knew exactly which part of her was screaming for his touch. Savannah knew he believed that Mae had brought them together with something exactly like this in mind. And maybe that was how it had happened. It hardly mattered, because it felt right. It felt as if she was exactly where she belonged with exactly the right man. Fate or Aunt Mae—it hardly mattered which—had brought them to this moment.

She was breathing hard and barely able to stand when he finally paused to take a breath. "Come upstairs with me," she said, then hesitated, suddenly uncertain. "That is what you want, isn't it?"

"Darlin', I've never wanted any woman more than I want you right this second," he said with flattering sincerity. "Are *you* sure, though? I don't ever want you to regret this."

"I've made mistakes and I have my share of regrets, but this won't be one of them," she said with total conviction.

She held out her hand and Trace took it. Together they walked up the stairs, past the floor of guest rooms and on to the private quarters on the third floor. In recent years Mae had kept a small room for herself on the ground floor, but Savannah had opted for the privacy upstairs for herself and Hannah. She led Trace to her room, which had a panoramic view of the mountains lit by moonlight glistening on the snow.

She walked to the window and stood looking out. "Every time I look at this view, I feel this amazing sense of peace come over me. It's so incredibly beautiful."

She felt Trace come up behind her, his arms circling her waist.

"I think you're more beautiful," he said softly, his breath whispering against her cheek.

His hands slid up to her breasts, cupping them. As if the exquisite sensation weren't enough, the reflection in the window of his hands exploring her so intimately doubled the sweet tug deep inside her.

She was already shivering when his fingers slid beneath her sweater to caress bare skin. Eyes closed, she leaned back against his chest as he made her body come alive. Her breasts were heavy and aching before he undid the zipper on her jeans and repeated the delicious torment between her legs. She shuddered at the deliberate touches, each more intimate than the last, each coming closer to sending her over the edge.

She could feel the press of his arousal against her backside, could feel the heat radiating from him in waves. When she risked another look into the glass, she saw the tension in his shoulders, the hooded look in his eyes as he pleasured her. She'd never known a man could give so much without demanding anything in return.

The complete lack of selfishness inflamed her even beyond the effect of Trace's touch. Savannah turned in his arms, then slipped from his embrace. Her gaze locked with his, she stripped her sweater over her head, then let her already-unhooked bra fall to the floor. She knew the precise instant when he saw the reflection of her actions in the window, when that image merged with the one before him and deepened his desire.

She shimmied out of her jeans and panties, then reached for the hem of his sweater. She slid her hands over his chest, which felt like a furnace in the chilly room.

"One of us has way too many clothes on," he said in a husky growl as he tried to push her hands aside to relieve her of the task of ridding him of his sweater.

"Oh, no, you don't. I get to do this my way," she challenged.

A smile curved his lips. "By all means," he said. "Just hurry it up, will you?"

"Some things should never be rushed."

"And some things can't be stopped," he said, drawing her to him, bending down to circle each throbbing nipple with his tongue in a way that had her gasping.

The gesture pretty much destroyed her intent to torment him. Instead, she began to rush the task that only moments before she'd planned to draw out until he felt the same urgency she felt. Within seconds, they were both naked and moving toward the bed, knees weakened by exploring hands, desire ratcheted up to a height Savannah had never before experienced.

When Trace finally entered her, she was already crying out with the first explosive climax. He stilled while the pulsing sensations slowly died away. Then he began to move deep inside her, stirring her all over again, turning restless need into a demanding urgency that stretched every muscle taut with anticipation, until at last, with one sure, deep stroke, he took them both tumbling into a whirlpool of shuddering sensation.

Finally, still cradled in his arms, she fell into the first dreamless sleep she'd had in months.

Trace's heartbeat was easing, his pulse slowly quieting as he gazed down at Savannah. Such a sweet, innocent face to pack so much heat. If he hadn't been enthralled before, the last few hours would have been a revelation. She had a wicked, wanton streak that could lure a man into the fires of hell. Who would have thought it?

The strength and resilience he'd seen in her from the beginning took on new meaning when it came to making love. She'd all but exhausted him, yet he couldn't seem to stop looking at her—touching her—long enough to fall into desperately needed sleep.

Her porcelain-fine skin was still flushed, her hair tousled. Her chest rose and fell with each breath she took, drawing attention to breasts so perfect they took his breath away. Amazingly he wanted her again. In fact, he suspected that after tonight there would never come a day when he didn't want her.

Forever? The word he'd always avoided like the plague popped into his head and wouldn't go away. Forever meant commitment. It meant compromising, joining his life with someone else's, putting her needs above his own. Was he capable of such a thing? Or was he his father's son in that regard? His father had certainly never considered for a second what his irresponsible choices meant for the rest of the family. Trace had always made sure that there would be no one in his life to be affected by the choices he made.

Oh, really? This time when he heard the voice in his head, it was Mae's. More than once she'd scolded him for such self-deprecating comments. She'd pointed out that he had hundreds of employees who counted on him for their livelihoods, that he'd never once let them down, that he'd never let *her* down.

He let his gaze linger on Savannah. Was it possible that he could give her everything she needed? Everything she deserved?

And what about Hannah? Being a stepparent wasn't easy. Oh, they got along well enough now, but what if the rules changed? What if he were here all the time? Would she balk at any attempt by him to take the place of her father...in her life or in her mother's?

He chided himself for getting way ahead of himself. Just because he and Savannah were compatible in bed, just because they'd spent a couple of incredible days that felt magical, didn't mean there was a future for the two of them. She might not even want that. Hell, *he* might not want it. If ever there was a time for clear, rational thought, for not looking beyond the moment, this was it.

Just then, Savannah sighed deeply and snuggled more tightly against him. Heat shot through him. Heat and need. The need went beyond sex, he realized. He needed what she represented— steadiness, love, family—things he'd never imagined himself wanting.

It was his turn to sigh then, his turn to tuck his arms more tightly around her. Maybe morning was soon enough for answers. Maybe tonight was simply meant for feeling fresh, new, enticing emotions.

He breathed in her scent—flowers with a hint of musk— then pressed a kiss to her shoulder. In minutes, he was asleep.

Savannah lay perfectly still, her eyes closed against the brilliance of the sun and against whatever she might discover in Trace's expression. It had been so many years since she'd experienced a "morning after" that she had no idea what to expect. Awkwardness topped the list of possibilities, though.

"You're playing possum," Trace teased, his voice low and husky and warm as it whispered against her cheek.

"Am not," she denied, feeling a smile tug the corners of her mouth.

"Come on, Sleeping Beauty, wake up. We have a million things to do today."

"I don't suppose any of them include staying right here in bed?" she asked wistfully.

"Afraid not."

To her relief, he sounded as disappointed about that as she felt. "And once Hannah's back under this roof, I suppose any more nights like this are out of the question, too."

"Your call, but I'd say that's the sensible way to go."

She opened her eyes then and met his gaze. Fighting against the uncertainty spilling over her, she asked, "Then this was a one-night thing?"

His gaze never wavered. "Not if I can help it," he said emphatically. "I think that's something we need to discuss in detail, don't you?"

Actions seemed vastly preferable to words in Savannah's current frame of mind, but he was right. Talking was definitely indicated, someplace and at a time when temptation wasn't inches away.

"I suppose there's enough time for me to do this," he murmured after a quick glance at the clock on the bedside table. "And this."

Kiss followed kiss until Savannah was writhing and crying out for him to slide inside her. The sweet urgency, the rush for one more taste, one more touch, made their joining even better than any they'd shared during the night before.

"Now we really do have to get up," Trace said with obvious regret. "The caterer will be here in an hour, and I've got to polish the dining room floor and be out from underfoot when he gets here."

"I'll fix breakfast," Savannah said. "And clean up the kitchen."

Trace's heated gaze roamed over her. "Or we could take a leisurely shower together, and to heck with breakfast and polishing the floor."

She grinned. "I think breakfast is highly overrated anyway."

"Not a sentiment you should be sharing with prospective guests," Trace advised as he scooped her up and carried her to the shower.

They were still damp and barely dressed when the doorbell rang.

"Nick of time," he said with a wink. "I'll get it. You might want to see if you can tone down that blush before you meet Henri. He's French and considers himself an expert on the nuances of romance. One glimpse of you, and he'll be offering more unsolicited advice than you ever dreamed of."

"Heaven help me," Savannah said wholeheartedly. "I'll be down in a minute…or an hour. However long it takes."

When Trace had gone, she sat down at her dressing table and studied her face in the mirror. He was right. She was flushed in a way that was entirely too revealing. Even so, she couldn't seem to stop the grin that spread across her face.

"Get a grip," she told herself firmly. "Tonight's too important for you to be frittering away time up here."

But no matter how important tonight was, she had a very strong hunch it wouldn't hold a candle to last night, especially if Trace refused to share her bed again.

By eight-thirty, Savannah knew that the open house was going to be a roaring success. Neighbors were crowded into every room, sharing holiday toasts, commenting on the delicious food as Henri basked in their compliments. Again and again, they had paused to welcome her and Hannah and tell them how delighted they were that Holiday Retreat would be reopened.

"My parents honeymooned here," Donna Jones confided when she caught up with Savannah during a quiet moment in the dining room. "My mother claims I was conceived here, since I was born almost nine months to the day after their wedding night."

Savannah grinned. "I'll bet I know which room," she said. "Aunt Mae always referred to it as her honeymoon suite because it's the largest room here. Want to take a peek? The decorating isn't finished, but I painted it yesterday."

"Oh, I'd love to," Donna said, following her upstairs.

At the door of the freshly painted green room with its white antique iron bed, she turned to Savannah with a gleam in her eyes. "It's going to be beautiful." She moved to the window that faced the mountains. "And the view is fabulous. I wonder if I could convince my husband to sneak off here for a weekend sometime."

Savannah heard the wistfulness in her voice and considered it thoughtfully. "You know, it might not be a bad idea to offer an introductory weekend getaway special for locals. People get so used to living in a place like this, they forget that the tourists who come here see it entirely differently."

"And it seems silly to spend money to stay just a few miles from home," Donna said enthusiastically. "But if it were a special promotion, I'll bet you'd be jammed with reservations. There's no better way to build word of mouth. People would start sending all their out-of-town guests here. It could fill in the slack once ski season dies down."

"I'm going to do it," Savannah said, delighted by the whole idea. "And for giving me the idea, your stay will be free."

"Absolutely not," Donna protested. "That's no way to start a business."

"Sure it is. You'll tell everyone you know how fabulous it is, so when I offer the promotion, it will be sold out in minutes."

As they walked back downstairs, Donna regarded Savannah

with open curiosity. "So, what's the story with you and Trace Franklin? I'm sorry if I'm being nosy, but everybody in town remembers his coming to visit Mae. A handsome, single man who owns his own company is bound to stir up comment. Have you known him long?"

Savannah felt a now-familiar flush creep into her cheeks. "Only a few days," she admitted.

"My, my," Donna teased, "you work fast! I know a lot of women who tried to get to know him on his prior visits, and he never gave any of them a second glance. Last night he couldn't take his eyes off you, and, if anything, he's watching you even more intently tonight."

"We're just—"

"If you say you're just friends, I'll lose all respect for you," Donna teased. "Any woman who doesn't grab a man like that ought to have her head examined."

"Talking about me, by any chance?" Trace inquired, stepping up beside Savannah and slipping an arm around her waist.

Savannah felt her face heat another ten degrees. "We were talking about—" she frantically searched her brain for a suitably attractive, sexy bachelor "—Kevin Costner."

Trace regarded her with amusement. "Oh? Is he in town?"

"No, but we do like to dream," she said, as Donna coughed to cover her laughter.

Trace leaned down to whisper in her ear. "Liar," he said softly.

"I think I'll go chat with my husband and tell him about your offer," Donna said. She grinned at Trace. "Nice to see you again. Merry Christmas."

"You, too," he said.

When Donna had gone in search of her husband, Savannah lifted her gaze to meet Trace's. "I think the party's a success. Thank you for talking me into it."

"It's been fun," he said, as if that surprised him just a little. "Mae's introduced me around before, but this is the first chance

I've had to really talk to some of the locals. They're good people, and they really are delighted that you're reopening the inn. Not only has this place been a boon to the economy, its history and charm provide something that the chain hotels can't. I didn't realize that in its heyday, Holiday Retreat employed several full-time people on staff and that the dining room was open to the public for dinner. Is that part of your plan, as well?"

"Eventually," Savannah said. "I'm going to have to take things slowly, so that I don't get overextended financially. Once all the rooms are ready for paying guests, then I can start thinking about whether to offer more than breakfast. I can cope with making eggs or French toast—I'm not so sure I could handle gourmet dinners. And I know I can't afford any help yet."

"Your spaghetti was pretty good," he said.

She frowned at him. "Somehow I doubt that's up to the standard the guests would expect. Remind me and I'll show you some of the old menus. Mae stopped doing the dinners about ten years ago, when it got to be too much for her, but she saved all the records. Since she left the file right where she knew I'd find it first thing, I'm sure she was hoping that I'd open the dining room again in the evenings."

The rest of the party passed in a blur. Soon guests were putting on coats, thanking Savannah for having them over and leaving for the Christmas Eve services planned by the local churches. When the last guest had departed, Hannah found Savannah and Trace standing on the front porch.

"Mom, this was the best. I must have met everybody in my class at school. I can't wait to start after New Year's. And there's going to be an ice-skating party in a couple of days and I'm invited. Isn't that totally awesome?"

"Totally," Savannah agreed.

Trace grinned. "Then you're back to being happy about living in Vermont?"

"Absolutely," Hannah said. "Can we go to church now?"

Trace glanced at Savannah. "What about it? Are you too tired?"

"I'm tired, but exhilarated. Besides, going to Christmas Eve services was always part of the tradition. I'll grab my coat."

Trace drove into town, which was teeming with many of the same families who had just left Holiday Retreat. They were all walking toward the various churches within blocks of the town square. Bells were ringing in the clear, crisp air.

As they entered the same little white chapel Savannah had attended with her family so many years ago, the scent of burning candles, the banks of red poinsettias by the altar, the swell of organ music, all combined to carry her back to another time. A wave of nostalgia washed over her.

How had she let moments like this slip away? As a child, she'd had no choice, but she could have insisted on coming back as an adult, even if she'd had to leave Rob behind to sulk in Florida. His mood had always been sullen around the holidays anyway. What would it have mattered if it got a little worse because she was sharing an experience like this with their daughter?

Ah, well, those days were behind her. She glanced at Hannah and saw the wonder in her eyes as the choir began to sing "O, Holy Night." Trace slipped his hand around hers as the familiar notes soared through the tiny, crowded church.

Savannah's eyes filled with tears at the beauty of the moment. Trace regarded her with such a concerned expression that she forced a watery smile. "Merry Christmas," she murmured.

"Merry Christmas, angel."

Hannah heard the murmured exchange and beamed at both of them. "Merry Christmas, Mom. Merry Christmas, Trace. I don't care if we don't have presents. This is the best holiday ever."

Gazing into Trace's eyes, Savannah couldn't help but agree with her daughter. It was definitely the best one ever.

NINE

Savannah was hearing bells. Convinced it was a dream, she rolled over and burrowed farther under the covers.

"Mom! Mom! You've got to see this! Hurry!" Hannah shouted, shaking Savannah.

Groaning, Savannah cracked one eye to stare at her daughter. "This had better be good." She and Trace had sat up talking until well past midnight, and if she wasn't mistaken, the clock on her bedside table said it was barely seven. Even if it was Christmas morning, she had counted on at least another hour's sleep, especially since Hannah wasn't expecting Santa's arrival.

"It's not just good," Hannah said, clearly undaunted by her testy tone, "it's fantastic. Come on, Mom. Hurry. I'm going to wake up Trace."

"Wait!" Savannah shouted, but it was too late. Hannah was already racing down the stairs screaming for Trace. Savannah heard his groggy reply, which amazingly was far less irritated than her own had been. In fact, he sounded downright cheerful.

Even with all that commotion right downstairs, Savannah could still hear those bells, louder and more distinct now. She tugged on her robe and went to the window, then stood there, mouth gaping at the sight that greeted her.

There was a huge, horse-drawn sleigh coming through the snow toward the house, the bells on its reins jingling merrily. The back was piled high with sacks and wrapped packages. And the driver was... She blinked in disbelief and looked again. Nope, no mistake. The driver was Santa himself.

Savannah whirled around and headed for the stairs, pausing only long enough to run a brush through her hair and take a swipe at scrubbing her face and teeth. She met Trace at the second-floor landing. Hannah was already downstairs with the front door thrown open to allow in a blast of icy air.

Savannah studied Trace's expression, looking for evidence of guilt. "What do you know about this?"

"Me? I have no idea what you mean."

"Santa? The sleigh piled with gifts? It has your name written all over it."

"Actually I don't think you'll find that's true," he said, giving her a quick kiss. "Stop fussing and go down there. Santa's a busy fellow. I doubt he has all day to hang around here."

"Trace!"

"Go," he said, waiting until she led the way before following along behind.

They arrived downstairs just as Santa trudged up the steps toting two huge sacks. Still filled with suspicion, Savannah stopped him in his tracks. "Are you sure you have the right place?"

"Holiday Retreat?" he said, edging past her. "You're Savannah Holiday, right? And that young lady out there by the sleigh is Hannah?"

"Yes."

"Then this is definitely the place. Even after such a long and busy night, I try not to make mistakes. Sorry about not squeezing down the chimney the traditional way, but if I go home with this suit all covered with cinders, Mrs. Claus will have my hide."

Savannah barely managed to suppress a chuckle. "I had no idea Mrs. Claus was so tough on you."

The jolly old man with a weathered face and white beard, who looked suspiciously like Nate Daniels, rolled his eyes. "You have no idea. Now, where would you like these gifts?"

"Under the tree, I suppose."

"And that would be?"

"Inside, in the living room on the right."

Santa carried two loads of packages inside, declined Savannah's offer of hot chocolate, then left with a cheery wave and a hearty "ho-ho-ho" that echoed across the still air. Hannah stared after him, still wide-eyed.

"Mom, do you think that was really Santa?" she asked.

Savannah exchanged a look with Trace, trying to gauge from his reaction whether her guess about Nate Daniels was correct. Before she could respond, Trace spoke up.

"Looked exactly like Santa to me," he said. "And you said you weren't going to have presents this Christmas, so who else but Santa would bring them?"

"Oh, I have some theories about that," Savannah muttered under her breath, but she kept her opinion to herself. She might have a few words for Trace later in private, but she was not going to strip that excitement from her daughter's eyes. "How about breakfast before we open gifts?"

"No way!" Hannah protested. "I want to see what's in the boxes, especially that great big one. Santa could hardly get it up the steps."

"You know that Christmas is about more than presents," Savannah felt duty-bound to remind her.

"I know, Mom, but these are here and some of them are for me. I checked the tags."

"Only some? Who are the others for?"

"You, silly. And Trace."

"Me?" Trace said, looking more shocked than he had at any time since this incredible morning had begun.

Savannah studied him intently. His surprise seemed genuine. Was it possible he wasn't behind this? Or at least not all of it? Curious to find out for sure, she acquiesced to Hannah's pleas and followed her into the living room.

"Big box first," Hannah said, rushing over to it. "Okay?"

"Your call," Savannah agreed.

The big box turned out to contain skis and ski boots. Hannah immediately had to try them on. "These are so totally awesome," she said, then wailed, "but I don't know how to ski."

"Maybe Santa thought of that," Trace suggested, his expression innocent.

Hannah's expression brightened at once. She began ripping open her remaining presents in a frenzy, *oohing* and *aahing* over each toy, over a new ski jacket and finally over the certificate for ski lessons that came in a deceptively large box.

Though a part of Savannah wanted to protest the degree of excess, she couldn't bring herself to spoil the moment.

"Your turn now, Mom," Hannah said, bringing her a comparatively small box that seemed to weigh a ton.

"What on earth?" Savannah said when she tried to lift it. She began carefully removing the wrapping paper until Hannah impatiently ripped the rest away, then tugged at the tape on the box. Inside, nestled in packing chips and tissue paper, was a tool kit, painted a ladylike pink but filled with every conceivable practical tool she could ever possibly need.

Her gaze shot to Trace. How had he guessed that she would prefer a gift like this to something totally impractical?

"It's perfect," she said, her gaze locked with his.

"Santa must know you pretty well," he agreed.

"Mom, there's a huge box here for you, too," Hannah said, shoving it across the floor.

This time she discovered a floor polisher, precisely the kind she would need if she was to keep the inn's floors gleaming. For most women, an appliance on Christmas morning would have been cause for weeping, but Savannah's heart swelled with gratitude.

"Wait, Mom. There's something little tucked inside with a note," Hannah said, her expression puzzled as she handed it to Savannah.

At the sight of the jewelry-size package, Savannah's breath caught in her throat. Her gaze shot to Trace, but he looked as puzzled as Hannah had. Then she caught sight of the handwriting on the envelope. It was Aunt Mae's.

Tears stung Savannah's eyes as she opened the note.

My darling girl,
I hope you are happily settled in by now and that you will love your new home as much as I have over the years. I've done what I could to be sure you find joy here.

Here's something else I hope will bring you happiness. It belonged to your great-great-grandmother.

With all my love to you and Hannah. I wish I could be there with you this morning, but please know that wherever I am, I will always be looking out for you.
Mae

Savannah sighed and blinked back tears. Finding Mae's present tucked amid all the others made her question everything. She'd been so sure that Trace had sent them, but now? Recalling Santa's resemblance to Nate made her wonder if Mae hadn't been behind this whole magical morning.

"Aren't you going to open it?" Hannah asked, leaning against her and regarding the box with evident fascination.

Savannah slipped off the wrapping paper, then lifted the lid of the velvet box. Inside, on a delicate gold chain, was an antique gold cross. The workmanship was exquisite. The gold seemed to glow with a soft light of its own. She could remember Mae wearing this cross every day of her life. She had always said it symbolized faith itself—so fragile yet enduring.

She opened the delicate clasp, slipped on the necklace, then fastened it. The gold felt warm against her skin, as if it still held some of Aunt Mae's body heat. Once more, her eyes turned misty. She felt Trace take her hand and give it a squeeze.

"Merry Christmas," he said quietly.

"Wait!" Hannah said. "There's another box. It's for you, Trace."

Once more, he looked completely disconcerted. Hannah gave him the present. He handled it gingerly, studying the large, flat box with suspicion.

"What does it say on the tag?" Savannah asked, curious herself.

"Just Trace," he said. "No other name."

"Must be from Santa, then," she teased.

He slipped open the paper, then pulled out the box and lifted the lid. The grin that broke over his face was like that of a boy who'd just unexpectedly received his heart's desire.

"What is it?" Savannah asked, trying to peer over his shoulder.

"It's the biggest, mushiest card I could make," Hannah said, grinning. "And Mrs. Jones took me to get it framed so Trace could hang it on his office wall."

Trace stared at her, looking completely mystified. "But I lost the bet."

"I know," Hannah said delightedly. "But I could tell you really, really wanted the card, so I made it anyway." She threw her arms around his neck. "Merry Christmas!"

To Savannah's shock, there was a distinct sheen of tears in Trace's eyes as he hugged her daughter.

"It's the very best present I ever received," he told her with such sincerity that Hannah's whole face lit up.

If this didn't stop, Savannah was going to spend Christmas morning bawling like a baby. She was about to head for the kitchen to start on breakfast, when Trace grabbed her hand and halted her.

"Wait. I think there's one more present for you, Savannah," he said, pointing Hannah toward a flat box beside the chair where he'd been sitting earlier. "Bring that one to your mom."

The box weighed next to nothing, but when Savannah tore off the paper and looked inside, her mouth dropped open. "Stock certificates?" she asked, turning to Trace. "In Franklin Toys? I can't possibly accept such a gift from you."

"It's not from me," he said firmly. "Not directly, anyway. These were Mae's shares of the company. She gave me power of attorney to vote them for her during the last weeks of her illness, but she told me I'd know what to do with the shares after her death." He looked straight into Savannah's eyes. "I think she would want you to have them."

"But she left me the inn," Savannah protested. "And Franklin Toys is your company."

He grinned. "I hope you'll remember that when you vote, but in many ways the company was as much Mae's as it was mine. She'd want you to have the financial independence those shares can give you."

"But I don't know anything about running a corporation."

"You can learn," he said. "Or you can sell the shares back to me, if you'd prefer to have the cash. The choice is yours."

Savannah sat back, still filled with a sense of overwhelming shock and gratitude. And yet... She studied Trace carefully. "Is this really what you want to do? She gave you her power of attorney, not me. I think she wanted you to control these shares."

"She wanted me to do the right thing with them," he corrected. "And I think that's turning them over to you. They're yours, Savannah. My attorney took care of the transfer yesterday."

Once again, Savannah looked at the certificates. She had no idea what each share was worth in today's market, but it had to be a considerable amount. The thought that she would never again have to worry about money was staggering.

This truly was a season of miracles.

Christmas morning had been incredible. It was everything Trace had imagined, from the awe and wonder on Hannah's face to the amazement on Savannah's when she'd realized that her financial future was secure. Trace had given the two of them everything he knew how to give. He'd been deeply touched by their gratitude.

Somehow, though, it wasn't enough. He wanted more, but he had no idea how to ask for it, or even if he had the right to, especially after knowing the two of them for such a short time.

Struggling with too many questions and too few answers, he wandered into the kitchen where Savannah was just putting the turkey into the oven.

She turned at his approach, studied him for a minute, then gave him a hesitant smile. "Everything okay?"

"Sure. Why wouldn't it be?" he asked, feeling defensive.

"I'm not sure. You seem as if you're suddenly a million miles away."

"I've got a lot on my mind. In fact, if you don't need my help right now, I was thinking of taking a walk to try to clear my head."

"Sure," she said at once. "It'll be hours before the turkey's done, and everything else is set to go in the oven once the turkey comes out." She continued to regard him worriedly. "Want some company?"

Trace shook his head. "Not this time. I won't be gone long," he said, turning away before the quick flash of hurt in her eyes made him change his mind. How could he possibly think about what to do about Savannah if she was right by his side tempting him?

He heard her soft sigh as he strode off, but he refused to look back.

Outside, the snow was a glistening blanket of white. The temperature was warmer than it had been, though still below freezing if the bite of wind on his face was anything to go by. He almost regretted the decision to take a lonely walk when he could have been inside in front of a warm fire with Savannah beside him.

He headed for the road, then turned toward town. He'd only gone a hundred yards or so when Nate Daniels appeared at the end of his driveway. He was bundled up warmly, an unlit pipe clamped between his teeth. He paused to light the tobacco, then regarded Trace with a steady, thoughtful look.

"Mind some company?" he asked, already falling into step beside him.

"Did Savannah call you?" Trace asked.

"Nope. Why would she do that?"

"I think she was worried when I took off."

"She called earlier to wish me a merry Christmas, but that was hours ago," Nate said. He regarded Traced curiously. "Funny thing, she seemed to have the idea that I was over there this morning playing Santa. Where would she get a notion like that?"

"Santa did bear a striking resemblance to you," Trace said.

"You didn't tell her, though, did you? You let her go on thinking that Mae was behind all the gifts and that she was the one who conspired with me to bring them."

"Oh, she suspects I had something to do with it, but there were enough surprises to throw her off." He glanced at Nate. "So, if Savannah didn't call, what brings you out into the bitter cold?"

"The truth is, I was all settled down with a new book my

son gave me for Christmas when I felt this sudden urge to go for a stroll."

"Really? A sudden urge?" Trace said skeptically.

Nate nodded. "Finding you out here, I'm guessing Mae put the thought in my mind."

Trace kept his opinion about that to himself. Maybe Mae did have her ways even from beyond the grave.

"Something on your mind?" Nate inquired after they'd walked awhile in companionable silence.

Okay, Trace thought, here was his chance to ask someone older and wiser whether there was such a thing as love at first sight, whether a marriage based on such a thing could possibly last.

"Do you think there's such a thing as destiny?" Trace asked.

Nate's lips didn't even twitch at the question. "'Course I do. Only a fool doesn't believe there's a reason we're all put on this earth."

"And that applies to love, too?"

"I imagine you're asking about you and Savannah," Nate said. "Now, granted I've only seen the two of you together once or twice, but looked to me as if there was something special between you. It's not important what I think, though. What do *you* think?"

"I don't know if I even believe in love," Trace said dejectedly.

"Well now, there's a topic with which I'm familiar," Nate said. "You know about Mae and me, I imagine."

Trace nodded.

"You probably don't know so much about me and Janie, my wife. Janie and I met when we were kids barely out of diapers," he said, a nostalgic expression on his face. "By first grade I'd already declared that I wanted to marry her, though at that age I didn't really understand exactly what that meant. Not once in all our years of growing up did I change my mind. Janie was the girl for me. We married as soon as I graduated from college, settled down right here and began raising a family."

He glanced at Trace. "Now that should have been a story-book ending, two people in love their whole lives, married and blessed with kids. But Janie's nerves started giving her prob-lems. The kids upset her. Anytime I was away from the house for more than a few hours, she'd get so distraught, I'd find her in tears when I came home. The doctors checked for a chemi-cal imbalance. They tried her on medicine after medicine, but slowly but surely she slipped away from me."

Tears glistened in his eyes. "The day I had to take her to Country Haven was the worst day of my life. I told her she'd be home again, but I think we both knew that day wouldn't come. She's happy at Country Haven. She feels safe there. But there's not a day that goes by that I don't miss the carefree girl I fell in love with."

"It sounds as though you still love her deeply," Trace said.

"I do," Nate said simply.

"Then what about Mae?"

"After Janie went into the treatment facility, Mae helped out with the kids from time to time. They adored her. They stopped by the inn every day after school, and she always had cookies and milk waiting for them. Soon enough, I took to stopping by, too. Mae was a godsend for all of us during that first year."

He met Trace's gaze. "It's important that you know that nothing improper went on between us. I considered myself a married man and I loved my wife. But I loved Mae, too. Since you're not even sure if love exists, I don't know if you can un-derstand that it's possible for a man to love two women, but I did. If I had thought for a single second that my friendship with Mae would hurt Janie, I would have ended it. But the truth was, there were times when Janie didn't even seem to know who I was, didn't seem to care that I was there to visit. That never kept me from going, but it did make me see that I didn't need to lock my heart away in that place with her. I gave Mae every bit of love I felt free to give her. I also gave her the freedom to choose whether to love me. I admired her too much to do anything less."

He sighed. "Given the way of the world now, a lot of men would have divorced a wife like Janie and moved on. That wasn't my way. I'd made a commitment, and I honored it in the only way I knew how. And whether you believe it or not, I honored my commitment to Mae the same way."

"I'm sorry you were in such a difficult position," Trace said. "It must have been heartbreaking."

"Having Mae in my life was one of the best things that ever happened to me. I can't possibly regret that it couldn't have been more, except for her sake. She deserved better."

"I think you made her very happy," Trace told him.

"I hope so," Nate said, then paused and looked directly into Trace's eyes. "There's a reason I'm telling you this. I always believed that one day Mae and I would be able to be together openly, that we'd marry and spend our remaining years together. Maybe even do a little traveling. We never had that chance."

Trace understood what he was saying. "This is your way of reminding me that life is short and unpredictable."

"Exactly. If you love Savannah, don't waste time counting the days until it seems appropriate to tell her. Don't fritter away precious hours planning for the future. Start living every moment. I've lived a good long life, but I'm here to tell you that it's still a whole lot shorter than I'd like."

They'd circled around and were back at Nate's driveway. "Think about what I said," he told Trace.

"I will," Trace promised. "Would you like to join us for Christmas dinner?"

"I would, but I'll be going out to see Janie in a while. She seems to like it when I come by to read to her."

"Thank you for sharing your story with me," Trace said, genuinely touched that Nate had told him.

"Don't thank me. Take my advice." He grinned. "Otherwise, I have a feeling Mae will find some way to give me grief for failing her. That woman always did know how to nag."

Nate was still chuckling as he walked slowly toward his house. Trace watched to make sure he didn't slip on the icy patches, then walked back to Holiday Retreat, his heart somehow lighter and more certain.

TEN

For the life of her, Savannah couldn't read Trace's expression when he got back from his walk. She thought he looked more at peace with himself, but had no idea what that meant.

She was also still puzzling over his magnanimous decision to give her Aunt Mae's stock. Had that been his way of making her financially independent to ease his own conscience and rid himself of some crazy sense of obligation to look after her? Was that going to make it easier for him to pack his bags in a day or two and walk away? When he left, would he go with no intention of ever looking back on her or Holiday Retreat as anything more than a pleasant memory? If that happened, it would break Hannah's heart.

It would break Savannah's heart, too.

"How's the turkey coming?" Trace inquired, peering over her shoulder to look into the oven. "It certainly smells fantastic."

"Another hour or so," she told him, wishing he would stay right behind her, his body close to hers.

She stood up and turned slowly to face him, relieved that he didn't back away. She reached up and cupped his cheeks. "You're cold. How about some hot chocolate? Or some tea?"

"I'm fine," he said, slipping his arms around her waist. "I'd rather have a kiss. I'm sure it would do a much better job of warming me up."

Savannah tilted her face up for his kiss. His mouth covered hers and brought her blood to a slow simmer. She couldn't be sure if it was working on Trace, but her body temperature had certainly shot up by several degrees. She sighed when he released her.

"Warmer now?" she inquired with forced cheer.

"Definitely," he said, his eyes blazing with desire. "Too bad we can't send Hannah for a ski lesson right this second."

"Are you sure we can't?" Savannah inquired hopefully.

"Nope. They're all booked up at the lodge."

She stared at him, biting back a chuckle. "You actually checked?"

"Of course. I always like to know my options."

"Do we have any?"

"Afraid not."

"Oh, well, once we've eaten, I have it on good authority that the turkey will put us straight to sleep. Maybe when we wake up, we'll have forgotten all about sneaking upstairs to be alone."

"I doubt it," Trace said, his expression wry. "Besides, I promised Hannah we'd all go for a walk after dinner."

"Why on earth would you do that? You just got back from a walk."

"Which taught me the distracting power of exercise," he said. "Besides, maybe we can have another snowball fight, and I can tackle you in the snow."

Savannah laughed. "Now there's something to look forward to."

"Sweetheart, a frustrated man is willing to take any contact he can get."

"Interesting. I would think the chill of the snow would be counterproductive."

"I think I'd have to spend a month outdoors in the Arctic before it would cool the effect you have on me," he said with flattering sincerity. He tipped her chin up to look directly into her eyes. "By the way, let's make a date."

"A date?"

He grinned. "You know, a man and a woman, getting together. A date."

"Out on the town?"

"Or alone in front of a cozy fire."

"Okay," she said with a surge of anticipation. "When do you want to have this date?"

"Tomorrow night?" he suggested.

The level of relief Savannah felt when she realized he intended to stay another day was scary. She had a feeling she wanted way too much from this man. Asking for a date—even making love—was hardly a declaration of undying devotion. She really needed to keep things in perspective and not get ahead of herself.

"Tomorrow would be fine. Maybe I'll see if Hannah can spend the night with Jolie again."

Trace grinned. "Best idea I've heard all day."

Savannah's heart beat a little faster at the promise beneath his words. The memory of the last night they had spent alone in this house brought a flush to her cheeks.

"Then I will definitely make it happen," she vowed. Because she was desperate for another one of those sweet kisses despite the risk of Hannah walking in on them, she backed away from Trace and moved to the stove, opening lids and checking on things that were simmering just fine only moments ago.

"Trace," she said without turning around, "if I ask you something, will you tell me the truth?"

"If I can," he said at once.

"You did make all the arrangements for Santa and the presents, didn't you?"

"Do you really want to know?" he asked, sounding vaguely frustrated. "Wouldn't you prefer to think it was part of the Christmas magic?"

She turned to face him. "Sure," she said honestly. "But I also believe in giving credit where credit's due. I'm not an eight-year-old who still believes in Santa, at least when it suits her. I know the kind of effort and money it takes to make a morning like the one we had happen. The person responsible should be thanked."

He shrugged, looking as if her persistence made him uncomfortable. "Look, it was nothing, okay?"

"It was more than that and you know it. You made Hannah's Christmas, and mine."

"I'm glad," he said. "Can we drop it now?"

"Why do you hate admitting that you did something nice?"

"Because I didn't do that much. I just made a few calls, ordered a few little things. Nate was more than willing to play Santa, especially since he had that gift from Mae for you."

"Which was wonderful of him to do, but you bought me a floor polisher and a professional-quality tool kit, for heaven's sakes."

"A lot of people would say that gift explains why I'm still single," he said.

"And I say it explains why I find you so completely and utterly irresistible," she said.

"Irresistible, huh?" A grin tugged at the corners of his mouth. "Come over here."

"Oh, no, you don't. We agreed that any more fooling around with Hannah underfoot would be a bad idea."

"Did we agree to that?"

"We did," she said emphatically.

"Does one kiss qualify as fooling around?"

"Probably not with a lot of people, but in my experience with you, it has a tendency to make me want a whole lot more."

His grin spread. "Good to know. I'll have to remember that tomorrow night."

Savannah met his gaze, her own expression deliberately solemn. "I certainly hope you do."

Trace woke up in a dark mood on the morning after Christmas. Rather than inflict his foul temper on Savannah or Hannah, he made a cup of coffee, then shut himself away in Mae's den and turned on his computer.

Even though he'd given his staff the week between Christmas and New Year's off, he checked his e-mails, hoping for some lingering piece of business to distract him. Aside from some unsolicited junk mail, there was nothing. Apparently other people were still in holiday mode. He sighed and shut the thing off, then sat back, brooding.

He'd spent the whole night wondering if he hadn't made the biggest blunder of his life the day before by giving Savannah that stock. It wasn't that he thought it was the wrong thing to do or that Mae would have disapproved. In fact, he was certain she'd known all along what he would do with her shares. No, his concern was over whether he'd given Savannah the kind of financial independence that would make her flat-out reject the proposal he planned to make tonight.

He was still brooding over that when the door to the den cracked open and Savannah peeked in.

"Okay to interrupt?" she asked.

"Sure," he said, forcing the surly tone out of his voice. "Come on in."

To his shock, when she walked through the door, she was wearing some sort of feminine, slinky nightgown that promptly shot his heartbeat into overdrive.

"On second thought," he muttered, his throat suddenly dry, "maybe you should change first."

"Why would I do that?" She glanced down. "Don't you like it?"

"Oh, yeah," he said huskily. "I like it. Maybe just a little too much."

Apparently she didn't get the hint, because she kept right on toward him. The next thing he knew, she was in his lap and his body was so hard and aching, it was all he could do to squeeze out a few words.

"What are you up to?" he inquired, staying very still, hoping that his too-obvious response to that wicked gown of hers would magically vanish. "Where's Hannah?"

"Gone," she said, brushing her mouth across his.

"Gone?"

"For the day," she added, peppering kisses down his neck.

"The entire day?" he asked, suddenly feeling more hopeful and a whole lot less restrained.

"She won't be home till five at the very earliest," Savannah confirmed. "I have Donna's firm commitment on that. She couldn't keep her tonight, so we compromised."

"I see," he murmured, sliding his hand over the slick fabric barely covering her breast. The nipple peaked at his touch.

"Sorry my present's a day late," she said as she proceeded to unbutton his shirt and slide it away.

Trace gasped as her mouth touched his chest. "Oh, darlin', something tells me it will be worth the wait."

Savannah had never felt so thoroughly cherished as she did lying on the sofa in Trace's arms, a blanket covering them, as a fire blazed across the room. In a few short days, she had discovered what it meant to be truly loved, even if Trace himself hadn't yet put a label on his feelings. She wondered if he ever would.

She turned slightly and found him studying her with a steady gaze.

"You're amazing, you know that, don't you?"

She shook her head. "I'm just a single mom doing the best I can."

"Maybe that's what I find so amazing," he said. "You remind me of my mother."

"Just what every woman wants to hear when she's naked in a man's arms," Savannah said lightly.

He gave her a chiding look. "Just hear me out. You're strong and resilient. You've had some tough times, but you haven't let them turn you bitter. You've just gotten on with the business of living and making a home for Hannah. When I was a kid, I don't think I gave my mother half enough credit for that. I spent too much time being angry because she didn't tell my dad to take a hike. I realize now that she didn't see him the same way I did. She loved him, flaws and all. It was as simple as that, so she did what she could to make the best of his irresponsible ways."

Trace caressed Savannah's cheek, brushing an errant curl away from her face. "So, here's the bottom line. I meant to do this with a bit more fanfare, but since our date has turned out to be a little unorthodox, this part might as well be, too."

He sounded so serious that Savannah went still. "What's the bottom line?" she asked worriedly.

"Will you marry me? I know we've just met and that you're still recovering from a divorce, but I've fallen in love with you. I talked it over with Nate—"

Savannah stared, sorting through the rush of words and seizing on those that made the least sense. "You what?"

"Now don't go ballistic on me," Trace said, then rushed on. "I ran into him yesterday. He saw that I had a lot on my mind, because I had all these feelings and I thought they were probably crazy, but he put it all in perspective for me. He said life is way too short to waste time looking for rational explanations for everything. I'm not all that experienced with falling in love, but apparently it doesn't follow some sort of precise timetable."

Savannah's lips twitched at his vaguely disgruntled tone. "No," she agreed. "It certainly doesn't."

"Then again, I'm used to making quick decisions. And I do think it's exactly what Mae had in mind when she insisted I come here for Christmas." He met her gaze. "And just so you know, with these quick decisions of mine, I rarely make mistakes."

"Is that so?" Savannah said quietly. "Well, it's certainly true that Aunt Mae was an incredibly wise woman. She hasn't steered me wrong so far."

"Me, either," Trace said, regarding her warily. "So?"

"So what?"

"Bottom line? I've fallen in love with you. Something tells me that if I don't reach out for what I want with you now, it will be the biggest mistake of my life."

"Then reach," she said softly, her gaze locked with his.

Trace held out his hand. Savannah put hers in it, and for the first time in her life, Savannah felt as if she were truly part of a whole, something real and solid, with a future that was destined to last forever.

"There's something about this place," she said with a sense of wonder. "It must be Aunt Mae." She lowered her mouth to Trace's. "She always did get me the best gifts of all."

★ ★ ★ ★ ★